CIRCUMFERENCE OF SILENCE

JACQUIE HERZ

Black Rose Writing | Texas

ISBN: 978-1-68433-710-1
PUBLISHED BY BLACK ROSE WRITING
www.blackrosewriting.com

Printed in the United States of America
Suggested Retail Price (SRP) $19.95

Circumference of Silence is printed in Calluna

*As a planet-friendly publisher, Black Rose Writing does its best to eliminate unnecessary waste to reduce paper usage and energy costs, while never compromising the reading experience. As a result, the final word count vs. page count may not meet common expectations.

In memory of my mother, Lola Lesser, and my mother-in-law, Rena Herz, whose stories have inspired me to write this novel, and for my children and my children's children to always remember.

CIRCUMFERENCE OF SILENCE

"Memory that is intelligent, reflexive, is not limited to the past, but allows you to define the reality and project the future. Otherwise, why would we even need memory?"

–Piotr Mateusz Andrzej Cywiński
Director of the Auschwitz-Birkenau State Museum

CHAPTER I

October 26, 2014

Mali Feuer stands outside her mother's door, struggling to fit the key into the lock. The narrow, carpeted hallway is dim, stuffy. Talk show voices bark unintelligible words at her from inside the apartment next door. Now the key is in, but won't turn. With an impatient huff, she yanks her messenger bag off her shoulder and, along with her mother's mail, drops it to the floor. Unencumbered, she tries again, this time pulling the door in tight and turning the key at the same time. The bolt clicks back; the door gives way.

Through the window, at the opposite end of the living room, a strip of the East River glimmers, winking at her in the sunlight. She deposits her mother's keys and mail on the little table in the entryway, slings her bag across the back of a dining chair, and heads for the balcony. She pushes the door wide open, letting badly needed air into the place; exactly, she realizes—shaking her head and smiling—as her mother would have done; and steps outside.

In the sunshine, she takes a deep breath and leans against the railing, mesmerized by the cars, the buses, and the people below her: everything in miniature from this nineteenth-story height. Mali closes her eyes. A silky ribbon of air caresses her face and, as if directed by a ghostly messenger from the past, she is transported years back and miles away.

She was six or seven. Her mother had sent her out to play in the garden. But it wasn't too long before Mali tired of winning at a game of hopscotch against her imaginary friend, Kemma, or of drawing pictures with colored chalks on the asphalt of their steep, uphill driveway. So she went to sit on the red-tiled step, by the glass-and-wrought-iron front door of their house, and watched the cars and double-decker buses rumble up and down Finchley Lane, a busy road in north west London.

Funny that this particular recollection of living with her mother, who was absent from most of her childhood, should still be with her some sixty years later. She wonders how she has remolded this and other memories over time. How her ever-changing emotions, kneaded into the hard-baked facts, have become as indistinguishable from each other as flour is to dough.

She turns back to the apartment, half expecting a change. Of course, nothing has. Except that the leaves of the philodendron, animated now, flutter with the breeze from the open door. Though not Mali. She's feeling even more dazed and disoriented than when she first arrived. She inhales deep gulps of air. Could it be any other way? The living room is too calm; the leather couch, so sad and forlorn looking with only a blue, woolly throw draped untidily over one arm to occupy it. Fallen petals litter the coffee table around the vase of long-stemmed yellow roses; their heads shriveled and drooping, as if they, too, are too spent to stay up. Even the crammed floor-to-ceiling bookshelves appear neglected. The crumbling, leather-bound volumes of Goethe, Schiller, and Heine are arbitrarily squeezed between hardcover spy novels, paperback love stories, and the European history books that had belonged to David, her mother's husband. Those old, tattered German books stand out in Mali's mind as the remnants, the reminders, of a stolen time and place.

Sorting through the mail, Mali finds nothing urgent. Only bills. Bloomingdale's, Con Ed, and a letter from the landlord releasing her mother from her lease. At the bottom of the pile, she recognizes one from the United States Holocaust Memorial Museum. A similar letter had come to her own mailbox at home a few days ago. She had thrown it away, unopened, never thinking more about it, until the following morning when she walked down the driveway to collect her *Times*. There, right in her path, staring straight up at her, was an envelope with the words, WHAT YOU DO MATTERS. As she picked it up, a sudden strange feeling came over her. Had those words been purposefully put in her way? An omen, perhaps.

Unable to throw the envelope away, she left it on the table by the front door, the words jumping out at her each time she passed by. That evening, she showed it to her husband, Michael. He laughed. A raccoon had gotten into the garbage, he said. He thought he'd cleaned it all up, but the envelope must have escaped him and been blown to the driveway by the wind. She laughed then too. And although she admitted a little foolishness to herself, she couldn't quite let go of the thought that what you do *does* matter, and she brought the pledge card downstairs, adding it to her stack of bills to pay.

On the threshold to her mother's bedroom now, she hesitates at the door for a moment before going in. The sheets on the bed are pulled back, still unmade from the night last week when the paramedics had come to take her mother to the hospital. A thick book lies open on the bed, the jacket's flyleaf folded over a page, as if waiting for her mother to return and continue to read where she'd left off. It's Vikram Seth's *Two Lives*. She had given it to her mother a few months ago. Picking up the book, she sits on the carpeted floor with her back against the bed and begins to skim its pages, mostly looking at the photographs. The memoir had originally interested her because of their families' coincidental connection with the same two cities. First there was Berlin in the time prior to World War Two, where Vikram Seth's great-aunt and great-uncle had lived, and Mali's mother had grown up. Then, Hendon, the area of north west London they had all settled in afterward.

She stands, sets the closed book on the bed.

Blue jeans, a brown leather belt hanging from them, and a blue and white pin-striped man's shirt—just what her mother had always liked to wear—lie neatly draped over the white wicker chair next to the bed. The clothes look oddly deflated to Mali, as if the body that once inhabited them has been spirited away by the wave of a magic wand. A few small white pills dot the bedside table.

Before she leaves the bedroom, she stops to look at the photographs crowding the top of the chest of drawers. Most of them are of Julia and Steffi, Mali's two daughters, in various stages of growing up. Then, as mothers themselves, with their own young children. Behind the children's photos, a faded wedding portrait of herself and Michael, their faces so young and serious. On the opposite side, a loose snapshot, its wavy edges curling inwards, rests against a framed, formal sepia of her grandmother. Mali sits on a park bench, in this photo, and her mother stands behind her, leaning in, so that their faces appear stacked, one above the other. As she smooths out the picture, trying to remember when and where it was taken, she studies the two faces in the glossy print. Apart from the color of their eyes, a similar grey-green, they never did look alike. She leans the picture back up against the one of her grandmother, and turns away.

Her cell phone rings, the sound muffled in the back pocket of her jeans. It's Michael.

"Hey, how's it going?" he says.

"Okay, I guess."

"Do you want me to come into the city?"

Still preoccupied with the photographs, Mali doesn't answer him right away. How these prints flatten and compress her years, she thinks; perhaps, not so differently from beach stones polished smooth and shiny by the sand and sea.

Finally, she says, "Only if you want," though she wishes he would.

Silence.

"But you don't have to." And when she hears a slight sigh of relief through the phone, she adds, "I can't imagine I'm going to be here all that long anyway. I'm really tired."

"Let me know what train you're catching, and I'll pick you up from the station."

After hanging up, she quickly checks her email before slipping her phone back into her pocket. She doesn't want to be bothered with work at the moment but finds she can't keep herself away. The business will survive one day without you, her mother would always say when trying to get Mali to spend time with her in the city. Logically, she knew her mother was right, of course. Though the truth of it—and what she could have never told her—is that she's a consummate worrier, always imagining disaster lurking around the corner, a fiery monster clawing at the fringes of her existence.

So, what were those things her mother had wanted her to keep? The big glass ashtray that had belonged to Mali's grandmother? Or the wrought-iron candlestick, the only object her mother said she'd taken from her parents' Miami Beach apartment after her father's death? Where will she find these? Mali closes her eyes. Tears gather beneath her lids. She holds them back. Slowly, and to her surprise, she realizes how, despite everything she's thought until now, she will miss her mother terribly. But this shouldn't surprise her. Hasn't she spent most of her life, one way or another, longing for her?

A sudden blast of sirens from the street below gives Mali a start. She goes out to the balcony, only to catch the tail end of flashing red, yellow, and orange lights, as they race up the avenue toward their emergency.

The sun has begun to set. Mali feels a slight chill in the air after the warmer-than-usual October afternoon. Rubbing her arms, she comes back into the living room. At the small secretary, she switches on the light and notices a large manila envelope resting against the cubbyholes at the back of the desk. Shocked to see her own name in over-sized, black-marker letters scrawled in her mother's childlike script, she rips open the envelope. Dozens of odd sheets of blue, yellow, and cream-colored paper fall out, all torn from various-sized spiral-bound notebooks. "Oh my God," Mali whispers, stunned, as she gathers up the handwritten pages and rearranges them into their numbered order.

The familiar handwriting distracts her and she's unable to take in the words at first. Instead, she can only see the blue airmail letters of her childhood, stubbornly stuck in her mind's eye, like a patchwork of fallen leaves in grounded chaos. *My Dearest, Darling Mummy,* was how she had always begun hers, as if, in doubling the words of endearment, she could make up for their separation, could suck up the ocean between them and diminish the vast emptiness her eight-year-old, aching heart had tumbled into, the day her mother left.

Mali sets aside the letters and goes to the window. She stares down at the street once again. Even from this height, she can hear the cars and buses rumbling along the avenue, their honking horns, their squeaking brakes as they slow to stop for the traffic light at the corner.

But suddenly, she is overwhelmed by an aching curiosity to know what her mother had been writing to her, and she comes right back to the couch, where the letters sit, waiting for her, just the way she'd left them. Careful not to disturb the vase of yellow roses and the dried petals that keep floating to the dark, polished wood of the coffee table, she puts her feet up, slips on her reading glasses, and looks at the first page. But this time, before she can even focus on her mother's words, a strange eeriness grabs ahold of her. It's her mother—reaching up to Mali from the grave—her words tight and trembling in her fist, as if for the final say.

CHAPTER 2

October 5, 2014

My Dearest Mali,

You might wonder, my darling, why I couldn't have just sat you down to talk, to explain myself, the way I imagine any other ordinary mother would, to her daughter. I don't have a good excuse to give you. Only that, whenever we sit face-to-face, the right words escape me; they evaporate, as if clouds, into the thickness of the air between us. And to be honest, writing has always come so much more easily to me. It offers me the time to think, to make sense of our worlds, without my worrying and wondering, as we sit across the table from one another, at the expression in your eyes.

Perhaps then, you'll imagine how surprised I was to find the old stories I'd written long ago, of my early years, hiding beneath a mound of outdated paperwork, in the bottom drawer of my little desk. It was as if I'd cracked open that part of my life, come face-to-face with my ghost, the dead, and long forgotten part of who I'd been, both in what I'd already written and what I knew I still had to record.

So, my darling daughter, I took a giant breath, crossed my fingers for good luck, and plunged into chronicling the rest of my life for you. I can say, it's not been an easy task. Some days, my memories spread before me in my thoughts, as if battling warriors edging each other out of the ring. Other times, I see your face, and I want to shred my words into tiny pieces, fearful of what you might think of me. Maybe you wish I'd had the guts to sit and talk to you in person. Perhaps I do as well. But this—this writing— I've come to realize, is the surest, the only way I know how to give you my own uninterrupted side of the story.

Think of it, too, as my way of forging a path back to the eight-year-old child you were when I left, when our writing to each other—our only means of regular communication back then—was the core of our relationship. I remember how you used to begin each of your letters to me when you still lived in the red-brick, bay-windowed house in London, and I, banished by your father, lived here in New York City, three thousand miles away from you, at first with my own parents, then later with a new husband.

You'd always begin with My Dearest, Darling Mummy, as if dearest by itself, or even darling, seemed incomplete somehow, like a kiss blown into the air. But the words dearest and darling together felt weighted, like a tight bear hug, ensuring I'd never underestimate your love for me. Your handwriting too, so beautiful in those days. Do you remember? I hope so.

With all my love, always.

CHAPTER 3

October 26, 2014

The telephone rings, disturbing the quiet of the apartment and startling Mali. She puts aside her mother's pages, takes off her eyeglasses, sits up, plants her feet on the floor, and tries to stand. But a force inside her keeps her down. She feels like a prisoner: Gulliver in Lilliput. After the third ring, there's silence. Then her mother's voice—shocking and jolting in its unexpectedness—projects from the answering machine, her words drawn-out and measured: *Please tell me, slowly and clearly, your name and your number and I will get back to you as soon as possible.* Suddenly Mali recalls the first time she'd spoken to her mother over the phone. It was the summer she'd turned sixteen and had just come to live with her mother in New York. Off at the Central Park Zoo one afternoon with her newly made friends, she had called from a pay phone, probably to say she'd be home later than expected. What had struck her for the first time was her mother's German accent. Mali had found it so odd that she'd never noticed it before then.

"Eva, where are you?" A man's voice cuts into her thoughts.

She should answer his call, be the bearer of sad news, but she can't. This gluey lethargy won't let her. She holds her breath and listens for the click that tells her he's hung up.

Restless, her concentration broken, Mali paces the living room. The walls are crammed with paintings and lithographs. Marble and wood Buddha statues in many sizes sit on the shelves and end tables. Primitive figurines stand in corners around the room. Mali stops in front of the closet in the small entryway by the door. At first reluctant to open it, she then reminds herself that, sooner or later, she will have to anyway. A dozen or so coats for winter, spring, and fall hang from the railing. Mali reaches to the shelf above. She finds plastic rain hats, the kind beauty parlors hand out on rainy days, a navy-blue beret, its oversized made-in-France label sewn on the inside, woolen hats and gloves, and a collection of vinyl totes promoting cosmetic companies collected from Bloomingdale's, her mother's favorite store. An assortment of shoes, boots, and sneakers form neat lines on the closet floor. She's about to close the door, when she notices a large cardboard box tucked away in the back behind the coats. She tugs at it. It doesn't budge. She pushes aside the coats and shoes and with both hands pulls the box out of the closet, then drags it through the living room to where she has been sitting on the couch.

A sudden loud knock at the apartment's door startles her. She tiptoes through the living room. Her heart hammers at her ribs as she peers through the spy hole in the door. Elizabeth. At first, she's annoyed at the intrusion, but when she opens the door and her mother's friend stands before her, a rueful smile on her kind face and arms outstretched to embrace her, she's glad for it.

"I was just coming home when I noticed the lights on in the apartment and figured maybe you could do with the company."

"That's so nice of you." Mali ushers in her mother's younger friend, closing the door behind her. "Can I offer you something?"

"I can't stay long. I'm meeting Barbara at Petaluma's for dinner at 6:30."

"Ah, Petaluma's, my mother's favorite haunt. If I ever went back there again, I think I'd have to bring a spare chair to the table and pour an extra glass of wine to honor her, as we do for Elijah at the seder."

Elizabeth takes off her gabardine coat, drapes it over a dining chair, follows Mali to the kitchen and stands in the doorway, watching as Mali fills the kettle and puts it on the stove.

"I'm brewing myself a cup of coffee. You sure you wouldn't like one too?"

"No, thanks, really. . .you know. . . I loved your mother," Elizabeth says, a little quiver in her voice and tears welling up in her eyes.

"She loved you as well." Mali's answer, though she means it, sounds too quick, the words almost mechanical. She takes a step toward Elizabeth, puts her arms around her bony shoulders.

Elizabeth nods, wiping away her tears.

"Sometimes," Mali says, pulling a tissue from the box of Kleenex on the counter and handing it to Elizabeth, "I think you were more of a daughter to her than I was."

"That's ridiculous," Elizabeth says through a stuffed nose. "You do see that, don't you?" She blows her nose, dabs her eyes.

The kettle whistles and Mali pours the boiling water over the ground coffee in the cone-shaped filter of the Melitta one-cupper.

"Let's go sit," she says, once the coffee has dripped through to her cup, and she leads the way from the small kitchen to the living room.

"Wow!" Elizabeth stares at the pages spread out on the couch next to where Mali has been sitting. "She really wrote a lot."

"You know what this is all about?"

"Sort of. I mean . . . you remember when David was so sick all those years ago, and she was crazy and frantic with worry and petrified of how she would live her life alone?"

"Yes, of course."

"Well, I'd read in a magazine back then how writing about your feelings and anxieties can be a great comfort. It helps organize and clear the mind. And if you write as though you're writing a letter to someone, it's as good as pouring your heart out to a friend. And in some cases, even better."

Mali laughs, as she gathers her mother's pages together, and stacks them on the coffee table next to the small mound of yellow rose petals.

"I think I have her whole life story here, all of it in letters to me."

"What a great legacy. I never guessed there'd be so much. Obviously, she had things she needed to tell you."

"Or herself. Too bad she couldn't have given them to me while she was still alive. Then we could've talked it over."

"She must've had her reasons."

Mali looks away from Elizabeth for a few moments, remembers her coffee, picks up her cup, and takes a sip.

"You sure I can't get you something?" she says.

Elizabeth shakes her head. Mali turns sideways on the couch, brings her legs up, and crosses them beneath her. She's facing Elizabeth, who's staring straight ahead at the lights in the dark, outside the window. Mali studies her profile. Although she's a ready smiler, and only a little older than Mali, she finds her hard to read. And Mali has often wondered what stories her mother confided to Elizabeth about their mother-daughter relationship.

"Actually," Elizabeth suddenly says, breaking the stillness, and looking back at Mali. "I think I've changed my mind. If it's okay with you, I'll help myself to a Scotch."

"Of course, please do. You most probably know, better than I do, where everything is."

Mali watches Elizabeth walk to the kitchen. She listens to a cabinet door open and close, a glass put down on the countertop, a sigh of suction as the freezer door opens then closes, and the clinking of ice cubes in the glass. She hears another cabinet door open and close, a slight groan from Elizabeth as she unscrews the tightened top of the bottle, then a hissing and a cracking sound as the Scotch is poured over the ice.

"Well," Elizabeth says, coming back to the living room. She sits across from Mali, takes a long swallow of her Scotch, sets the glass on the polished table, and continues: "There are a few things she might've kept from you."

"Oh?"

"Yes . . . you see it all started . . . perhaps a month ago."

"Started? What started?"

"Well . . . one evening, your mother came up to my apartment for a chat and a drink, as she so often did. Since I was on the phone with my daughter, Emma, trying to help her work out a situation she was having with her husband, I poured your mother a Scotch, mimed that I needed a few more minutes and pointed to the day's *Times* on the kitchen table. After I got off the phone, I found your mother engrossed in an article. It was one of those profile pieces they run from time to time. You know what I'm talking about?"

Mali nods.

"The guy profiled was Philip Schwartz. Ring a bell, by any chance?"

"The little boy my grandparents adopted from the Jewish orphanage in Berlin?"

"Exactly right."

"Wow! She must've been ecstatic to have found him. What serendipity! She loved that little boy."

"Yes, she was super-excited at first," Elizabeth says, reaching for her glass.

"Why only at first? Was it definitely him?"

"Oh, yes, for sure. In the interview, he even spoke of his experience at the Jewish orphanage in Berlin, and the incredible luck to have been adopted at the age of six for a family in Detroit. How many could've fit that bill so perfectly?"

"True," Mali says. "But why was he being interviewed?"

"His memoir, published just a few weeks ago."

"Impressive. But then why was she only excited at first? What happened?"

"Not sure," Elizabeth says. "It was almost as though a switch inside her got turned off."

"Maybe he wasn't the right guy, after all?"

"He most certainly was the guy, all right. She'd even contacted his publisher."

"Really? Why wouldn't she have told me any of this?"

"Perhaps, she wanted to talk to him first. Whomever she spoke to at his publisher said he was away on a national publicity tour and sometimes hard to reach. Maybe she'd decided to wait for him to get back."

Mali shifts her legs from underneath her and stretches them out. She rubs her calves. They feel numb.

"Come to think of it," she says after a few moments. "A man called here a little while ago. I wasn't in the mood to talk, so I let the machine answer. He just said, 'Eva, where are you?' and hung up. He never left his name or his number. Do you think it might've been him?"

"He wouldn't have heard . . . I mean, how could he have known?"

"But something in the tone of his message implied that they'd spoken beforehand. It was too familiar sounding. Almost as though he already knew her," Mali says, turning to stare at the lights outside the window.

"I'm sure whoever he was, will call back. Especially if it was him. By the way, I still have the paper with his interview, if you're interested."

"Yes, I'd love to see it. I should get his book, too."

"I think he sent your mother a copy. It must be floating around here somewhere."

Has she already seen Philip's book in her wanderings through the apartment? She watches Elizabeth finish her drink, lean back in her chair, and stretch her long thin legs straight out, crossing them at the ankles.

"Do you want another?" Mali points to her empty glass.

"You've twisted my arm." Elizabeth laughs. "But then I must be going."

Mali listens for the same ritual sounds: the glass on the countertop, the freezer door released from its seal as it's opened, the ice pinging the glass, and the Scotch being poured.

"There's something else," Elizabeth says, coming back to her same seat. "Your mother was doing research on a girl she once went to school with, in Berlin. Have you heard of Stella?"

"Stella? Not sure."

"Well, your mother was trying to locate her family."

"What on earth for?"

"I think in some way she felt responsible for her death."

"That's crazy." The words escape her lips. They sound brittle. She can't help but feel hurt. How could she have been excluded from so much in her mother's life in recent months?

"Yes, I agree, really crazy, and especially after all this time. And believe me, I tried to convince her she was in no way responsible. But you know how your mother was, once she had an idea in her head, it was virtually impossible to change it. So, evening after evening, she'd show up at my apartment, armed with papers from the school she and Stella had gone to, her autograph books—the writing in them so beautiful they'd put the American kids' script to shame—and a bottle of Scotch. We'd go into my little den, sit by the computer and Google names and addresses until we were blue in the face, literally." She laughs.

"Did you find anyone?"

"Not a soul. Although I must admit, we did have a lot of fun searching."

Mali picks up her mug, finishes her coffee.

"I'm going to miss your mom," Elizabeth says.

"Me too." Mali clears a little space among the yellow rose petals and puts her empty mug back on the table. Then she turns to Elizabeth. "So what do you think made her obsess so about the past?"

"Her life passing her by? Wanting to make things right? You? Sometimes it's easier to dream backward than to imagine what the future holds. The past has a way of altering itself to suit us, if you get my meaning. In any case, I never had the heart to deny her those searches."

"You were such an incredible friend to her all these years."

"I told you. I loved your mother. And she was just as good to me. You better believe it."

Mali nods. She finds herself feeling jealous of Elizabeth's attachment to her mother. And like the outsider. As though she were the friend and Elizabeth, the daughter. Where does the blame lie for their relationship? Mali could easily fault her mother. After all, she was the mother, the beginner of it all—the chicken, not the egg. But perhaps something in Mali's nature has always made her put up barriers. Prevented her from an easiness she notes and envies in others. She looks around her—at the handwriting on the mismatched colored pages stacked on the table, the curled rose petals, and the box of photos from the coat closet—then settles her gaze back onto Elizabeth's face, more drawn and paler now than when she first arrived.

"You see this?" Mali points to the box. "It's crammed with old photos and papers."

"Maybe you'll find your answers in there."

"Mm. . . maybe."

They both look at the box.

"But tell me," Mali says, crossing her legs underneath her again. "Was she upset . . . or rather . . . did she ever mention to you or complain that I didn't come in to see her more regularly than I did?"

"Only to say that she knew how busy you were."

"And how she so appreciated you, right?"

"Well, yes."

"I must tell you; I'd come home to find messages on my answering machine, telling me to call and thank you for being there for her. I never understood why she couldn't have called me when she knew I'd be home. I have to admit I resented those calls. They made me feel like a rebellious teenager. Stupid, I guess. But, in any case, I'm sorry I never called you. I hope you know how much I've appreciated your always being there for her."

"Don't be silly. I told you. There's nothing, *nothing* to thank me for. It was always a two-way street with her. She was there for me as much, if not more, than I for her. It's the truth."

"I don't exactly believe . . ."

"Believe it. Your mother knew how to be a great friend, and I will truly miss her with all my heart."

Elizabeth looks around her slowly, seeming to take it all in and imprint everything forever in her thoughts. An expression of disbelief suddenly crosses her face, as though her sitting here, in her friend Eva's living room, without her, can't be her true reality. Her eyes close for a moment. When they open, she looks at Mali and smiles.

"I meant to tell you how lovely the service was. It truly captured her life. Everyone thought so."

"Thank you," Mali says and turns away. Inside herself, she shakes her head. No. She is embarrassed by the compliment. She'd said a few words at the funeral, then afterward regretted them. What she'd said was so inconsequential, so meaningless. A piece of fluff about their mother-daughter shopping at Bloomies. As though their relationship had been as simple as that.

"Well, you have your work cut out for you. I don't want to keep you."

"It's okay. I think I'll end up spending the night here. Aside from reading these letters, I'm trying to remember what my mother wanted me to keep—you know, for sentimental reasons. By the way, is there something of hers you'd like to have?"

"A small memento to remember her by would be great. Whenever you get around to it. No rush. But please, knock on my door if you need anything, or just want to talk."

Elizabeth gets up, leans over Mali, and plants a kiss on her cheek. Mali stands and follows her through the living room. They hug at the open door.

"Don't be a stranger," Elizabeth says, stepping into the hallway.

"I won't. And don't forget to tell me what you'd like of my mother's."

After she hears the elevator door slide shut with her mother's friend safely behind it, Mali slowly and quietly closes the apartment door.

Back on the couch, she pulls the box of photographs closer and begins to look through them. Something about the haphazard way they lie in the box, makes her think of layered rocks on ancient cliffs: the geologic history of the world melded together, layer upon primeval layer. But these pictures represent so many parts of her mother's history, her life remembered with random cuts through the years of the once young, then older, and finally aged and lined faces.

Here's one of her mother and grandmother. They're sitting together at a table. Her mother, a teenager of sixteen or seventeen, is pouring the tea, English style. It's summertime. They're outside. Her mother wears a tartan, short-sleeved blouse. Her hair is half up and half down, pouffed up in the front, as was the fashion in the mid-1940s. Her grandmother has on a white, collared shirt under an open jacket. One side of the collar is tucked in untidily, the other sticks out. Her hair is also pouffed up in the front, but Mali can't tell if her hair has been swept into a bun or cut short and combed back. Her grandmother looks rumpled, beaten, worn-out in this picture, as though these past frightening years of her life have etched themselves on her face: an indelible tattoo of horror and insanity. What also strikes Mali about this photograph is the expression of complete disbelief, almost disgust, in her grandmother's face, as if she has just said to Eva, "What the hell are you thinking, child?" And Eva, for her part, looks calm, her face almost expressionless, as she pours the tea. What has this teenage Eva told her mother? That she will marry Hirschel, a Jewish man eight years her senior and a refugee as well, but this one originally from Poland?

In the picture, there's a beautiful old, ivy-covered mansion behind them. Mali thinks this must be Selsdon Park, a place they used to frequent on the weekends when her mother was still married to her father and living in London.

But no. When she picks up another photo—this one, of two women smiling, with the same house in the background—and turns it over, the inscription on the back reads: *Eel Pie Island, 1944. To remind you of happy days in an unhappy time.*

CHAPTER 4

May 5, 2014

Just checking in—those first words when you call, my darling Mali—strike me as such a funny way to begin a conversation. They seem so strained, so business-like. But as we talk, your voice unwinds, your words soften, and you begin to open up. Not much is new on your end, you tell me. Both Julia and Steffi are doing fine, busy as usual with their work and their children. And of course, business could always be better, you say. I might describe a shirt I found on sale at Bloomingdale's, tell you the latest gossip about certain people in my building, or the new, good, and inexpensive restaurant on First Avenue, Elizabeth and I recently discovered. We'll have to try it for lunch the next time you come.

After this, our talk invariably turns to the news of the day: eighty people killed and one hundred twenty wounded in retaliation for the killing of Osama bin Laden in Pakistan; a march in the capital of Nigeria, calling for the release of schoolgirls abducted by the Boko Haram; Obama pressing for Israel to go back to her pre-1967 borders. The state of the world is not good.

Today, after we hang up, I decide to take your advice and stay in. It's rainy out and unusually cool for May. A perfect time for sorting and clearing out the drawers in my little desk, a job I've been meaning to tackle for quite some time. As always, CNN blares in the background. I'm quite a news fanatic, now that I've reached the ripe old age of eighty-seven. I remind myself of your father in the old days. And how ironic, I think, that just as he watched their fathers and grandfathers, I find myself drawn in anguish to this new generation of angry Egyptians gathering in the streets of Cairo. The only difference: dazzling Technicolor. The spilled blood is a brilliant red—no more shades of grey to tax the imagination.

With an eye to my own messy drawers, I know there is something I can do regarding *this,* and I begin. In the first drawer, I find a few colored photographs from a vacation trip David and I once took. God knows when or even where we were. Stashed behind the photos are a few loose checks, customized with my previous address from a bank that is no longer, and in the next drawer is the strongbox with my will and financial papers you are going to need when I am no longer. But in the third, I find a large manila envelope I don't recognize at first. I open it and pull out the sheets of lined paper nestled inside.

And then remember. I'd resorted to writing my life story for you.

I skim through my handwritten pages. Perhaps composed in fury or maybe only in haste, my rag-and-bone memories seem to dash across the lined paper, like sprinters in a race. David was dying then. I'd felt so alone and afraid.

What will I think of these memories now? What will you?

The mess in my drawers needs to wait for the time being.

I should turn off the TV, I say out loud to myself, as I move from my desk to the couch, the pages back in their manila envelope and clutched to my chest. But I can't bring myself to do it just yet. I'm stuck. Bombs explode on the screen. Refugees pour out of Syria by the thousands and find themselves held in makeshift camps in neighboring Turkey and Lebanon.

And here in New York City, the rain outside my window is heavy. Lightning streaks the sky, shimmering the river for a few seconds at a time. Thunder growls in the distance.

A reporter on the TV says the camps barely provide enough shelter from summer's heat or winter's cold—never mind basic hygiene, education for the young, or enough food for all. I wonder what will become of these refugees, their children, their children's children. More generations of underprivilege and hatred? I'm sickened. Squalor has a color too.

I switch off the TV. Settling on the couch, I wrap the blue, woolly throw around myself, put on my reading glasses, and empty the contents of the manila envelope into my lap. Everything seems to be coming back around. Or is it that nothing ever really goes away?

• • • • •

November 9, 1988

Mali, the other day, a review in the Arts Section of the *New York Times,* caught my attention. It was for an exhibit at the New York Public Library called, "Jews in Germany under One Thousand Years of Prussian Rule". Although the review of it was so-so, it sounded perfect to me, right up my alley. I thought of calling you to see if you'd come with me, but since I never know David's condition from one day to the next, planning is almost impossible. Besides, I was afraid you might worry about me and, as you so fondly like to call it, my deepening obsession with that morbid, depressing, ancient history.

I'm sure you must be aware that this day marks the fiftieth anniversary of Kristallnacht. Fifty years. I can hardly believe it. I was eleven then, even younger than your children, my grandchildren, are now.

I've been listening to, or I should say, I am riveted to the stories the Holocaust Survivors have been telling on the radio. Perhaps you've heard one or two. I listen to them all. So many, sounding too close to my own.

And I find myself returning to my childhood and wanting, somehow, to tell you all about it. From the beginning. For you to know. Then always to remember. And pass down. Never to be forgotten.

So, here I am, my dearest, darling Mali, fifty years later and back at my desk, a chronicler once again, just like the writer I aspired to be when I was a young girl growing up in Berlin.

In agreement with my parents, or most probably because of them, I always thought of Hitler's rise as an aberration of history; a quick and violent thunderstorm on a bright summer's day. But after walking through the exhibit, which I managed to get to this afternoon, I must admit I'm totally turned around.

Although I searched, I couldn't find any gaps in this one-thousand-year history, any signs—on the makeshift walls zigzagging along the center of the library's exhibit room—to say that the hatred was isolated, or that it happened a long time ago, or that it only materialized when Hitler came to power. Instead, I found those black-and-white montages, as they wound their way through the room, one after another, a revelation of constant uncertainty and dread.

In the beginning, printed proclamations on parchment paper tacked onto tree trunks in village squares and on castle doors, announced the favor, the disfavor, the citizenship, the expulsion, and then the favor again of the Jews. It seemed to me to run in five-, ten-, or twenty-year cycles—as repetitive and learned as the tilling and the sowing and the laying fallow of the soil on the land they were prohibited from owning. But Jews came back into favor when kings and emperors needed money to fight far-off wars. And worst of all, they became the usurers and tax collectors because Christians were forbidden to lend money.

What was it about them, Jews like me, who invited so much hatred and hardship into their lives?—I kept wondering, as I examined the old-fashioned, fancy lettering printed on those proclamations.

By the time I reached the twentieth century, Jewish life was teeming in the German cities. But photo enlargements from the 1920s showed rioting in the streets of Berlin and anti-Semitic posters displayed all over town.

As I approached the section on the 1930s, and the closer I came to my own time, my own memories, a heaviness began to wash over me—as if my body had become a receptacle for all the losses and tears of my generation and of those before me. I used to believe the present automatically rolled itself into the future, a runaway train to watch from afar as it made its twists and turns. I never understood, when I was married to your father, how he could read three or four newspapers every day and watch so many news programs on television. And I wondered, did he honestly think he could single-handedly change the future or protect us from it? I can still see him as he was then: eyeglasses perched low on his nose, a steaming lemon tea on the glass-topped table in front of him, his legs crossed, his arms folded at his chest, and his intensity worn like the tightly knitted lines embedded in his face.

Perhaps humankind has become more sophisticated over the years, but I don't believe we have really changed. Given certain sets of events and situations, this history will probably happen again and again. But tell me, how do I help stop that runaway train?

Here, before me, an all too familiar scene. A boycott lodged against Jewish businesses. In the background of the blown-up photograph is a large Star of David whitewashed onto a shop window, and in the foreground, uniformed stormtroopers stand guard in the street, handing out anti-Semitic pamphlets to the curious passersby. From what I could see, not many people tried to cross their line, break their boycott.

Mesmerized, I stood looking at this photo for a long time. I peered into the faces of the German crowd; the faces that looked so ordinary. What were they thinking? Had storm troopers been stationed in front of my father's boycotted car dealership on Kommandantenstrasse, prohibiting his fellow Berliners from buying the latest model Fiats from him? I was only six in 1933. If my parents worried for our future then, I never knew.

Next was a blowup of the headline on the front page of Streicher's anti-Semitic weekly, *Der Sturmer*. "Jewish murder plot against non-Jewish humanity revealed." Underneath the headline, a cartoon pictured two repulsive-looking Jewish men with exaggerated hooked noses. One was plunging a knife into the bodies of pretty blond children, while the other was holding a bowl beneath them to catch their blood. This old superstition, from the early thirteenth century, was begun by a pious pope who believed the Jews needed the blood of small Christian children to make their matzo at Passover time.

Then there was the nineteenth century Prussian historian, Heinrich von Treitschke who said: "The Jews are our misfortune."

Can you imagine?

Now I came face-to-face with a picture of Berlin's Great Synagogue engulfed in flames. Firemen on the scene turn their backs to the fire, pointing their hoses, instead, to the cool, untouched buildings next door. This was Kristallnacht. Fifty years ago today.

Another new edict: Any debt owed to Jews was no longer considered a legal transaction. Two SS thugs hadn't paid my father for a jeep they'd bought at his *Motorwagen Vertrieb*. On November 10, 1938, they arrested him, and sent him to Sachsenhausen, a concentration camp, about thirty kilometers outside of Berlin. Now those thugs owed him nothing.

I didn't have to read a thing about the next photographs, the ones that showed cattle cars, human faces staring out between cracks in the walls, deadened eyes sunk into gaunt faces, sick, skeletal bodies, tall fences of electrified barbed wire, long-coated, black-booted machine gunners, and the high towers they watched from, as if the compound were the stage, the killing its slow, cruel play.

The exhibit's very last photo showed an almost life-sized, black-and-white photograph of two half-naked men. According to the printed message on the wall, the liberator-photographer had brought them to this dusty patch of road, where they posed for him in front of a tall pile of corpses, a mountain of skin and bones. As if to defy that mountain—their skinny arms wrapped around each other, their matchstick legs hardly big or strong enough to keep them standing—proud, wide, invincible smiles of camaraderie stretched their sunken, paper-thin cheeks.

I wanted to go back around the exhibit, look at everything one more time. I wanted desperately to change the thought that these pictures before me, these grainy black-and-white blowups were somehow a culmination, an inevitability of those one thousand years of Jewish life in Germany. How was it I hadn't realized this before? What had I missed in the stories I'd been told? What had my parents missed in their telling? And then, if this history, these one thousand years, pointed to this as its inevitability, I can't help but wonder if it excused the end in some respect.

On my way home, the two Auschwitz survivors came back to me. Was there a straight line from that earliest time, one thousand years ago, to this? Was it, I wondered, like some ancient cable buried deep beneath the debris of history and only unearthed after it was too late? Surely, this exhibit wanted me to think that Hitler hadn't just fallen from the sky—a nasty aberration of history—but that we'd all had these one thousand years of warning.

That night I dreamt of Stella.

CHAPTER 5

October 26, 2014

Mali lays her head back against the couch, closes her eyes. She has to stop reading. She needs a break. Putting her mother's pages aside, she stands, looks around the living room—for at least the hundredth time today—and leaves her place to go and sit in the armchair directly across from the couch. A change in focus might help, she thinks, as she sinks into the chair, stretching her legs far out and folding her arms in a tight knot over her chest. From this vantage point, she can see the whole living room. What else is hidden here? What would these walls tell her if they could talk? Perhaps if her mother had been brave enough to let her know about the exhibit, had planned a date, suggested a time, for them to go—even if it were tentative and subject to change at the last minute because of David— and view it together, and to know that afterward, they'd have walked away from it, and would have talked of luck and terror in the same sentence— for without the one, there would've been, without a doubt, the other. Perhaps their talk might have broadened to include her mother's young anguish at that time—the uncertainties and, later, the changes and disruptions she'd had to live with and overcome.

And wouldn't the words Mali spoke at her mother's funeral have had more depth, more meaning?

This change in focus isn't working, she decides, and gets up. She goes back to the couch and stands there, looking at her mother's pages.

All the things her mother had thought of and written about and collected through the years from those far-off places that compete for space here on these walls, tables, and shelves in this apartment, Mali is the one now, the only one, left to sort through it all—to decide what to keep, what to give away. "But tell me," she says aloud, pointing a finger to each of the overcrowded walls, "what am I supposed to do with all your memories now?"

CHAPTER 6

November 9, 1988

Beautiful, graceful Stella. We met in the autumn of 1936, when we were nine years old. She had been transferred to our school from one of the local Catholic schools recently closed by the Nazis. We took to each other instantly and became the best of friends, even though quite opposite in almost every way. Stella had long, blond, silky hair that swung across her back as she walked. Mine, on the other hand, a mousy brown, wavy, and cut short, would surely stay in place, once brushed, in the windiest of hurricanes. Stella excelled at school, never less than ninety-five on any of her tests. I, by contrast, always had to face an angry, disappointed father with my report cards. Good marks in school, she'd say to cheer me up, belonged to the boring, the unexceptional. But to have flair like yours, Stella said to me, was to be special. To tell you the truth, I never understood what flair she thought I had. Stella was the special one. She had the knack for finding the good in everything, even when there was truly nothing good to be found.

I'm trying to regain my way back to our good times. I see the heavy brown leather satchels strapped to our backs, the blue ink stains from our dip pens that won't wash off our index and third fingers, our disheveled hair, and our grey knee socks inched down our shins and bunched up around our ankles. We often walked home from school together. We giggled a lot. Some days we stopped at the bakery up the street from school for a snack. They baked delicious butter cookies, and Stella, I remember, loved anything with chocolate.

But as the days and weeks drew on, our school days became more intolerable. Ostracized by friends, made fun of by teachers, we were eventually excluded from all activities in and out of school. Stella believed that as long as we had each other, we would be safe.

She was dead wrong.

Stella became the Jew-lover and I, the dirty Jew. We were bullied mercilessly. I began to believe our tormentors and imagined myself a form of lower life, the disgusting vermin they said I was. Every afternoon when I got home from school, I rushed to the bathroom. Behind the locked door, I'd rip off my blouse and stick my nose under each arm. Then, sitting on the toilet, I'd bend my head down as far as I could to catch the smell, that *Jew girl smell* they said I stank of.

I never told Oma about my troubles at school. I couldn't bear to hear the sigh, the glazed look in her eyes, the slump of her shoulders, as she tried to explain what she couldn't understand herself. Then tears would begin to fill her eyes. You learn quickly, as a child, when your parents prove just as vulnerable and helpless as you. Besides, I understood their preoccupation with the boycotts on Opa's business, their keeping up with the latest day-to-day prohibitions against us Jews. In comparison, my problems seemed insignificant.

As I write this for you, Mali, I find myself using Oma and Opa to talk about my parents. It's how I always spoke of them to you, how you spoke of them to me.

In 1938, after I turned eleven, a new law barred all Jewish children from attending German schools. Special Jewish schools were set up. I was sent to the Lesslerschule near to where we lived in the Grunewald. So relieved, at first, to be away from the bullying, I hadn't even thought of my separation from Stella. Then, a few days later, we bumped into each other outside the bakery. I began to cry. Don't, she said, a sharpness to her voice I didn't recognize. It's easier without you. At least I'm no longer the Jew-lover. And with that, she walked past me. Stunned, I stood watching her golden, silky hair sway from side to side across her back, until she disappeared from my sight. I never got to ask how she was. Nor the chance to tell her I missed her. Or to find out if she still believed in the teaching of her God. A teaching, I once told her, I could never accept. An eye for an eye always seemed more just or sensible to me than turning the other cheek. But, always so good at heart, she let those horrible words splash off her back. Don't think about them, she'd say, they're only words.

That chance meeting was the last I ever saw of Stella. I only learned what had happened to her when I ran into the lady from the bakery, one day shortly before we were to leave Germany.

There had been lots of snow that winter. As usual, Stella was walking home from school by herself. A group of boys suddenly surrounded her. They began shouting out names, obscenities. Nothing she hadn't heard before. Even now, so many years later, I can imagine her on that slippery snow-covered street—her long legs in woolly stockings, quick footsteps in thick, black lace-up boots, her head bent against the biting wind—and her golden, silky hair dangling beneath her brown knitted cap, long and straight and dancing across her back.

What slanders did the boys shout at her before they got the idea to hurl snowballs? Was it in the name of the Führer, or in the name of *Deutschland über Alles* that they began to pack the snow in their gloved hands tighter and tighter until the balls became hard as rocks? Was it in the name of everything they believed good in Germany that they stoned her with them? Stoned her until all grace had gone from her body and she lay discarded in the snow, like a broken doll. By the time she was found, the lady from the bakery said, her angel face had been so badly bashed black, blue, and bloody, she was hardly recognizable. How could she have kept walking, ignoring them?—I wanted to know. Had she dutifully turned the other cheek the way her God had instructed her to do?

I can't help but wonder, as she lay there helpless, if her trust and beliefs had begun to cool and clot in her heart as her blood had cooled and clotted in the snow. What if I'd been with her that afternoon? Was she killed for being a Catholic or for being a Jew-lover? Or was she simply on the wrong side of the street at the wrong time, the boys revved up from some Hitler Youth meeting they had just returned from, inhumanity and sadism the prime order of the day? It's horrifying to think of their twisted minds, their behavior so encouraged. Can't we teach kindness and acceptance of our differences instead? Or are we humans just more monstrous than angelic?

I didn't remember much of my dream about Stella. Only that I awoke the next morning with an image behind my still-closed eyes of her walking away from me, her blond, silky hair, dancing from side to side across her back.

CHAPTER 7

October 26, 2014

Mali pulls off her eyeglasses, lets out a long, loud sigh, and sets aside the pile of her mother's letters, putting them next to her on the couch. She pinches the inside corners of her eyes, gets up with a groan, and stands by the window. She peers down at the street again, for just a moment, then turns back to inspect the living room. It seems unfair that her mother left all this for her to discover when she can only talk back to the picture-filled walls of the apartment.

"Goddamn," she says aloud, and stares at the abstract painting on the wall just outside the kitchen. Something about this painting—the rough and thickly brushed orange and yellow circles—has always struck her as a picture of a mother and child. Perhaps it's just the warmth of the colors. Or the circles' different sizes. But mainly, she thinks, it's because the larger one sits a little higher up on the canvas and even though the smaller circle hangs below it, it slightly overlaps the lowest portion of the larger one as if to show there's still a connection between the two. To Mali they even appear to bend into each other. Being a mother isn't easy, she knows. But at least she has always been there for her girls. That, in itself, must stand for something.

At the kitchen sink, she fills the kettle again, then puts it on the stove. On the countertop, she lines up the one-cupper Melitta filter, the coffee mug her children had once bought for their grandmother, and the can of Maxwell House.

Waiting for the water to boil, she first leans against the sink, then goes around the small kitchen, opening and closing the few cabinets. A calendar hangs on the side of one. Her mother always marked the date boxes to remind her of when her bills were due. Doctor and dentist appointments too. Tomorrow, the twenty-seventh, at 10 a.m., she's due at the lab for a blood test.

God, her mother's spirit permeates the very air she's breathing. This atmosphere is all around her, and Mali seems to keep bumping into it with every movement she makes in this tiny room.

The kettle's whistle startles her out of her reverie. She pours the boiling water over the coffee and waits for it to drip into the mug. A sort of numbness is spreading inside her chest, the air has become too heavy to breathe. She tears off a sheet from the roll of paper towels and brings it along with her mug, into the living room. She folds the paper towel in half, puts it on the wood table, and after taking a sip, places the mug on top of it, then leaning back on the couch, closes her eyes, confusion crowding her sight. And pictures her mother in the chair opposite.

Wearing her jeans and favorite man's collared shirt, her legs are crossed, the top one swinging back and forth ever so slightly. Size-ten socked feet are clad in clean white sneakers. An unlit cigarette is clamped tight between her front teeth, and, with her eyes screwed up in concentration, she searches around the vase of dying, yellow roses for the table lighter. "So, my darling," she says, bringing the flame to her cigarette. "What can I get you?"

Mali glances at the stack of letters piled on the pillow next to her. She shakes her head, then looks up and away. Her eyes are glazed. Everything is blurred. Even the phantom of her mother that she's conjured up.

Of course, she knew this day would come, but now that it's here, she can scarcely believe it. Even as a child, when she missed her mother, until it hurt more than she could bear, she always knew, deep in her heart, that she would see her again, feel her arms tight around her, hear her voice. But now... now there were only her things—the paintings, photographs, knickknacks—to keep her close. And these written words. Is her mother right, she wants to ask, can she really be that difficult to talk to?

She reaches again for the letters sitting next to her. Picks them up, fans through their pages. Then notices each letter has its own date and understands that her mother must have purposefully arranged the way they were placed in the manila envelope; not necessarily in chronological order, but back and forth in time, as her memories dictated.

CHAPTER 8

May 5, 2014

My Darling Mali,

As I read through these pages, the many bittersweet memories I'd long forgotten and now remember, so overwhelm me I can almost taste them. As I've written, 1988 was a very difficult year. I'm sure I must've burdened you with my worries about David and how I would manage after he died. I remember calling you every so often to ask you to come into the city to meet me for lunch. I tried not to call you too often. Hopefully, I succeeded in that, at least.

The rain has stopped, but a thick grey mist hangs over the river. I put on a record, a Chopin piano sonata, turn on my little lamps in the living room to brighten things up a bit, make myself a cup of mint tea, and go back to reading my old chronicles.

. . . . .

November 12, 1988

My routine used to be that I'd sit in the armchair—the one I'd dragged from the living room to our bedroom and parked next to David's side of the bed—and skim the *Times* for easy articles to read to myself or out loud to David. For the times he dozed off, I had a stack of the latest Holocaust memoirs to keep me busy. I always think I might recognize a schoolmate from the Lesslerschule in Berlin. What an experience that would be.

But I soon became restless and my back ached from the steady sitting. I needed something physical to do, something to relieve this pent-up energy knocking at my insides. Then, a few days ago, as we sat together surveying the bedroom that has become his only place of residence these days, David gave me a brilliant idea. I was making small talk, or most probably complaining about messy closets and the lack of space for putting things away. He suggested I keep him company and work at reorganizing our bedroom at the same time.

Now my new morning routine, after my coffee and a casual glance at the paper, is to clear out anything unused or unworn in the last year or so. It's quite cathartic, I must say. We laugh at the clothes I find buried, the old fashions we find weird today. The wigs I used to wear on days when my hair was an impossible mess. I try on dresses that are at least twenty years old, dresses I've loved so much I couldn't have given them away. Of course, they barely fit these days and besides, are much too short for me at my age.

"Tell me, what's the point of keeping them?" he says.

"Maybe one day I'll be thin enough to wear them again." I look away to hide my smile.

"But not young enough." He chuckles. At least he can still do that.

Yesterday, I found the fake ugly buck teeth he bought one Halloween. We were going to a party. He wore one of my curly-haired wigs, which looked more Afro than curly and went dressed as an old hillbilly woman. And I? I think I must've been an old hillbilly man. Not very creative, I know. But then I've never been a fan of fancy-dress parties. Today is different though. While he snoozes, I will pop the crazy teeth into my mouth, put on the Afro wig, and sit in my chair and wait for him to wake.

Thank God the elections are over. Dukakis and Bush preened like two peacocks in full regalia. I tried to keep up with the issues, but soon became bored, and then annoyed at how much money and press the candidates are afforded. The unfortunate part is that nothing momentous seems to change anyway. Before David got sick, we would spend whole evenings, martinis in hand, discussing the issues. David had been in business. For him, everything had a cost attached to it. I was on the side of the bleeding hearts. He loved to argue with me, to show me how wrong I was, how our government would never have the money to pay for the programs I wanted for the refugees, the poor, the disadvantaged. In the end, when he couldn't win me over, he'd just throw up his hands, plant a kiss on my nose, and tell me how foolish I was. Why, he wanted to know, would I want to give away the store? No one had done that for us when we first arrived here. Maybe, I reasoned, it's because I lived through those times and remember how hard we all had it.

In England, I worked diligently at trying to fit in with the English girls, to push myself beyond my refugee-girl-ness.

Nowadays, it's the exact opposite.

As with a moth to light, I'm drawn to the films and books and stories relating to the Holocaust. Although, I must admit, it's tough keeping up with the many articles in the newspapers and magazines commemorating the fiftieth anniversary of Kristallnacht. It was Hitler's trial balloon, they say. Was my life worth no more than a few puffs of air? And how would I have turned out if there had been no Hitler? I often think about that. I know it makes no sense. I mean, what's the point? Can I go on complaining about my inadequacies forever? Blame Hitler and the Germans for my lack of schooling? My insecurities? My too-early marriage? My divorce? I could go on with the litany. But I won't. I can hear you, Mali, breathe a sigh of relief. I do have to take full responsibility for what I've done, or not done, in my life. I understand that.

But I must tell you how I often daydream, nowadays, about our flat in the Grunewald district of Berlin. I think of my little bedroom there and of the makeshift desk just under the window, where I could sit and stare out at the garden for hours at a time. It wasn't a particularly well-kept garden. But I liked it better for its unruliness. It felt more natural, less interfered with. Aside from the bowl of colored pencils on my desk, I had a set of watercolor paints. Some of the colors were almost completely worn away, the metal of the box showing through. Use the paints sparingly, Oma had warned. She had no idea if she'd even be able to buy me more. A notebook lay on my desk as well, its pages filled with my made-up stories and poems, all written very neatly on the lined paper. I remember I'd wanted to be a writer when I grew up, figuring I wouldn't have to be good at math to make up stories.

How differently my life has turned out.

Elizabeth is coming to David-sit for me this afternoon. I need a couple of hours to run errands. She's such a good friend, I don't know what I'd do without her. It's true, I can call you, but she's right here in my building, and you have your work.

While I'm out, I leave the errands until the very last possible moment. I just want to walk and walk—it doesn't matter to where. I want to lose myself. Can you understand that?

The sun dazzles, and the sky, a brilliant blue, is the color of winter's crisp and clear air. My cheeks prickle, my eyes tear with the gusts of wind. After being cooped up in the apartment for the last few days, I feel the air sweep through my body, brushing away so much of the meaningless drivel crowding my thoughts.

By the time I return home, I am alive again. David seems happier too, entertained by Elizabeth's zany stories, which we're never quite sure are as real as she claims. I make a pot of coffee, pile the butter cookies I've just bought at Grace's Market, onto a plate and bring them all on a tray into the bedroom. We prop David up with three extra pillows behind his back and his head. Elizabeth and I sit at the small wicker table by the window. For a little while, the coffee, the cookies, and the conversation and laughter make me forget how ill David is.

After Elizabeth goes home, David falls asleep and I'm back at his bedside, the buckteeth in my mouth, the Afro wig on my head. I read, or I should say, scan the paper. The economy is slumping. Global warming is on the rise. A mother, Rachel Ginsberg, and her three children are burned alive on a bus in the West Bank—a terrorist attack. Her husband, their father—I just can't imagine his terrible grief. Israeli planes attack Palestinians in Lebanon. Why are people so destructive to one another? When will the world stop hating the Jews? Will there ever be a heartwarming story on page one—an account to lift our spirits, remind us of our humanity, if humanity really is the good part of us? I turn to the Arts Section, hopefully less depressing. A play by Emily Mann is reviewed. The play, *Annulla, an Autobiography*, is about a Holocaust survivor. It opened in Brooklyn on the fiftieth anniversary of Kristallnacht. Funny, I can't tell if the reviewer thought it good, or not. Too bad I can't go.

"You trying to cheer me up?" David says, looking at me now in my wig and teeth.

"Or perhaps myself," I say. "How do you feel?"

He grunts in response. I take out the teeth, pull off the wig, and run my fingers through my hair, reminding myself that I need a dye job and a cut in the worst way.

"Anything new?" He points to the paper.

"Only the usual suspects, a warming world, a cooling economy, and a terrible, burning terrorism in so many places."

"Well, at least I won't miss much . . ."

"Don't," I say and put a finger to his lips to silence him. "I read a cute story in the *Metropolitan Diary.* Do you want to hear it?"

He nods and closes his eyes.

I read him the story about a middle-aged couple crossing Second Avenue on their way to JG Melon's for cheeseburgers. It's an unusually warm day for November. Their coats are unbuttoned and flapping against their sides as they walk hand in hand. Just at the midpoint of crossing the avenue, an elderly woman coming toward them smiles and says, "You two look great, you look so happy." The man and the woman, taken by complete surprise, smile back at her, thank her, and walk on, a new spring in their step as they cross the rest of the avenue, reach the curb, and go through the door of the restaurant, each thinking a treat of an extra topping or two on their burgers would certainly be in order after such a compliment.

"The way we were." David's voice is flat, his eyes still closed.

"I've been going through my memorabilia box," I say, trying to keep the tears out of my eyes and David engaged. "You know, the one I keep behind the coats in the closet. And look what I found."

I hold up a paper scroll with a tattered yellow ribbon tied around it. David opens his eyes for a moment. I untie the ribbon and smooth out the paper.

"It's a verse of English poetry," I say. "I must've copied it from a book. There's no date, but looking at the handwriting, still so very German-like, it must go back to early days when I was first evacuated from London and attending that miserable school in Bedford. Look at those beautiful yellow roses I painted to go around the words. The verse is very short, only four lines. Shall I read it to you?"

David touches my arm, nods, and closes his eyes again.

I read: "*The kiss of the sun for pardon, / The song of the birds for mirth, -- / One is nearer God's heart in a garden / Than anywhere else on earth.*"

"Pfff!" David exhales loudly. "You don't actually believe in all that God crap, do you?"

"Not God exactly, no. But I remember how the poem always reminded me of the view from my bedroom window in Berlin. It seemed to connect me to everything I'd had and lost—if that makes any sense."

David reaches out for me again. "I'm sorry."

I've made him feel sad. Or is it that I've just made myself feel sad?

"You'll never believe what else I came across," I say, laughing. "It's Hirschel's old Will and Testament from 1956. It was in the same box."

David opens one eye and looks at me.

"I don't know why I still have it," I say. "It was a nasty will. He wanted to make sure I got absolutely nothing. Not that there was that much to get, mind you."

"Ancient history," David says, his arm lifting in an attempt at a wave of dismissal.

"Yes, ancient history."

But then I think of all those archaeological digs where the bones and fossils and shards of pottery, long buried deep in the earth, have charted their course upward to the muddy surface of yet another common era. How long does it take to uncover layer upon archaic layer until we're all the way back to the beginning? And what would we find there, at that very beginning?

CHAPTER 9

October 26, 2014

Curious, Mali goes in search of her father's old will. She wonders how it ended up in her mother's possession. He must have given it to her. A joke, maybe. And she imagines him laughing, the will not making a bit of difference to either one anymore. She looks through the cardboard box. She doesn't find the will but instead sees a mess of photographs. She scoops up what she can hold and lays them on the table next to the yellow petals. Here's one of Mali and her mother. Thanksgiving 1988. Her mother was on an emotional roller coaster, frantic with worry one day and in complete denial the next. But looking at the photo, you'd never know it. Mali and her mother are standing, arm in arm, in this living room. How young they both looked: Mali's dark hair an unruly, curly mess, her mother's, blonde and coiffed. Her mother had tried so hard, then, to be optimistic about David. She believed his strength and his will to live would prevail and get him through. Just as those surviving voices she'd heard on the radio did. *Remember. Never forget.*

But David was dying. And the time, like a thick and heavy protective coating that had hung between her childhood years under Hitler and her aging life here in New York, was in terrible danger of thinning out.

Mali paces the floor in front of her mother's bookshelves. That year—1988—proved to be a difficult year for her too. She stares at the books as if they can organize the chronology of events, jumbled and shapeshifting in her mind, a kaleidoscope of colored designs.

She can see the synagogue up the street from her house. The fifty-year Kristallnacht commemoration. Her daughters, Julia and Steffi, teenagers then, comfortable among their noisy, giggling peers. And she and Michael, harboring a strange sense of disconnection from this American interpretation of what their families had been through.

She wanted to yell out: Both your great-grandfathers were sent to concentration camp on this day fifty years ago, their freedom snatched away, their lives, a living, walking nightmare. If they hadn't gotten out . . .

But great-grandfathers . . . sounded so far away. Like trying to look behind the eyes on a face in an old, worn photograph. Two men they'd never met. What could this generation carry forward if all they knew were shadows and ghosts?

The synagogue up the street was a modern building. The sanctuary had floor-to-ceiling windows along two of its sides. Mali had never cared for it. Too modern, she always thought. Too cold and antiseptic for a place of worship. They hadn't been members since Steffi's bat mitzvah the year before.

The rabbi began the service. He talked, it seemed to Mali, without passion, without conviction. He told his congregants—from the safety, the comfort of this small suburban town—that their children had put this service together.

One by one, two by two, the children made their way up to the *bima*, lit a candle, and recited words from a poem, a memory, or a story someone else had written. Totally uninspired, the children in the audience talked and giggled among themselves, her children included. Mali felt embarrassed.

The last child to light a candle introduced a small elderly woman in a black pantsuit with a black beret over her short curly grey hair. I'm a Holocaust survivor, she said, beginning her story. I was originally from Essen, Germany, and I'd just turned fifteen the week before Kristallnacht.

The voice, the accent with the rolled *r*'s, the clipped way of speaking, sounded so familiar to Mali. It was as though this woman were a member of her own family, her words, and sighs, all too recognizable. Mali listened and tried to imagine the uniformed men in black boots, pushing their way into her house—her place of security, safety—and forcing their way across the physical boundary that protected her from the outside world.

In bed, later that night, she'd lain awake for a long time. She'd listened to the rain drum on an empty flowerpot outside her bedroom window, the radiator's knocking as the heat came up. Her thoughts wouldn't stop; they whirred around in her mind like wet clothes thudding in a spin dryer. What was the lesson to impart from this? To be guarded, protective, prepared for the inevitability? After all, history showed them that time after time, man's thirst for scapegoating would never be fully quenched. It would happen again . . . and again. But even as she thought of the odds, she couldn't quite grasp them. She couldn't truly put herself in her Oma's place; her own imagination stopped dead. It wouldn't, it couldn't make the leap.

As Mali scans her mother's bookshelves for Philip's memoir, she notices in the small space on the floor, between the couch and the bookshelves, a few paperbacks stacked up in a pile, as though in hiding. She lifts them out. Are these the books—*Crystal Night; Writing and the Holocaust; Topography of Terror; The Night Trilogy;* and *The Last Jews in Berlin*—her mother had devoured when David was so sick? When commemorations for the fiftieth anniversary of Kristallnacht were broadcast on the radio, with stories told by voices all too familiar sounding to ignore? Mali brings the books to where she's been sitting and puts them on the table next to the roses. Why didn't she know, then, how obsessive her mother was becoming? Did her mother think Mali wouldn't understand her pining for that other life, so easily undercut, stolen, appropriated, as though they who'd lived it were no more? Or was it simply an issue of not wanting to be burdensome?

CHAPTER 10

November 12, 1988

David is back to sleep again, and I'm at my little writing desk to continue where I left off. My writing papers are strewn on the floor, all around me. I have to admit, I'm a slow writer. I know what it is I want to tell you, my darling, but I agonize over how. And I must say, trying to organize my life in retrospect when it feels as though my memories have come up to the surface in a random muddle—just like those layers of bones and fossils and shards of pottery from ancient times—is much more difficult than I would have thought before I started. In any case, I find myself wandering back through those layers, the archaeologist of memory, digging deep into the labyrinths of my mind. I hope you will excuse that my stories may not be in perfect chronological order. I've discovered my memory is not so trustworthy.

·   ·   ·   ·   ·

You remember Stella, the Catholic girl I'd been in school with. Well, I had noticed my life changing in many other ways then too. In 1935, when I was eight years old, the world as I had lived it was disappearing day by day. My nanny had to be let go. She'd been with us since I was a baby. I remember how we'd both cried. She begged Opa to let her stay. She'd work for nothing if he couldn't afford to pay her. It wasn't the money, he said. The new law prohibited German women under the age of forty-five to work for a Jewish family. This devastated my poor nanny. We were her family, she had argued with Opa. Nothing doing. It was the law, he argued back. And provided we obeyed it, no matter how crazy, he felt positive that eventually, *eventually*, our lives would resume some semblance of normalcy. In the end, though, we had to move too, from our large apartment on the Prinzregentenstrasse in the Wilmersdorf section of Berlin, to a much smaller one on the Hagenstrasse in the Grunewald.

I remember liking my new room. It had a shelf that housed my collection of dolls from all nations and another one for the books I was supposed to be reading. Besides the box of paints and the glass bowl of colored pencils, my makeshift desk, which had been our old kitchen table, also held a globe of the world, my notebook of lined paper, and a large drawing pad. As I've told you, I was a very bad student at school, but I used to love to draw pictures and write stories.

By Kristallnacht, hardly any teachers remained in our Jewish school, and every day fewer and fewer children showed up. They were the lucky ones. After Kristallnacht, our school closed permanently. Once back home from Sachsenhausen, my father tried tutoring me himself. I still remember his geography lessons. He'd come into my room, make a beeline for my desk, pick up the globe of the world, and spin it on its axis. When it stopped, he'd point to an area and quiz me—continent, country, city? Obsessed with this game of geography, he would tell me a little about each of the places on the globe facing us after the spinning had stopped. It was like a game of roulette: place your bets, countries please. I didn't realize he was preparing me for our future. Who knew which countries would issue us visas? It was all a crapshoot. We could have ended up in cities at the other end of the world, such as Kingston, Buenos Aires, or Shanghai. And in any of those cities we would have been lucky, very lucky indeed.

At around this same time, I had become more aware of the Gestapo, a word I found synonymous with the darkened, closed looks I began to see in the faces of the people I knew.

And while our parents' conversations grew more and more frantic with worries as to how to get us out of Germany, my best friend, Marion, and I talked about emigration as though planning for a holiday abroad. We found our parents' huddling around the radio behind shuttered windows and drawn drapes—desperate for any news from the outside world— and later their whispered conversations with each other, very exciting. It was like living inside a spy thriller.

Until October 6, 1938.

On that day, the Polish government decided that in twenty-five days, it would revoke all Polish passports whose bearers had lived abroad for more than five years. Marion's father, Wolfe, had emigrated from Poland just after World War One. He'd come to Berlin, where he met Lily, Marion's mother, at a Jewish Youth Group sporting event. They had fallen in love and married, much against the wishes of Lily's parents, who came from a well-to-do family and, although Jewish too, looked down on Wolfe, the poor Jewish immigrant boy from Eastern Europe. Lily's parents considered themselves even more German than the Germans themselves. Anyway, Lily and Wolfe settled in Berlin. I don't know how our parents met each other—perhaps when Marion and I were babies in the carriage. I imagine your Oma and Opa out for a stroll one day when a smile of recognition came from the couple across the road, also pushing a baby carriage.

Oma had never met Lily's parents but detested them all the same. She'd been furious that they never helped Lily out with a little extra cash from time to time. Sadly, or perhaps ironically, their arrogance would become as useless a currency as their son-in-law's revoked Polish passport; ultimately, they could trade neither their Jewish money nor their feelings of German superiority for their Jewish lives.

On October 27, 1938, after some back and forth between Germany and Poland, regarding the fifteen thousand or so stateless Jews living in Germany, the Germans decided not to wait for the 31st cut-off date, but to expel them all within forty-eight hours. They deported Wolfe, leaving Lily and Marion alone in Berlin.

Marion relived the day her father was picked up and repeated the sequence of events for me, over and over again. It was on a Thursday, I remember, an ordinary, if unusually freezing cold October day.

She told me that her father had just come home from the Jewish Center. The place was packed, he'd said to Lily and Marion, kissing their warm cheeks hello. You wouldn't believe the pandemonium, he'd said, tipping a spoon into the pot of vegetable soup bubbling away on the stove. So many frightened people, he added, slurping a spoonful of broth into his mouth. He shook his head, put the spoon into the sink, left the kitchen, and went to the bathroom.

A loud banging at the door startled Lily and Marion. Marion ran down the hall. She thought her mother had invited my parents and me for dinner and forgotten to say. She only just got the lock unlatched when two men from the Gestapo pushed it open and barged past her, shouting for her father. She stood by the open door, motionless, as if playing a silly game of Statues, and watched the telephone wires being pulled from the wall. Lily came rushing out of the kitchen, her hands over her opened mouth, her face crumpled and grey. Her body looked so fragile, Marion said.

Then in a flash a brilliant idea came to her. And before she'd even had the chance to think it through, she found herself leading those men, their shined black boots stomping heavily behind her, along the darkened hallway to the back door—the one that opens to the garden behind their apartment—thinking she could get them to leave before they found her father.

At first, they followed her, laughing and joking with each other, knocking pictures off the walls, and opening and slamming shut doors as they went. But suddenly a cone of light spread out into the hall, and she heard her father's voice rise above the din of boots and laughter. The men turned back. Her father stood at the opened bathroom door, the top buttons of his shirt undone, suspenders off his shoulders and loose by his sides. The men lunged for him. Each grabbed an arm. Her father struggled against his captors, kicking out his legs, waving his arms, shouting out curses. Lily began to plead with the men. Then one of them, anxious to shut him up, reached over the sink, snatched the porcelain toothbrush holder from the shelf above, and hit Wolfe over the head with it. A loud clatter rang out as it crashed into the sink in shiny broken bits. For a few seconds, an eerie stillness prevailed. Then Marion became aware of her mother's stifled whimpering as the men dragged off her father, limp and bleeding and barely held up between them.

Lily and Marion rushed to the window. A truck waited outside. "It's the deportation," Lily said. "They're going to send all the Polish Jews to no-man's-land."

Marion ran from the apartment. She knocked on her neighbor's door, where the kind lady who always brought them her home baked

Pfefferkuchen lived. No answer. She could hear the radio playing behind the closed door. She knocked again. Still no answer. She began to bang on the door, yelling for her to open up, to please help. Still no answer. She ran up the next flight of stairs to another neighbor. Again no answer. Marion said she was so frantic, she raced to the top floor, where the crazy lady lived. We called her the crazy lady because she dressed in long flowery skirts and fringed shawls and looked like a gypsy. She wore thick white pancake makeup on her face, to cover up her wrinkles. She rouged her cheeks, reminding us of a clown's, streaked her eyelids blue with shadow and her mouth bright red with lipstick. Out on the street, we often saw her muttering loudly to herself.

But today the crazy lady was just a kind old soul. She answered her door, let Marion in, hugged her, dried her teary cheeks with a perfumed lacy handkerchief, offered her a coffee and cookies, and then pointed her in the direction of the telephone. Marion called the police. They said they'd be right over.

What silly hopes she'd had.

When she got back to her apartment, Lily hadn't moved from the window where Marion had left her. She was too dazed and frightened even to cry.

Lily felt truly lost without Wolfe. While Oma went from embassy to embassy, Lily only stood in line at the Polish Consulate. She'd heard from Wolfe. He was in Krakow. Lily was desperate to leave Berlin to be with him. As long as they were together, she'd said, everything would be fine. But Marion was scared. She had terrible headaches and stomach upsets every day. She had trouble eating and sleeping. I tried to comfort her, but I was just as heartbroken as she was at the prospect of her leaving.

Only two weeks later, and Opa would be gone too, not because he was a Polish Jew, but because of the actions of another young German Jew whose parents had also been deported back to Poland.

November 10, 1938. A day that lives in my memory like a lodger refusing to leave. We were let out of school early. Sometime in the morning, I seem to remember. Yes, the morning. The headmistress came around to all the classrooms to say there'd be no more school until further notice. Sudden bedlam broke out through the whole school: excitement and terror. Our headmistress instructed us, in a very somber voice, to pack up our belongings and leave for home right away. Go two by two, she warned, not in groups. And go straight home.

I didn't pay any attention to her. Instead, I walked Marion home. We only lived a couple of blocks away from each other. Her apartment was on the second floor of a building with a beautiful circular staircase and a front garden as well as the *Hinterhof* in the back. In the summer, wildflowers filled the garden. Now, in November, it was barren.

I don't remember exactly how we got home that day, or even what we saw on the way. I can visualize our coats and hats slung across the desk chair in her room, our satchels dropped to the floor, and the two of us slouched on her bed, talking. But not as usual. In the old days, we would've gossiped about our favorite movie star, Clark Gable, or giggled over our latest sighting of Viktor de Kowa, the actor who lived in our neighborhood. But since Marion's father's deportation to Poland, we weren't much in the mood for gossip.

Then Lily walked in.

"Are you mad?" she screamed, looking from one to the other of us. "Eva, what are you doing here?"

She pulled me off the bed. Grabbed my coat, my hat, my satchel, threw them at me, and told me to get home. To run home. I flew out of there, so scared. For the first time that morning, I could smell burning in the smoke-filled air.

As I rounded the corner of my street, I saw Oma. She wore no hat, no coat, her short hair flying every which way. She had Schani, my handsome white poodle, on his leash.

Wrapping me in a tight clasp, she said, "Thank God, you're safe. I've been so worried. It's your father . . . he was picked up earlier this morning."

Picked up. Two little words I had become all too familiar with. These were the words they'd used for Herr Goldmann from across the street who, whenever we crossed paths, would pinch my cheek, smile, and call me *Süsse.* But, as I'd rationalized to myself then, he was an old man, living alone, no wife, no children. Besides, I remember how he'd smelled of oldness. What about Marion's father? He'd been picked up. No, deported. Different, in my mind.

Now the words *picked up* had become synonymous in my young head with never heard from again. Suddenly, my whole life began to feel *picked up.* And dropped upside down. My thoughts were like the splinters of shattered glass in the shop windows I saw later that day: sharp-edged, painful, and impossible to see through.

Oma said it had happened so quickly. She never had a chance to help him. She just stood watching; an idiot, doing nothing.

"Good God." She began to cry. Schani seemed to understand and began to whimper.

I put my arm around my mother and buried my face in her shoulder. She stroked my hair. She was at a loss, she said. She didn't know what to do, where to go. And I remember thinking, wasn't she the one who always made the best out of any situation? Eternal Optimist. That's what Opa had always called her. She'd laughed back at him. But what had she been so optimistic about? Impossible things, Opa had said.

"You should've come right home after school. I got so frightened. I thought something had happened to you too."

We walked the rest of the block very quickly. Too quickly to talk. I can remember how everything seemed to have a thick greyness to it—the street, the buildings, the cloudy sky, the acrid smoky air—as though we were inside a film noir. I had to run to keep up with her. And I kept scrambling for consoling words to say. I hated to see her tears.

In the hallway outside our apartment, Oma put the key into the lock, turned it, opened the door a crack and closed it again. "I'm so sorry. I haven't had . . ." She didn't say anything more, just opened the door again, and walked in.

The apartment looked as if someone in a terrible hurry had rifled through the rooms, spilling our belongings out of drawers and cupboards. In search of something? But what? And then wasn't it enough they'd found Opa?

"I don't understand," I finally managed to say. "What were they looking for?"

"Weapons. At least that's what they told us," Oma said. "But really, it's all a pretense. They're looking for valuables to steal."

I picked up the little telephone table that had been knocked over.

"But we don't have anything so valuable, do we?"

"No idea what those brutes consider valuable."

She tiptoed over the debris they'd made of our lives and stopped in the middle of the living room, her hand cupped over her forehead, her eyes half-covered.

Opa's precious books had been pulled from their shelves. Goethe, Schiller, Ibsen lay piled in a heap on the polished parquet floor, as if fodder for a bonfire.

Oma walked around the room, picking things up, crying, muttering, and shaking her head.

"Look at this," she said, dabbing her eyes with a handkerchief. Fragments of the brilliant black 78s lay scattered all over the room like some giant devil's confetti. She bent to pick up some of the shards of shiny black. "Mozart's Requiem smashed to pieces. Your father's favorite."

The doors and drawers of the sideboard hung open. Tablecloths, napkins, silver forks, knives, and spoons littered the floor. Highball glasses lay on their sides in between papers and notebooks and old photo albums. One album lay face up, a muddied boot print on the exposed page with unglued photos curled and strewn all around it.

I found a photo of myself at a very young age. I brought the picture to Oma and sat beside her. "When was this?"

"You must've been about two," Oma said, smiling at the memory. "We were at the zoo. Look at your chubby little legs in those woolen leggings."

I had on a matching cardigan and hat. But looking at my face, I wasn't happy.

"You'd just had a temper tantrum," Oma said. "And your father, he couldn't bear to see you cry so he bought you those two balloons. Look how tightly you clutch the string in your little fist."

Oma put her head back and sighed very loudly. Deep black crescents of kohl eyeliner smudged the skin beneath her glassy, blue eyes. She looked exhausted.

"We should've left in '36," she said, her eyes closing. "I kept telling him, begging him, but he wouldn't listen."

You see, your Opa thought if we obeyed all those idiotic rules and regulations, the Nazis would eventually run out of ideas for new ones and we'd return to our normal life again. Or at least as normal as possible under the circumstances. All just a matter of time, he'd say, sure of it. The

German people would never allow this to continue. And hadn't pogroms similar to this happened many times in the past?

Suddenly, Oma stood. She paced the room again, folding and unfolding her arms, moving her head this way and that, as if she were a little kid carrying on a conversation with an imaginary friend. "There must be something we can do," she said in a husky voice.

At the window, she parted the curtains, looked out at the street. Then she turned back and stared at the jumble of things strewn across the carpet. She shook her head and began to cry again.

"When are the police coming?" I asked.

"They told me ages ago they'd be here. It's useless. They're all in cahoots."

I sat still on the sofa and rubbed my sweaty palms on my skirt.

"But do you know why they arrested him?" I said.

"I've heard that thousands of Jewish men, from everywhere in Germany, have been picked up in the last twenty-four hours. They don't seem to need reasons. Laws don't protect us anymore. Hooligans run this country now."

I couldn't hold back my tears anymore and I began to cry. Schani nudged his nose into my lap, and Oma wrapped her arms around me. We both cried. After a few minutes, Oma let go of me, walked over to the cupboard in the front hall, and pulled out Opa's best overcoat, the one he only wore for special occasions, such as going to the opera or to the theater. She held the coat close to her, hiding her face for a moment in its big furry collar. Then she ripped open a tiny portion of the red, silky lining, took money from her handbag, and stuffed the bills, one by one, into the space between the lining and the soft cashmere of the coat. She glanced at herself in the big gilt mirror, shook her head in disbelief, and turning away from it, quickly walked down the hall to the bathroom, shutting the door behind her.

I hated the sound of the door closing. It startled me. I felt very alone and frightened. I tiptoed over to where Opa's coat lay and touched it ever so gently, afraid to disturb the spirit residing inside. Opa had looked so handsome, so tall, strong, and invincible.

A few minutes later, Oma strode from the bathroom, her face freshly made up.

"Get your coat on," she said, picking up Opa's and folding it over her arm. "Hurry up. And if you dare say a word . . ."

"Where are we going?"

"To bring *Vati* his overcoat."

Out on the chilly street, it had already turned dark.

While we walked, I imagined other children busy with their homework. Mine, tucked away in my satchel at home, seemed as remote to me at that moment as was my father, suddenly and inexplicably gone. I heard someone playing the piano in one of the apartment buildings we passed. The music sounded good. But so did the sound of the traffic in the street, the sound of normal everyday life.

All at once Oma stopped and turned to face me. Her bright red lips appeared black against her white face in the lamp-lit street. Her blue eyes, dull and puffy.

"There it is," she said, pointing to an old majestic-looking building, the huge swastika flags lit up and waving in the night air. "You're shivering. Here, let's put this around your shoulders, it'll help."

She unfolded the coat and wrapped it around me. She gave me a little squeeze and a hug, for courage or good luck, and when the traffic cleared, we crossed the road.

"Don't let the coat drag."

"What will you say?" I said, clutching the hem so it wouldn't touch the ground.

"I haven't figured that out yet, but we must find out where he is. He needs a warm coat. This is November, for God's sake."

All the windows in the building were lit. I could see men in uniform walking around inside.

"Ready?"

My heart thumped in my chest, as if it were a bird gone wild in its cage. We climbed the long set of stone steps to the front door.

Inside, bright lights shone in the toasty warmth. Chandeliers hung from the vaulted ceiling, paintings of fat little cherubs and genteel ladies lined the walls. I could see a fuzzy reflection of myself in the highly polished white marble floor. Feeling too warm, I unwrapped Opa's coat from around my shoulders and suddenly caught his warm, sweet, smoky smell. It was so pungent; he could've been standing right next to me.

"Excuse me, please," Oma said to the man at the desk.

He didn't look up. He was busy scribbling his signature on the papers piled before him.

"I'm sorry to disturb you," she said, her voice high-pitched, sweet. "It's my husband, you see. When he was taken away this morning, he forgot his overcoat. I'm sure you must think me silly, but you know how we German women worry for our men."

She took the coat from me, held it up for him to see.

I concentrated on the scuffed toes of my shoes. I sucked in my cheeks and widened my eyes to stop a case of the giggles beginning to bubble up inside me. The man looked at Oma, then at the coat and without saying a word, went back to signing his papers. At first, I thought he hadn't understood. But then, after a few moments, he picked up the receiver, dialed a few numbers, and barked to whomever was on the other end to come to the front desk immediately.

"Stand over there," he said and pointed without looking at us. "Someone will come and help you shortly."

My legs trembled as I walked across the large foyer. If only we could just leave the coat right here on the floor and run out. But then guilt engulfed me. How would my father stay warm?

A tall man with curly black hair, wearing the same uniform as the man at the desk, came toward us.

"What can I do for you?" he said in a pleasant voice, a smile on his face, his eyes a deeper blue than I'd ever seen before.

My mother explained again about the overcoat. "I wonder," she said. "If you could tell me where he is so I can bring it to him?" She smiled.

"I wouldn't worry, lady. He won't need a coat where he is."

"Won't need a coat?" Her face turned white.

Picked up, the words that echoed through my head, again and again.

"Now, why don't you take your daughter and go home. You can't help him by being here."

"Won't need a coat?" Her voice louder now, and shrill.

"Lady, lady, please, you must calm yourself," he said in an almost whisper. He put his hand on her arm. "Your husband has been issued a uniform to wear. Now, please, take your daughter and go home. There's nothing you can do for him here."

"It's all a mistake. He's done nothing wrong. You must believe me. Please, let him come home."

The same pleasant smile played on the man's lips.

Oma held up Opa's coat.

"Look," she said, pointing to the rip in the lining. "You take it."

He took a step back, shook his head. He stopped smiling. His mouth closed into an even, straight line. He turned away from us, walked to the front door, his tall, shiny black boots stamping loudly on the polished floor, and opened it wide. He stood watching us from the open door until we got halfway down the stone steps. Then, as the door slammed shut, the steps went completely dark.

"Here, let's put this around you again," Oma said when we got to the street. "My God, you're shaking like a leaf."

The coat felt good over my shoulders. I nuzzled my face into the soft furry collar to get another whiff of Opa's sweet cologne. But all I could smell on that frigid night were the bonfires; books burning on every corner and buildings all around us up in flames.

Oma's arm came around me, her ungloved hand squeezing my arm. I dropped my head onto her shoulder and wrapped my arm around her waist. Our hips bumped as we walked and Opa's best overcoat, slung over my shoulders, trailed the ground behind me. It didn't seem to matter anymore. We had no words. And that didn't matter either. So long as I felt Oma's body—snug, warm, and comforting—next to mine as we walked. So long as the slammed door wasn't her shutting me out, then the feelings of loneliness and helplessness didn't seem quite so dense and unremitting as the night sky above.

•   •   •

A few days after Opa was picked up, my best friend, Marion, and her mother, Lily, received their necessary exit papers to leave Berlin. Oma and I accompanied them to the railway station. We hugged, we kissed, we promised letters, and photos, and eventual visits back and forth. Once we get settled in Krakow, Lily said. Once the political situation subsides, my mother said.

Marion and I stood on the platform, arms around each other, her scratchy woolen coat rubbing against my cheek, the smell of smoke and tar in my nostrils. A jangling clatter of sounds—hissing, barking, screaming, and yelling—came in and out of my consciousness, like the ebb and flow of ocean waves. We were freezing and couldn't stop shaking—as much from nerves, I'm sure, as from the icy wind blowing through the station. We didn't say very much. I think we were afraid to even look at each other. We watched the stationmaster with his flag instead, knowing that at any moment he would raise it, the signal for the train whistle to blow and for the passengers to board. Oma stuffed a few marks into Lily's pocket, as I'd seen her do many times before, and when the flag went up and the whistle blew, Lily and Marion turned from us and climbed the steep steps of the train. They went into their compartment, pulled down the window and, as the train—destined for the East—pulled out of the station, they half-hung out of their window, blowing kisses and crying and saying over and over, "See you soon, see you soon."

But of course, we never did see them soon. We never saw them again. Perished is the word people use now. It isn't died, it isn't murdered, and it isn't killed. It's always perished in the Holocaust: a whispered, ghostly word.

November 12, 1988

My darling, enough of 1938 for now. I gather my papers together, click off my pen, throw off the cozy blanket I have draped around my shoulders, and go to the bedroom to see how David is doing. The TV talks. Its blue light flickers in the dark. But he's fallen fast asleep. I look at the once handsome face, his colorless skin so smoothed out, his wrinkles almost all gone. His eyes have sunk inward. Dark circles underline them. I find myself checking for his breathing, looking for the rhythmic rise and drop of his chest.

Here's another goodbye about to happen. Will I have advance warning? Or will he be here one minute, gone the next? No chance for a goodbye, for an 'I love you.'

I stroke his forehead, bend to kiss it, bring the bedcovers up to his chin, turn off the light and the TV, and tiptoe out of the room. It's only nine o'clock. I'm so lonely. My writings have become my solace. I admit, I'm still addicted to the pen and the smell of fresh paper.

CHAPTER II

October 26, 2014

Mali rubs her eyes, stinging with fatigue and sorrow. She lifts the baby-blue blanket from the yellow couch, wraps it around her shoulders, and goes out to the balcony. The cool wind, soothing to her hot cheeks, blows through her thick, dark, curly hair. She paces the ten feet of outdoor space and concludes that nothing makes sense to her anymore. She feels like screaming at the top of her lungs. How could her grandparents have come back from this? How did they learn to trust again?

She stops pacing, looks down at the street's ordinary comings and goings. Then, as though a scrim is dropped over the scene, a different view of these familiar city blocks is in front of her. She's in another reality. Men in uniform uphold a new decree. Her life, the way she has always known it, is suddenly outlawed for her. The takeout place across the street bars her entrance. The restaurant around the corner doesn't seat her. The shoe shop on First Avenue prohibits her from buying a new pair. The sign in the dress shop's window, next door, forbids her to come in. Taxis don't stop for her. Her Metro card no longer gains her access to public transportation. Her savings account has been confiscated, stolen. It now belongs to someone else. Her house has been seized, her business too. She will be deported. Destroyed. After all, she is a Jew.

Impossible to even think about.

The picture of a railway station comes to her. A jumble of suitcases, leather knapsacks, cloth duffel bags. Confused and frightened faces. Men in overcoats and hats. Women clutching handbags. Children listless, dreamy. Deportations. Truckloads of Jews in the East. Cattle cars for Jews in the West. A parade of women and children, fresh off the train at Auschwitz, huddles past. Skin, hair, eyes in every shade from light to dark. Body types: fat, thin, skinny, beautiful, ugly, old, and young. No matter. There's only one common denominator.

Steamy grey smoke rises into the darkness from the power plants across the East River. Speckles of reflected light jiggle in the rapidly moving currents of the water, as if a shaky hand points the light. No stars shine in the sky, but it doesn't matter. The city needs no help, it sparkles all on its own. More sirens screech from somewhere out of sight. She watches a driver, up the street, struggle with parallel parking. A dog barks. A woman laughs. A baby cries. Brakes squeal as a car stops short for a red light. Drumbeat sounds boom from another, then fade as the light changes to green, and vanish as the car speeds off. Mali shivers and draws the blanket closer around her, burying her nose in its warmth. She doesn't want to go back in, not just yet. She needs the cool night air and the space away from her mother's haunting words to think.

But out of the darkness, another night in her own life begins to take shape in her mind.

Not long after the commemoration at their synagogue, Mali had given Julia *The Night Trilogy* by Elie Wiesel to read. She'd felt compelled to impress some seriousness, some weight, upon her sixteen-year-old daughter. She wanted her to know the terror, the frightening times their family had gone through, and finally their luck and strength in having survived.

But her lesson backfired in a way she could have never imagined.

One night, while Mali and Michael were watching *Hill Street Blues* on TV, she heard Julia shout out, "I have a headache. I'm taking a shower." Mali caught a glimpse of her daughter's reflection in the dark of the window, heard the water run for a while, and after a few minutes, Julia's slow shuffle back to her bedroom. Mali thought nothing of it.

Then, what seemed like quite a while later, the phone rang. Mali jumped. It was already ten to eleven. She must have fallen asleep. She picked up the receiver.

"Hello, my name is Tony," the voice on the phone informed her. "I'm calling from the crisis center. Your daughter has just taken aspirin, Tylenol, Dimetapp. Take her to the ER. Have her stomach pumped. Take her now. Tylenol is toxic."

Mali said nothing. Little beads of sweat began to form on the surface of her skin.

"Tylenol is toxic," he repeated. "You must take her to the emergency room immediately."

She still couldn't respond. She understood what he was telling her, but because of her silence, he didn't know that. She began to shake. Michael looked over at her, concern, and confusion in his face.

". . . the hospital right away . . ." the voice on the phone insisted.

"Yes, yes," she was finally able to say and hung up.

"She's taken pills," Mali said, throwing off the warmth and comfort of her blanket and running toward Julia's room.

Wrapped in just a white terry-cloth robe, Julia stood at the back of the room next to her old upright piano, as if she could will herself into shriveling up and disappearing from her parents. Her long, brown, curly hair hung wet and stringy. Her hazel eyes, large, scared, were filling with tears. As if in a shrine to some strange god, there—spread out over a sheet of newspaper on the floor—were the aspirin, Tylenol, Dimetapp, a glass of water, a business card from the crisis center, and the telephone.

"What the hell have you done?" Mali said, in a high-pitched scream. "What the hell . . .?"

Julia cried, telling her nothing.

Michael repeated the question more firmly, his face grey with pain and anger.

Nothing.

"No use now," Mali said. "We must get her to the hospital."

"You take her," he said, his anger spilling out through his voice. "I can't . . . I just don't think . . . Anyway, one of us needs to stay home with Steffi."

"Here, let's get you dressed," Mali said to Julia, ignoring Michael, as she looked for a pair of sweatpants and a shirt in the clean laundry pile that was supposed to have been put away in her chest of drawers days ago, and trying her hardest to focus on her daughter, and not the chaos in her bedroom.

The lights were bright in the emergency room, the questions routine, almost business-like: What did you take? How much? How long ago?

Not why.

They answered, at first with apprehension, then as though talking about a sprained ankle or a broken arm. Of course, Mali realized, her child was not the first they'd seen in these circumstances. One nurse brought Julia to a cubicle, while another plied Mali with more questions regarding insurance, pediatrician, allergies. After the inquiries, Mali slipped through the nurses' station and found Julia already in a hospital gown, her clothes lying in a heap on the only chair. Mali tied the little cloth ties together at the back of the gown. Then Julia got into bed and they waited in silence for the nurses to begin their routine. One came to take blood. Julia looked away and winced as the needle went into her arm. Another came to take her blood pressure, her temperature. Mali felt in the way, sitting on the chair, Julia's clothes still warm from her body, in a heap on her lap. She expected one of the nurses to ask her to please step out into the waiting room. No one did. She said she felt queasy, whenever she watched someone throw up. They ignored her. They inserted the IV into Julia's right hand and started the bottle dripping. Mali watched it to make sure it dripped at a regular rate, whatever that was. She longed for a cigarette. She longed to leave the cubicle. She debated with herself. Would Julia feel abandoned if she left her for a few minutes? Would the nurses think her a cold mother? In the end, she said, to no one in particular, she'd be back shortly.

Out in the waiting room, she called home.

"Hi," Michael said, his voice sounding gentle, tired. "How's it going?"

"They're giving her ipecac right now."

"Did she say anything to you in the car?"

"No. She said she didn't want to talk about it. Not now. I told her she had to—if not to me, then to someone. I told her this is it. This can't go on."

Mali felt a sudden anger rise in her, like bubbles in boiling water.

"How are you doing?" he said.

She wanted to tell him to come and be with her.

"You know I once tried," she said instead. "I once took six aspirins and afterward went to bed and cried my eyes out because I really didn't want to die."

But what had she wanted? She remembered envisioning the life she knew, but without herself, and had pictured her mother, her father, their grief, their guilt. If only . . . she imagined them saying to each other. She was eighteen then. In a state of self-pity.

Michael didn't respond. Her attention glazed over the drab ER waiting room, the fluorescents stinging her tired eyes.

"We must talk," she said into the silence.

"Not now," he said. "I can't right now. There's nothing for me to say."

"Nothing to . . .? Your daughter is in some sort of crisis and you have nothing to say about it?"

"No, not right now. I can't."

"Well, in that case, I'm hanging up." She slammed the phone back into its cradle, fighting off new feelings of self-pity, and the tears that would inevitably come with them.

As she walked away from the pay phone, she had a memory of being eleven and in Paris for Christmas with her stepmother's brother. Someone had given her a diary and she'd begun to write her thoughts on the clean white pages. Disappointment had crept into her heart there. Nothing concrete, just a wispy discontent she could neither name nor understand. She imagined her diary being found, imagined the sorrow the finder would feel, the pity the finder would shower on her. But since her diary was not surreptitiously found and read, she'd brought it to Fleur's brother instead. They'd sat together on the couch in his living room. After he finished reading it, he turned to her and asked if she wanted to go back home to London. Of course, that wasn't what she'd wanted. But what had she wanted? She really hadn't any idea. In the end, she'd just felt foolish. There was no other word for it. Ever since then, she'd tried to avoid the snake of self-pity. Except for the day when she'd lain in her bed, years later, crying her eyes out, because she really was afraid to die.

Mali thought of these things while she sat in the ER's waiting room.

Then, other times she'd sat here, came to her: stitches to mend a gash in a chin; a splint to protect a broken finger; a fractured arm. Time seemed suspended in here, unreal. She considered pulling out the notebook in her bag meant for her own jottings—but filled instead with shopping lists, dates to remember, telephone numbers—to help make sense of those bits and pieces of muddle inside her head. But it felt too difficult for her leaden body. So she went outside, lit up a cigarette and paced the sidewalk, wishing for someone she could call, someone she could talk to, someone to take away the loneliness. She sorted through her list of friends. She imagined how each of them might act if they were here with her, consoling, supportive, urging her to talk. She imagined herself with each of them. Not ready to open up. Too drained and confused. No one from her attenuated list could have done anything for her.

Mali found Julia propped up in the bed, a large aluminum bowl in her lap. She picked up her daughter's clothes and sat back down on the chair.

"How're you doing?" she said.

Julia screwed up her face. "Tell Dad not to speak to me about the six million," she said. "I mean, honestly. Am I supposed to stop and say to myself, Oh, I shouldn't be taking these pills because of all those Jews who died in the Holocaust?"

"Okay." Mali tried hard not to show her shock at so strange a statement. But then, she thought, it was too bad that Julia couldn't have stopped and said that to herself; even as strange and seemingly unrelated as it was.

Julia bent over the bowl again. Mali rose to hold her hair away from her face. She rubbed her back. This was his job, she was thinking. Changing diapers had always been hers.

"I need a tissue."

Mali twisted Julia's hair, so it lay in one long curl along the middle of her back and reached for the tissues. Julia spat into the bowl, wiped her nose and mouth, and looked over at Mali. Her eyes were swollen, her right hand black and blue from the IV.

"Here," Julia said, taking off the earrings she'd just gotten from a friend for her sweet sixteen party the week before. Mali took them and put them in her change purse for safekeeping. Julia then took off her gold bracelet, the one Mali and Michael had brought back for her from St. Thomas that winter and passed it to her. Mali put it on her left wrist with her watch. To have it felt good—a treasure Julia was giving her for safekeeping. But the aluminum bangle Julia had bought for eight dollars with the name of a

Russian Jewish family engraved on it remained, as she had promised, on her other wrist, until word came that the family had been freed.

Mali thought back to Julia's involvement with Russian Jewry and the school trip to Washington, DC, to march for their freedom. Michael and Mali had talked about the march, had talked about the kids who didn't go. Why their parents forbade it. Paranoia. Mali understood. But she didn't want to give in. Irrational, she told herself, as she pictured the Mall in Washington. Hundreds of thousands of Jewish kids, protesting out loud, carrying banners, proclaiming freedom. Hundreds of thousands of Jews gathered in one place. How easy it would be. How crazy to think of that now, here in America, in the land of the free.

"So, how do you think I should wear my hair for the prom?"

"I prefer it half up and half down," Mali said, relieved her daughter's thoughts had returned to living.

A picture of her—twirling in front of the full-length mirror in the shop, her eyes bright and clear, her face flushed with expectation, as she surveyed herself in the new pink, strapless dress—transported Mali out of this hospital cubicle for a moment.

"You won't tell anyone in the family, will you?" Julia said, a frown of worry crossing her puffy face.

"No. And you shouldn't tell anyone at school."

"I won't."

"Do you think your problem was worth all this?" Mali couldn't help asking, gesturing at the bowl in her lap, the IV dripping nourishment into the body Julia had wanted to vacate.

"No," she said too emphatically.

Mali wished she could've believed her.

The pediatrician came into the cubicle. Julia asked Mali to leave when he asked her about the suicide attempt.

What would Julia tell the doctor? Mali wished her daughter could turn herself inside out for him, show him what hurt so badly. But Mali knew her better. At best, only half-truths would dribble out.

After a few minutes, he emerged from behind the closed curtain of the cubicle and came toward Mali. They went into an unused room. Leaning up against one of the beds, they talked. He apologized for being so tired. He'd been up for countless hours and maybe not as coherent as he might've been earlier in the day. She laughed. She was tired too. The attempt was not overt, he said. She didn't take enough to hurt herself. But in any case, it was not to be ignored. In between talk of suicide, Mali and the doctor talked of life. He pointed to the gold hand—a good luck charm to ward off the evil eye—that hung on a chain around her neck and told her he'd once had one too. It was his way of letting her know he was also Jewish. And because it was so late at night and they were both so tired, they seemed to have bypassed a first-meeting formality. She liked this man, who now colored his conversation with a smattering of Yiddish words. He recommended a psychologist. And she's Jewish, he said. He wrote her name and number on a slip of paper and gave Mali one of his cards as well. She put them both in her wallet. Tomorrow she would call.

Mali went back to Julia. She held her hand through the bars of the hospital bed. She looked so small and vulnerable.

Julia smiled. Mali wondered what she was really thinking. How had they failed her? How had they come to be here? If only she could've bent down and kissed it better, as she'd done for a scraped knee when she was small.

"I'm sleepy," Julia said. "I wish they'd hurry. Can you open the curtains? I like to see what's going on."

Mali let go of her hand and got up to draw the curtains aside. They fell into silence, watching the activity at the nurses' station.

"Why don't you just lay your head back and try going to sleep?"

For a moment, Julia put her head on the pillow and closed her eyes.

Then opened them again. "This is bothering me," she said, pointing to the IV. "Do you think I'll have to have it all night long?"

"I'm not sure."

Mali tried to move the thin, clear tube out of the way. She stroked Julia's hair. Mali felt adrift, helpless. She loved this child. But why didn't she know it?

Sometime later, after Julia was settled in another bed, in another room, her eyes closing with exhaustion, one of the nurses came in and told Mali she should go home and get some rest herself. She would need her strength in the coming weeks. Mali kissed Julia goodnight, gave the nurse her phone number, saying she lived only five minutes away if anything came up, and then left the hospital.

Driving home, she turned up the volume on the radio and let her mind sink into the concerto for violin and piano she recognized but couldn't name. As she got closer to home, she wondered if Michael was still awake. She knew he must be but wondered all the same.

"Hi," she called out from the front hall, so relieved to hear the television going and the picture in her mind of him sitting in his black chair, his head back, his feet up on the hassock.

"How is she?" he asked as she plunked down into her chair across from his.

She told him bits and pieces that immediately came to her, too spent to think in chronological order.

"Ready for bed?" he said after a little while.

Mali called the dogs in from the yard, bribing them with a biscuit. He turned off the lights.

"You see," he said as he was getting undressed, "I don't believe in Judaism and I don't believe in God, but I do believe that Jews, above anyone else, *cannot, must not* commit suicide. Not after the Holocaust. It isn't right. Do you know what I mean?"

She crawled into bed. She remembers she couldn't answer him. It was three in the morning. She couldn't be sure what was right, or even what either one of them meant anymore. She just lay there and thought how odd that they both should've spoken of the Holocaust at a time like this. What was the connection? Too tired, too confused, she closed her eyes, surprised at how easily sleep was taking her over.

CHAPTER 12

October 26, 2014

Today, Mali is no less confused. She puts down her mother's pages, stands up, and stretches her arms overhead, her body aching from sitting in one position for too long. Not such a young chicken anymore, she hears her mother's voice echo in her head and imagines the smile of conspiracy on her face. Too bad I don't drink, Mali muses. A good stiff one might be just the thing right now. On her way to the kitchen to make another coffee instead, a photo above the TV catches her attention. It was Thanksgiving, a couple of years ago. In her mother's kitchen, the three of them—her mother, Julia, and herself—posed for a selfie over the crispy-skinned turkey just pulled from the oven. After David died, her mother always made the Thanksgiving dinner in her apartment, and Julia would spend the Wednesday night with her so that she could get up early the next morning to prepare the turkey. Mali didn't belong in that picture. She was the guest, the outsider, the odd one out, the piggy in the middle.

And how would she have learned how to mother? she wonders now, continuing a conversation she has been having with herself.

In the weeks following the night of Julia's suicide attempt, life had begun to resume some sort of normalcy, except that Mali felt compelled to keep a vigilant watch over Julia, know her whereabouts every minute of every day. If Julia were coming home later than usual from school, she had to phone Mali. That was the deal Mali had made with herself to keep Julia out of the country club of a hospital her therapist had recommended, and

Julia was desperate to go to—to be anywhere else but home, her daughter had said. One day Julia hadn't called. By the time she walked in the door, Mali was frantic and furious. She brought Julia into her study, sat her down on one of the red butterfly chairs opposite her desk. Mali kneeled on the floor facing her.

"How do I know you're not where you're not supposed to be, having done God knows what and . . .? Tell me. How should I know?"

Julia only glared at Mali; her eyes glassy with held back tears.

"Don't look at me as if I'm quite mad. You've put me in this position, this constant state of anxiety. I worry every time you leave the house. I worry when you say goodnight. I worry the minute I open my eyes in the morning. I worry all the time. God, I love you. The thought of life without you . . . I can't bear it."

Mali leaned forward and buried her wet face in her daughter's lap.

"Do you realize?" Julia whispered, stroking Mali's hair. "This is the first time you've said 'I love you' since last December. Do you know that you didn't even say 'I love you' on my birthday?"

Mali pulled back, sat on her heels, and stared into her daughter's face. Shock and grief and denial spun wildly around her, like planets on a collision course. She tried to think back over those last few months. But she could only think back on herself and wonder why those three little words—I love you—were so difficult to say. Why the words, the hugs, the kisses, didn't just roll out of her freely, uninhibited? Why Julia couldn't have been more like Steffi, able to come to her for what she needed.

"But I do love you," Mali said. "I've always loved you and I'm sorry I don't say it often enough. I guess . . ." and she stopped herself. What excuses could she have given? That this was the way she was? Would she have accepted that from her own mother?

Julia sat in silence.

"Listen," Mali said. "I need a promise from you. I have to believe that you won't do this again, that you won't take any more pills . . ."

"I can't guarantee you anything," Julia said, as matter-of-factly, as defiantly as if she were refusing to clean up her room. "I don't know how I'll be tomorrow," she went on. "Or next week or next month or anytime in the future."

Mali was stunned. She wanted to shake her up, keep shaking her up, like a Magic 8-Ball, until she got a better answer, one with a rosier, more solid view of her future.

"Look, I'd do anything for you. I want to help you. You're my child. We're on the same side, you know. Maybe it's difficult for you to see it that way right now, and maybe you won't really understand until you have your own kids. But I want you to be happy with yourself, and I want you, I need you, to tell me that you won't kill yourself, not for the six million, not for me, not for Dad, but for you. You have your whole life in front of you. Don't look at me that way. I know it sounds trite, but it's true. Things change all the time, including the way you feel. Please, you must believe me. I love you more than anything, Julia. And I'm so proud of you. You must, deep down underneath it all, believe that. You do, don't you?"

Julia nodded. The tears she'd so stubbornly held back now streamed down her cheeks. Mali leaned forward and pulled Julia up toward her, and embraced and kissed her, and felt a little less frightened than she had the week before when she and Michael were in the therapist's office. They'd sat next to each other on the couch, the therapist on a wooden rocking chair. A low glass coffee table—as if it were a barrier set up between patient and shrink—separated them. The therapist, Dr. Fischer, explained the results of the tests she'd administered to Julia: Rorschach, Minnesota Personality, et cetera, et cetera. Her recommendation: hospitalization and antidepressant drugs.

Their child was seriously ill, she insisted. Their child didn't live in this world: her reality was not their reality; her thoughts were too disconnected. Her reality was morbid, bleak, black, death ridden.

This was their child?

Mali sat there in that little room. Diplomas she could hardly read hung on the white walls. Slits of sunlight, the promises of a cheerier world outside, edged in through the closed slats of the Venetian blinds. A child's table and chairs placed neatly in one corner of the room, a bookshelf in another.

Mali listened to the words: inherent, genetic, constitution.

Don't worry, Dr. Fischer said. Fifteen out of seventeen questions on the test regarding suicide were answered in the positive. Don't worry, it's not your fault, she kept repeating. Don't go on a guilt trip.

Mali listened, felt iced-over inside. She began to shake. The therapist brought her a cardigan to wear. She gave Michael an apple juice. The cardigan didn't help. It wasn't her body that needed warming. Mali tried to recognize her daughter in the picture being drawn for them. She couldn't keep her thoughts together. They kept tumbling away from her.

After their session, Mali and Michael sat across from each other—he with a cup of coffee, she with a fruit shake—in a restaurant in the mall, waiting for Julia to finish up work at Victoria's Secret. The restaurant was empty. She could see the bar from where she sat and, from time to time, found herself watching the bartender wash glasses, put bottles away, wipe down counters, keep busy. Oldies music played. She began to feel warmer again. At least the shaking inside her had stopped.

But everything around her felt unreal. Perhaps nothing would ever be the same again. She stared at Michael's hands—hands that knew her so intimately. She traced the veins with her finger. *It's my party and I'll cry if I want to* . . . Leslie Gore bellowed from the speakers. He took his hand away to drink his coffee. After the first sip, he wrinkled up his face in disgust. Too weak, too old, or most probably both. She didn't have to ask. He gave her back his hand.

I'll cry if I want to . . . As though written for her, the song had fit her at eighteen so perfectly. Why did she feel embarrassed and amused whenever she thought back to her own teenage tragedies?

"Do you remember this song?" she asked him. "Do you remember what you were like then, what you thought, what you felt? Do you remember?"

"Some of it," he said. "Why?"

"I keep thinking that if I could remember exactly what I was like then, perhaps I'd be better able to understand what's going on with Julia now. It seems such a cruel trick, in a way, not to be able to conjure yourself up from another time in your life. I mean . . ."

She meant, how could she crawl back inside herself to find that younger, more insecure self who'd cried and listened to Leslie Gore sing her life as it was? And then, how could she claim to be the fortune teller, promising her daughter that she had everything to look forward to?

"How have we made such a mess of things?" he said.

"Maybe it is, as Fischer says, in her genetic makeup."

"I don't understand suicide," he said, anger rising in his voice. "What does it accomplish?"

As though watching someone else, Mali saw herself in her bed in the dorm room—alone, shivering, crying—six, ten aspirins in her belly. What had made her life so difficult? Why hadn't her imagination been able to make the leap to a future a little better, or even just a little different, from that moment?

"After Auschwitz," he said, the tone of his voice almost vigilant. "Especially after Auschwitz, no Jew has the right."

"Did you think of Auschwitz when you were sixteen? Did you think of your life then as a sort of blossoming out of the ashes? A reaffirmation, so to speak?"

What was she saying? A blossoming out of the ashes? A reaffirmation? What romantic notions were those? They lived, that was all. And when people lived, they did things like get married, have children. They carried on. For whatever it was worth, they carried on. Then why, when this child had everything, did she want to trash it all? Where was her strength? Where had her own strength been, back then? Mali remembered the terrible loneliness, curled up under the pile of blankets in that dormitory bed, with no one to call or speak to. Only the voice in her head enumerating all the things she would miss in the present and those she'd miss in the future. And what if she'd called her mother? Would she have understood? Would she have wrapped her arms around her, enveloped her as she must've when she was a baby? Or would she have stood apart from her, arms folded across her own chest instead, disbelief in her eyes, words flowing from her open, angry mouth. Words to pull at the straws of reason, words to say what is, and what has been, good in her young life? But her mother's words would have been so twisted and held back by fear, she would have only protected herself, not safeguarded Mali from Mali. But what could be so irrevocably bad in a young girl's life? The same words she found herself asking of the image of Julia, a beautiful girl, blossoming, in a new pink prom dress, twirling around and around in front of the store's full-length mirror.

Michael ran his hand through his curly hair. How grey it had become this last year.

"I don't think of my life in terms of Auschwitz now," he said. "And I don't remember what I was thinking back then. But I do know I've never thought of suicide."

"But I have."

"Why?"

"Not sure. It felt right at that moment, I guess."

"You don't remember?"

"No, not really."

"Do you think she's as sick as Fischer says?"

He leaned into the table and for a moment, his leaning in felt like a weight, a relinquishing—as though the choice, the decision, the weighing of life and death, depended on her, was her responsibility.

"I'm not sure," she said.

She couldn't keep her vision of Julia in her new pink dress, cheeks flushed, eyes bright, out of her mind's eye.

The waitress brought their check and asked if they wanted anything else before she deposited it face down on the laminated table. Mali watched her walk back toward the bar, say something to the bartender, and giggle. Then she was gone.

"But my question is," Mali said, "do I feel she doesn't belong in the hospital because I'm her mother and can't face up to having an emotionally sick child? Or is it, because I am her mother, I don't feel she belongs there? I don't know which way is right. I just don't know."

"Me neither," he said, letting out a long, loud sigh.

"As crazy as it sounds, though, I can't help but think her suicide attempt was a survival mechanism. Julia is a survivor. I believe that so strongly about her. She's a problem solver, like you. And look, here we are, rallying to her side, trying to help her, gathering all our forces."

"But what about this deep, black world Fischer says she lives in?" he said. "The results of those awful tests, her morbid thoughts? What do we do with those?"

"I can't reconcile those tests with the child I know," she said.

"Even though those tests show her . . .?"

"But look how she's functioning at school and at a job."

"I agree. Nothing seems to make any sense."

Michael looked at his watch and, taking money out of his wallet to pay the check, said they should be going. Julia would be out of work in a couple of minutes.

• • • • •

Mali stares out the window of her dead mother's living room, drawn again to the flickering lights of the city. She tries to think back over their daughter's life. What had they passed down to her? What had made her world so tenuous, so fragile?

Then another memory comes back to her.

One day, a few months later, when she happened to be in Julia's room putting away her clean laundry, she'd found Elie Wiesel's book lying open on the floor. She'd picked it up, annoyed at how it had been abandoned in that way. As she idly flipped through the pages from back to front, she was caught by a passage both highlighted and underlined. She sat on Julia's bed, stunned, breathless, the words punching her in the stomach: *I speak of society's attraction to violence on one hand and the temptation of suicide on the other. How can we explain the hate that burns in so many homes? How can we understand the despair that pushes so many young people to suicide if not in the context of the event? All roads lead us back there. Defying all analogies, Auschwitz institutes itself as a point of reference.*

How does the Holocaust get passed down? Does it become a part of this next generation, the way it did for Michael and Mali? Just by being? A sort of osmosis? A kind of absorption? Like water into a sponge?

As Mali turns back from her mother's living room window, she notices the miniature silver tea service on the windowsill behind the couch. A gift from her father for their fifth wedding anniversary, her mother once told her. It was one of the few things she couldn't leave behind when she left London. Badly in need of polishing now, the pieces are a dull grey. The lid to the sugar bowl is missing. A tiny wire has replaced the lid's hinge on the larger pot. A butterfly, its wings spreading upward as though ready to flutter off at any moment, rests as the knob on top of the tiny lid. Mali brings the tea service to the couch. She sets it on the cocktail table by the vase of parched yellow roses, adding it to the stack of Holocaust books she's found on the floor between the couch and the bookshelves.

She exhales a long sigh, brings her reading glasses down from the crown of her head to her eyes, and picks up her mother's pages again. But then she finds herself unexpectedly thinking of how her own words, written out of anger, and hurt, unintentionally changed the course of her young life long ago. She stares up at the blackness of the sky, forcing herself to change the trajectory of her thoughts and return them to her mother's.

CHAPTER 13

December 4, 1988

The more I go backward in my life, the more I remember. The old memories seem to be coming in fast and furious. I only wish I could say the same about David's recuperation. He sleeps most of the time when he's not in too much pain. We've talked about the hospital. The time has come for him to go, he says. It'll be easier for us both. I feel so badly, so ill-equipped. But he doesn't want the entire burden to rest on me. He says this to me again and again. Doesn't he realize that I need him here with me? Once he goes to the hospital, it'll feel as though he's already gone. And I know what it'll be like when I visit him. I'll be in the vinyl-covered chair by his bed, and while he sleeps, which he'll be doing most of the time, I'll try to read my book. I won't get very far because of the distractions all around me. People coming and going—nurses, doctors, lab technicians, volunteers, meals delivered on trays, the empties taken back, and on and on. Am I being selfish? Yes. And although I dread his being in the hospital, I realize I can no longer give him the nursing care he needs.

It's around nine in the morning. I've had my English muffin with butter and marmalade and drunk a good strong cup of coffee. Then, bundled up, I'm out on the balcony. I really enjoy being out here in all sorts of weather, especially now that I can't get out as often as I used to. I can feel connected to the world at large even though I'm just the observer from up high. We had a dusting of snow last night. Where the snow has stuck— on the window ledges and fire escapes—the buildings across the road look pretty, decorated, like a cake covered in frosting. Otherwise, the roads and sidewalks are messy and black with grime. I'm tired this morning. The frigid air is good for me. It revives me a bit.

David's still sleeping. Today we'll call his doctor to discuss our options.

I hope Elizabeth can spare me a little time later. I absolutely must go to the library. Then again, if David goes into hospital, I won't have to have someone here if I need to go out. This, the only plus side to my life right now.

I've come back inside, made myself another cup of coffee, and brought it to the dining table that has now become my writing desk. I've opened my latest notebook and read over what I wrote yesterday. I hate to do that. It never reads as well, the second time around.

• • • • •

After your Opa was picked up on November 10, 1938, and imprisoned in the concentration camp at Sachsenhausen, Oma would get up at five every morning, travel to one or another foreign embassy—it really didn't matter which one—and stand in line with thousands of other Jewish women. Everyone had money and jewels hidden in coat linings, in underwear, or in shoes to bribe embassy officials for exit permits, visas, or whatever else it would take for them to help release their husbands, fathers, brothers, or uncles, from the concentration camps, and guarantee them emigration from Germany. Poor Oma stood in line for hours, day after day, waiting to get an interview. At the end of the day, or even sometimes arbitrarily at noon, if the officials felt like it, the embassies would be shut down and everyone sent home. Then the women would have to start all over again the next day, and for most of them, the day after, and then the days that followed, until time ran out.

While Oma was away, I tried to be very brave for her. She was usually long gone before I even woke up, but I'd always find my roll-and-jam breakfast waiting for me on the kitchen table. To overcome my fear of the eerie stillness in the apartment, I hummed quietly to myself or talked or sang out loud to Schani. I can still see him now, his ears cocked as he listened to my off-key attempts at the songs Opa had taught me when I was very little. After my breakfast, I'd go into Opa's study, lock the door, wrap myself up in a blanket, and lie on the couch; Schani always curled in a ball at my feet. Then I'd close my eyes and pray that even if the Gestapo came knocking, I wouldn't hear them and Schani wouldn't bark.

Every evening at sunset, a huge sense of relief would wash over me. I knew it couldn't be too long before Oma would be home. My job was to prepare a footbath of warm water and scented bath salts for her. Without even giving her a chance to take off her coat, I'd put my arm through hers and guide her to the couch I'd been hiding on all day. Once she sat, I'd take off her shoes, rub her frozen feet, and sink them into the warm, soothing water.

As each day passed, her beautiful face seemed more haunted and gaunt to me.

Then one day, without any advance warning of his release, Opa was home. He just showed up one morning, as mysteriously and suddenly, as when he'd been picked up six weeks earlier. I happened to be looking out of the window when the taxi dropped him off. There he was. But he didn't look like my father. He looked like a beggar. Completely disheveled. His suit crushed and dirty. He even seemed smaller to me than I'd remembered him. His hair had been shaved, his bare skull, dead-like. After he'd been home and his hair had begun to grow back, it came in solid white. But that day, stuck by the window, I watched him walk from the taxi to the door of our apartment building. He moved very slowly. His shoulders were hunched. And then his hat. God knows why, but I remember his hat. Vividly. It was rumpled, as though it'd been squeezed through a wringer and it had shrunk and was now too small for his head. When he rang the doorbell, I ran to the bathroom, petrified. I locked myself in and wouldn't come out for a very long time. Later, I didn't dare look at him. He'd only been gone for six weeks and I couldn't recognize him as my father. I became obsessed with his hat, even dreaming about it at night.

I can't imagine how awful it must've been for him.

Because Opa had been so stubborn about leaving Berlin when it would've been very much easier to do so, we were the last of our family to make it out of Germany. In those harrowing months, from October 1938 to August 1939, we lived in a state of constant terror. The world had become an irrational and terrifying place. Normal, everyday predictability had been wiped clean from the slate of our lives. We never knew from one day to the next, what might happen to us; what new laws or edicts the Nazis would enforce. Our life, as we knew it, had been smothered, as surely as pillows put to our faces, our breathing to a stop. Telephone calls and ringing doorbells terrified me. I began to throw up every morning. As soon as I opened my eyes, I'd feel a lump rising from somewhere deep inside me and without warning, dinner from the night before would be in my mouth, lumpy, acidy, frightening.

I have a terrifying memory. I don't remember precisely when this was. But it must have been before Kristallnacht, before Opa had been picked up and imprisoned at Sachsenhausen. The day was beautiful, I remember. We were out for a walk in the Tiergarten. As usual, I trailed behind Oma and Opa, kicking at the loose dirt and stones on the path as I walked. At one time, I used to fantasize that if I were to slip behind a tree, or just run back in the opposite direction, Oma and Opa wouldn't even notice. They'd continue their walk, totally engrossed in their conversation, in themselves, and completely mindless of me. But on this day, Oma turned back. She came toward me, her steps quick and short in her long, narrow skirt.

"You really can't dillydally around here," she said. "It's much too dangerous."

She linked her arm through mine and led me to where Opa—a look of slight annoyance on his handsome, smooth-shaven face—waited with Schani. It was never that I had trouble keeping up with them, it was more that I enjoyed going at my own pace, listening to my own voice, not theirs. Oma and Opa's talk frightened me. Not intentionally, of course. But in those days, the only topics of conversation were focused on the SS, roundups in the dead of night, suicides, train stations, headquarters at Alexanderplatz, killings, robberies, and sudden disappearances. The many, never-ending fears.

After our walk around the Tiergarten, we got back into the car, Oma and Opa in the front, and I in the back with Schani, his sticky tongue licking at my face, tickling me. Oma suggested we stop at our favorite *Konditorei* on our way home. We told each other which pastries we were in the mood for. Always cream puffs for me. I had such a sweet tooth as a kid.

Opa parked right in front of the bakery. Oma and Opa went in. I stayed in the car with Schani, my protector. Suddenly, a green police car drove up and parked right behind us. Two men from the Gestapo got out. They were very tall. I slunk as low as I could in my seat without losing sight of them. Everything about the two men, from the buttons on their tight-fitting green uniforms to their polished belts and high, black boots, shone in the blinding sunlight. Schani lifted his head to the window and barked. The two men turned their heads toward us for a moment. I slid to the floor, pulling Schani down with me. I waited a few seconds, then peeped out of the window again. The two men looked at each other, shrugged, and went in.

Convinced they had followed us from the Tiergarten and were here to arrest Oma and Opa, I sat back up and kept a vigilant watch over the bakery. I didn't dare take my eyes off it for a second. Schani jumped on top of me. He thought we were playing a game. I watched an old woman in a long grey coat enter the shop. She was tiny and walked stooped over. The way her head bobbed up and down, she reminded me of a bird pecking for grains on the sidewalk. The thick, heavy coat she wore, so ill-fitting and oversized, must have belonged to her husband at one time. Although how she would have had a husband, my eleven-year-old self could not have imagined. The old lady carried a shopping basket. I envisioned it filled with the fruits and vegetables Oma was prohibited from buying. Schani nudged my thigh. He barked. He wanted to play. I put an arm around his curly, furry neck to quiet him, and resumed my silent, vigilant guard, all the while a knife-stabbing ache radiated through my insides.

What was taking so long?

Two schoolboys on bikes stopped at the bakery. They let their bikes fall against the shop window in a noisy clatter, the plate glass shimmering with the vibration. Laughing and shadowboxing with each other, they ran in. The old woman came out of the shop, a loaf of bread sticking out of her basket.

More nervous and scared by the moment, I began talking to Schani. What has happened to them? What was taking them so long? I thought the worst.

Schani licked the tears from my cheeks. I expected the two Gestapo officers to emerge with Oma and Opa under arrest, their arms held high in surrender, their box of pastries dropped to the sidewalk. And in my imagination, I saw them being brutally shoved into the back of the police

77

car as if they were common thieves. I worried. How would I get home from here? I didn't even have the money for a streetcar.

But just as my panic began escalating beyond my control, Oma and Opa, pale and shaken, were walking quickly toward me. Relieved and so happy to see them, I kept kissing and hugging Schani and didn't notice at first that they were as empty-handed now as when they'd first gone into the bakery.

"That was most unpleasant," Opa said as he got in behind the wheel.

"There was an old lady who went in after you and came out before you," I said, leaning over Oma's seat. "Do you remember seeing her?"

"We let her go ahead of us, pretending we hadn't made up our minds yet," Opa said.

Oma caressed my arm. "It would've been impossible to leave as soon as the Gestapo came in. Much too obvious."

"So, what did you do?"

"Your mother came up with a brilliant idea. She announced loudly how she'd stupidly left our money in the car."

"And we walked out," Oma said.

She closed her eyes and rubbed her arms to stop from shivering.

Opa slipped the car into gear. All of us were silent now, even Schani had settled down on the seat next to me and put his head in my lap.

As we pulled away from the curb, I turned back and saw the two Gestapo officers walk out of the bakery toward their car, stuffing over-filled chocolate éclairs into their mouths. They appeared so harmless at that moment, I remember thinking, and just like anybody else, laughing and licking the creamy white filling off their fingers and from the corners of their mouths. Just like anybody else, with their bodies bent forward, their legs spread wide apart on the pavement. Only they weren't. Even if the creamy white filling were to ooze and dribble over the front of their shiny-buttoned green uniforms and land in sticky dollops on the topside of their tall, shiny, black leather boots, they weren't just like anybody else.

• • • •

December 4, 1988

I can recall all too well that lump that pushes up from under my sternum, making it hard for me to breathe. Desolation, uncertainty, and loneliness, these, the only cards I can see in my future now.

David will be admitted into Mount Sinai tomorrow, December 5th. I am sure his death is coming soon. As each day ends, the inevitable seems so much closer to me than even the day before. I'm trying to steel myself. David insists I don't spend my entire day at his bedside. But I know I'd find it too difficult not to do that. So I will go to the hospital anyway. I'll pack a Bloomingdale's shopping bag with books and magazines, scrap paper and pens, an apple or two, a package of chocolate chip cookies to share with David's nurses, and always a pair of fresh pajamas for him. And thanks to you, I have a little contraption that lets me listen to music.

Shamelessly, I have been walking around Manhattan with the tiny buds stuck in my ears, while either Mozart, Beethoven, or Schubert keeps me calm and lets me lose myself. There are times, I get so lost I don't even hear the occasional car or truck honking at me as I blithely cross the street without looking. I've had a couple of near misses. And as I scramble back to the curb, I secretly laugh at myself, imagining a headline in the newspaper: Woman, with Husband Dying in Hospital, Run Over Crossing the Street. Ear Buds to Blame.

CHAPTER 14

October 26, 2014

Mali smiles. The little contraption was a Sony knockoff she'd found in one of her kitchen drawers, the one she normally reserved for odds and ends such as rubber bands, appliance how-to booklets, or bits of string. Her mother had thanked her profusely for it, and for the music tapes she had made for her. A lifesaver is what she had called her, and Mali could only laugh at the exaggeration.

Right around the time David was admitted to the hospital, Mali remembers going into the city to have lunch with her mother. They had agreed to meet at the clock in Grand Central Station, and rather than their usual window shopping up Madison Avenue, the plan was to head downtown for a change of pace, find a coffee shop, then go on to Macy's. On Fifth, they stopped every so often to look at the shop windows already decorated for Christmas.

"There'll be no holiday for me this year," her mother said, her voice sounding flat, matter of fact.

Mali steered her away from the glittery window in silence.

They continued their walk arm in arm, eyes squinting against the low-slung sun, bright in their faces.

"He'll never be good again." The words spilled out of her mother's mouth in a rush, as if they were unbearable and she was unable to hold on to them any longer.

"How can you be so sure?" Mali asked.

"You remember Oma?" her mother said and stopped walking to face Mali.

How could she forget her grandmother? Her blue eyes, the way they sparkled with laughter and complicity, as if she and Mali shared the secret to the world. Or how her hands flew up to her face in excitement as she talked, a lit cigarette pinched between her index and middle fingers, her nails painted a pearly pink. And her elegance and poise when she walked. But she could also remember her mother's angered impatience.

"Do you know what the doctor told me after Oma died?" her mother said a few moments later, squeezing Mali's hostage arm tightly. "He said she'd really committed suicide. The cancer had gone from her lungs to her brain. I knew it must've been true because by the end of her life, she did things backward, like take out her teeth whenever friends came to visit. Can you imagine?"

"No," Mali said, a sudden shiver of fear going through her.

"Opa," her mother continued, defiance in her voice. "He was a madman. He tried to protect Oma from herself—at least that's what he said—but honestly, I think it was himself he needed to protect. He didn't allow any of us to mention the 'C' word. You think she didn't know? All that weight loss and feelings of weakness?"

She made a clucking sound with her tongue and shook her head. Then she released her hold on Mali's arm and they resumed their slow pace along Fifth Avenue.

"She knew she had cancer?" Mali said.

"Of course she did. How could she not? But she didn't say anything because she didn't want to upset him. We all had to go along with it, play this dumb charade for him. What a selfish man."

Mali wasn't aware then, when she was younger and her own kids were small, that she could have been of any help to her mother, or that her mother might have even cared for it. Now, so many years later, she realizes that her own memory of the four months her mother had spent in Miami Beach with her dying mother is very vague. Mali thinks of her own two grown daughters. What does she expect of them? Like her, all those years ago, they are now preoccupied with family lives of their own: children and husbands, households, and work. It makes her feel lonely to think of them in their separate lives, as though they lived in a join-the-dots drawing, the family only emerging as true and whole after the dots have been linked and the connections made. But would that linking be up to her? Mali appreciates only too well the jealously safeguarded preservation of the family unit. Michael doesn't. He misunderstands her intentions, her laissez-faire attitudes, and accuses her of not caring, of being like her mother. Now that her mother is gone, will he continue to compare them? Or will she take over by proxy?

"So this is what I wanted to talk to you about," her mother began, once their coats were off and they were settled in a booth with glasses of water and menus on the table. "I don't know how else to put it," she added. "But I seem to be reeling backward in my life."

Mali remembers that she didn't know how to respond, sitting across from her mother in that coffee shop on Thirty-Fourth Street with its cheery, noisy anticipation of the coming holidays in the air, the cutout pictures of turkeys and pilgrims still plastered on the mirrored walls above the red vinyl booths, and the small silver Christmas tree decorated with red and green shiny ornaments.

"My past is swallowing me," she said, moving her menu aside and pushing up the sleeves to her sweater. "Parts of my childhood come back to me so clearly, it's like time has collapsed between then and now. Other times, I look back and the person I thought I was, is a stranger, belonging in some other life. Does what I'm saying make any sense to you at all?"

Mali understood perfectly. Whenever she went back to London to visit her father, she would always search for confirmation and clues to a place and time she could recognize as truly her own: a childhood, a past, a history that *she* alone came from and still felt a link to.

She could have never revealed her feelings of detachment to her mother, the childhood nightmares, the second-hand history so real, so palpable. She couldn't stand the traces of guilt in her mother's face, as obvious to her as the wrinkle lines marking her forehead the moment talk of her divorce or Mali's childhood would come up. And anyway, those talks would inevitably make Mali feel stupid for the self-pity that rose up inside her, heating her cheeks and worming its ugly way through the callous of old, scarred, battle wounds—ones that had never completely healed, even now.

Over bacon, lettuce, and tomato sandwiches, her mother told Mali about the dreams she was having of her early childhood in Berlin. They were so vivid, she said, that in the first few moments after waking in the morning, she felt disoriented, even paralyzed in a way. First, she felt let down, then terribly sad when she realized where she was, and what she faced with David's illness.

"And I keep going backward in my head," she said. "While needing to focus my thoughts on David, I find myself thinking of Oma instead. Young, vibrant, full of life."

"But that's okay, Mom. You don't have to feel guilty."

"And always filled with energy and raring to go," her mother continued. "One year, when we still lived in Berlin, Opa gave her a white two-seater Fiat for her birthday. It was the cutest little thing. She loved to tool around town, happy to pick up any one of her friends needing a ride. It meant that I had to sit with Schani in the open baggage compartment at the back. I never minded, really. Every afternoon she'd be waiting at the door for me to come home from school, dressed in her hat and coat, and ready to go out. If she happened to have a date with her sister and couldn't wait for me to get home, she'd call up the school and tell the secretary I had a doctor's appointment and needed to leave right away. Then she'd come and get me, even though the school day hadn't ended. She never worried about my homework. Bring it along, she'd say, you can just as easily do it at the Dobrin. That was the coffee house we Jews were still allowed to go to."

Her mother laughed at her memories. She took a sip of her coffee, then rearranged the plate and the water glass in front of her, seeming to need the time to formulate the rest of her thoughts.

"Coffee houses, the heartbeat of Berlin, lined the Kurfürstendamm," she went on. "And in pleasant weather, rows and rows of tables and chairs took over the sidewalks. Such a marvelous city in those days. Exciting, fashionable, cosmopolitan. And my mother, the lady of leisure, at least that's what Opa had always called her, was pampered. Not only did we have my nanny back then, but also a maid and a cook. But, of course, all this was before Hitler."

Mali remembers them being distracted suddenly by the clattering of dishes and silverware as the busboy cleared the table next to theirs. At a loss, she was relieved by the commotion. What words of consolation could she have found for her mother? Were there any? She didn't think so.

"Did I tell you about the dog I saw the other day on my way home from the hospital?" her mother said in an upbeat voice, as if she were going to tell a joke.

"No," Mali said. "What kind of dog?"

"A beautiful, white haired standard poodle. He was tied up to a parking meter. He reminded me so much of my Schani, I was thrown for a few moments."

"Ah," Mali said, reaching for her mother's hand.

"I had to pet him. I bent down, closed my eyes, and ran my fingers through his soft, white, curly coat. And on cue, so many random childhood memories began to click through my mind like a movie."

"Do you think seeing and touching the dog set you off on your backward slope, so to speak?"

"Maybe the dog is to blame for a bit of it, but not all. Anyway, how can I blame a poor innocent dog for all my troubles?"

"I'm not suggesting . . ."

"No, I understand," her mother said, and laughed. "But in all seriousness, I think it's because I've been so overwhelmed and scared for David. Then, on top of it, listening to those fiftieth anniversary Kristallnacht stories on the radio. Remember, I told you about them?"

"Yes," Mali said, "but why do you keep listening to the broadcasts if they upset you so?"

"Believe it or not, I can't help it. I am just so drawn to those stories. I don't know how else to explain it to you. I don't have the words for it yet."

"Yet?" Mali said.

"Never mind."

"Okay. Then tell me what happened with the dog tied up to the parking meter."

"It's a funny story," her mother said. "The dog began to bark."

"And?"

"Well, a youngish woman in sneakers and black spandex—you know the type—strode out of one of the stores and gave me a filthy look."

"Did she say anything to you?"

"No, thankfully. She just untied her dog and walked away with him."

"That's it? That's the story?"

"Yes," her mother said.

"She probably thought you were going to steal him."

"Maybe." They both laughed.

It was later than they'd expected when they left the coffee shop. Mali had a train to catch and her mother was due back at the hospital to see David. Macy's would have to wait for another day. They made their way back up Fifth Avenue mostly in silence, only commenting every so often on a shop window, or the way a person they passed in the street was dressed.

At Grand Central, they kissed each other goodbye, and before her mother let her go, she said, almost as an afterthought, "Opa was always such a law-abiding citizen. When the Nazis called for the Jews to give up their jewelry, their furs, their money to the German state, he properly complied. Meanwhile, everyone else around us smuggled their jewels and money abroad, sewing them into the linings of their clothes or packing them into the heels of their shoes. They also sent out valuables by hiding them in the felt flowers they fabricated, a common cottage industry at the time."

She kissed Mali, first on one cheek then the other, and said, "I love you. Take care of yourself. Kisses to Julia and Steffi, and to Michael, of course."

As Mali ran for her train, she wondered if, after all, she had missed something her mother had been trying to tell her.

CHAPTER 15

December 6, 1988

I've just finished reading Vikram Seth's *Two Lives*. Do you remember the book? I was fascinated by the life story of Seth's great-uncle from India and his Jewish great-aunt from Berlin. It brings back so many memories. What a coincidence that they'd lived in Berlin before the war, then in the same area of London as we did during and after. As I read, I wondered if we had ever crossed paths in Hendon: at the Gaumont cinema located next door to the Hendon Central tube station, for example, or in Hendon Park, across from their house on the Queen's Road, or at the library on the Burroughs, further up Hendon Road and across the Watford Way.

I'm sorry I didn't know them at that time. Perhaps we could have consoled each other.

•　　•　　•　　•　　•

When Opa still owned his *Motorwagen Vertrieb,* a very nice young man from India came into his automobile showroom one day. He looked at a Fiat. He explained to Opa how he'd arrived in Berlin from Delhi with his wife and two small sons only a couple of months earlier. He said he was interested in buying a car so that he could take his family away from the city on weekends, go on road trips around the country, explore. As Opa showed him the different model cars, their conversation inevitably came around to our plight—that of the Jews in Nazi Germany. The man was very sympathetic to Opa and asked him if there was anything he could do to help.

"I was dumbfounded," he said, home now, and coming into the kitchen. "No one has offered to help in any way since . . . God . . . I don't even remember when."

He stopped talking. Unfolded his arms. Shoved his hands into his trouser pockets, jingled keys, and coins.

I remember I'd just finished setting the table for dinner. Oma was cutting up the few vegetables she was permitted to buy and tossing them into the pot of water boiling on the stove. And Opa, he remained standing in the doorway, his arms crossed at his chest, his eyes focused on the floor. Was he searching for the perfect words to say what he intended and then the way in which to speak them?

"That's so thoughtful." Oma turned off the gas and came to give him a kiss hello.

"Here's the thing, though," he said. "It came to me that with two small children, he might like to adopt a very handsome, good-natured white poodle."

"No. Not Schani. You can't . . ."

"The nice young man was delighted with the idea," my father said, ignoring my outburst. "He told me to contact him when we're ready."

I ran from the kitchen to my bedroom, flung myself on the bed, and cried my eyes into two puffy slits, positive my heart would be irreparably broken if Schani were taken away from me. Why? I kept asking myself. Why was all this happening? Why were chunks of my life being chopped off, as if they were no more than the dead branches of a tree?

And my Schani, my playmate, confidant, love of my young life, to be given away to a family from India who lived in the east end of Berlin, the map showing it to be in the absolute opposite direction from the Grunewald, our West Berlin address.

If I knew the family's name, I don't anymore.

I should mention that the fateful day was precipitated, then cemented by a strange and frightening incident.

We had woods and a lake in our neighborhood and Oma always took Schani out for walks there. He loved the water and would run for the lake the moment Oma let him off the leash. No sooner was he out of the water than he'd be rolling around in the nearest patch of mud—his legs sticking straight up in the air, a teeth-baring grin spreading across his handsome face—until any sign of whiteness had disappeared from his fur.

On the day of the incident, Oma and Schani encountered a man with a large, fierce-looking Alsatian dog. The dog growled at Schani. Schani whimpered and dashed off. The dog chased after Schani, caught up to him a few moments later and bit him in the neck. Poor Schani cried out in pain and darted away again. Oma was frantic and began to run after him. The man who owned the Alsatian laughed at her.

He yelled, "Hey you! You, Jewish bitch. Don't let your Jewish dog run without a leash."

Oma was furious. And surprised at his audacity. After all, who was he to tell her what to do? Besides, his own dog ran off the leash, too.

"*I* may be Jewish," she shouted back at the man, "but my dog is most certainly *not*."

That ended the encounter and Oma forgot all about the incident until, a few weeks later when out of the blue, she was summoned by the Gestapo to be at their headquarters the following morning.

She and Opa stayed up very late into the night, going over every possible reason for the summons. By the time she left our apartment early the next morning, she still couldn't imagine what she'd done.

At the headquarters, she was brought to a large room with rows and rows of wooden chairs facing a long table that sat high on a dais. A multitude of swastika flags and banners surrounded the back of the table and hung from the walls.

She was made to sit on the cold marble floor facing the dais, still without a clue as to why she'd been summoned. Hours passed.

Finally, an officer came to her. "You've been summoned for insubordination to a high official," he said.

Stunned, she couldn't imagine what he was talking about.

"There must be a mix-up."

"No mix-up. Weren't you the one walking your poodle in the woods a few weeks ago?"

Her throat tightened; she couldn't swallow. How could she be detained for speaking up to a rude man with a vicious dog? That's crazy, she almost blurted out, then thought better of it.

Instead she said, "He wasn't in uniform. I had no idea of his high-ranking position in the Party. Naturally, I would've never talked back to him, had I known."

The officer told her to sit and wait.

She couldn't imagine they'd throw her in prison over this dog encounter. But the longer she sat there, the more she began to believe in that absurd possibility. She put her head down, closed her eyes to block the sight of the men and women around her, pleading, whining, and begging for their lives. She prayed she wouldn't have to become one of them. Eventually she lost track of time.

Suddenly, she felt a kick to her foot. She opened her eyes. Towering above her stood another uniformed man. He had a stack of papers in his hand. That's all she said she could remember about him.

"Get up," he said.

She scrambled to her feet, dizzy and faint for a moment.

"You're free to go."

"Free?" Oma said, but he had already gone.

"I think it's time," Opa said, once Oma was back at home and calmed. "I will call my friend, the kind young Indian man, and tell him we're ready for them to take Schani."

Petrified I'd never see Oma again, I didn't say a word. No choice in the matter. I knew the time had come. I'm pretty sure Oma never told us how really frightened she felt for her life at the Gestapo headquarters. I think she never allowed herself to imagine what could've just as easily happened to her that day.

Opa and I packed up the car with Schani's few possessions, the great big cushion he always slept on, his squeaky toys, his dog bowl, his papers. I attached the leash to his collar. Since he thought he was going out for a walk, it took me a little while to coax him into the car. Finally, he jumped in. I sat next to him in the backseat, rolled down the window. As usual, he stuck out his head, letting the wind blow through his curly white fur, a happy grin widening his mouth, baring his teeth.

Opa and I said nothing to each other in the car. The ride took thirty minutes. Even with the directions the nice young man from India had given to Opa, we had to stop and ask the way from local passersby.

Two young boys came running out to greet us as we pulled up outside the small row house. Their mother and father followed behind. The boys, shy at first with Schani, soon plucked up enough courage to pet him. His tongue tickled them. I showed them what Schani loved most of all. Belly rub, I said. And right on cue, Schani lay down, turned over onto his back, spread his legs wide, and shook his head from side to side in excited anticipation of my stroking his soft, white furry belly. The boys giggled, as delighted with the belly rub as Schani.

Smiling with relief that we'd reached the end of this awkward gathering; we shook hands and murmured wishes of good luck to each other. I gave the leash to the older boy and watched Schani walk the path through the little front garden and into the small house, his clipped tail bobbing away in oblivious happiness. He never did turn back, not even to look for me.

On our way home, I sat in the front next to Opa. I didn't know how I was going to survive without my precious Schani. He'd been such a huge part of my life for so long. I think I must've been around four when Opa surprised me with him one day. It was love at first sight. Everyone adored him. Schani was the best gift I ever got from Opa. He could have never predicted when he brought him home, how profoundly important that little ball of white fur would become to me.

Opa made small talk as he drove. It had begun to rain, softly at first, then more steadily. The windshield wipers sounded like a metronome, beating back and forth, and making me think of the one on my piano teacher, Frau Orloff's grand piano. I could tell Opa was trying to think of ways to cheer me up. Would I care for a piece of chocolate? He'd been saving it for a special occasion. I couldn't respond. I just sat there next to him, a lump. I watched the raindrops splash against the windshield. Then I let the steady ticktack of the wipers lull me into a daze. My eyes, open wide and staring straight ahead, couldn't focus on anything but the image in my mind of Schani, a boy on either side of him, walking away from me, his tail wagging in blissful ignorance and the question once again. Why was all this happening to me?

•   •   •

May 6, 2014
I must admit that this same question still haunts me. I've been digging into David's books on World War Two again, looking for some piece I can grab

onto, some fact that would define for me how it all came to pass. So far, I've found nothing, only a crazy, irrational hatred. Some people have said not to take it personally. After all, they say, it wasn't *me*, it was all of us. And I say back: But Hitler's feelings of hatred and loathing were personal at the start. Then his feelings got turned inside out and were made into public policy. Nobody seemed to care. Or was it that everybody agreed?

CHAPTER 16

October 26, 2014

Her mother's telephone rings out again in the silence. Before Mali has even got to her feet from the couch to the floor to stand, her mother's voice on the answering machine is suddenly cut short, mid-sentence. The caller has given up for now. Mali groans as she stands. She walks up and down the length of the living room. All these things, all these memories. She feels like crying. Her eyes fill, but the tears won't come.

She fishes her cell phone out of her back pocket and dials Michael.

"Hey," he says. "How's it going? Found any hidden treasures yet?"

"Ha! Ha!" she says, taking her mug and Elizabeth's empty scotch glass into the kitchen. "Just to let you know, I've done absolutely no sorting, no packing, so far, and I'm rapidly losing the energy to do anything tonight."

"Why? What's going on?"

"First of all, my mother left me a bunch of letters. Turns out they're the story of her life, and just as I was getting into them, Elizabeth—you remember my mother's friend, Elizabeth—stopped by here. In between her two Scotches, she told me that my mother found an article in the paper about the man, who turned out to be the little orphan boy my grandparents had adopted in Berlin in the 1930s, and who lived with them for a few months before he was shipped off to my great-grandfather in America."

"Where was the article? How did she find it?"

"It's a long story. I'll tell you all about it when I see you."

"And you had no idea?"

"No, none at all," Mali says, opening the fridge and finding the shelves almost bare except for a half-empty pack of English muffins and a tub of butter, then closing it again. "That's what makes it so . . . I don't know . . . maddening . . . and annoying. Why wouldn't she have told me? I just don't get it."

"Obviously, she must've had her reasons."

"Yeah, like what?" She peers into kitchen cabinets and finds a half-empty box of stale Ritz crackers, a can of Campbell's tomato soup, and an opened container of salted peanuts. She picks out one peanut and puts it into her mouth to test it.

"Oh, maybe just . . ." says Michael, "not wanting to make excuses for what happened, afraid of dredging up her whole childhood again?"

"But that makes no sense at all. She obsessed over everything to do with Nazi Germany and never seemed to care how her stories affected me in the past. So why now? And as for excuses . . ."

"Things change."

Mali leans against the kitchen's door jamb, looks out over the living room, and wonders how she'll empty the apartment of its bric-a-brac. She knows she won't have the heart to throw it all away.

"Have you decided, then, as to whether you're coming home or spending the night there?"

"I guess staying here the night makes the most sense. What do you think? Are you okay with it?" She grabs a handful of the peanuts, now that she knows they're not rancid, and pops them all into her mouth.

"Probably not a bad idea. It's getting late. At this rate, you won't be home before ten at the earliest."

"Then that's settled." And a sudden sense of relief washes over her. The thought of crisscrossing her way downtown to Grand Central and battling the crowds of commuters at the station exhausts her.

"The only thing is," she says. "There's absolutely nothing to eat here but half a can of peanuts and I'm suddenly starving."

"Isn't there a market across the street you can go to?"

"I guess I'll do that. And how was your day?"

"We got a few nice orders. Otherwise, nothing out of the ordinary."

"Well, that's good. Did you have a chance to talk to the kids?"

"Yes. They're doing fine. Sad, of course, but fine. They send their love and kisses."

"I can't believe it's already a week," she says, realizing, to her horror, that whenever she thinks of her mother now, she pictures her in a coma, her slack, dying face peeking above the tightly tucked, white sheets of the hospital bed.

"But not to put too much pressure on you," Michael says. "You do remember that we don't have all the time in the world to get out of the apartment. Unless, of course, you're willing to pay an extra month's rent."

"I'll get it together, I promise. What will you do for dinner?"

"Don't worry about me, I'll figure out something," he says. "So tomorrow I'll come into the city first thing and we'll tackle that jungle of an apartment together. But if you happen to get a second wind . . ."

"Yeah, I know. I'll start without you. Call me later, though."

He makes a funny kissing sound into the phone and hangs up.

Mali stares at her phone for a few seconds before sliding it into her back pocket again.

Will Michael think she's crazy when she tells him she'll want to keep the iron statuette of the Indonesian dancer or the fat white Buddha sitting on its little black stand or the clay figures from Peru with large heads and small, androgynous bodies? Or that, in fact, she wants to keep them all? Is it normal? she wonders.

Normal, that after all these years she still harbors a tiny sliver of doubt about her mother. That even now as she looks at these old photos of the two of them, she still has the need to scrutinize their faces for similarities, differences, and at the same time, tamp down the illogical fear that one day she might have totally ceased to exist for her mother.

Perhaps it's only the expectation, the anticipation, Mali thinks, that the people who claim they love you the most, will know instinctively how to make you happy. But mind reading is only for clever magicians. Disappointment muddies everything.

How many times had Mali told this to her own children when they were growing up? Steffi seemed to have understood and would appear in the kitchen many a night just before dinner, her blond hair coming loose from her lopsided pigtails, her socks bunched around her ankles, a look of worn-out frustration from too much homework on her beautiful, freckled face. Mali would be at the stove, stirring spaghetti sauce, or at the sink, rinsing lettuce leaves, trying to recapture an important moment in her own world when she'd see Steffi coming toward her out of the corner of her eye. Mali would then make believe she was taken by surprise. A little shriek, arms up in the air, eyes wide. Later it became a standard joke between them. Steffi would tiptoe up to Mali and bark "Boo!" to catch her unawares. And then after their laughter had subsided, Steffi would wrap her arms tightly around Mali's waist, lay her head on her stomach and whisper words of love. Mali would embrace her little girl back, bending to kiss the top of her head. I love you, she'd whisper. I love you, I love you, I love you, she'd whisper, again and again, to feel the power of the words, as though she could turn those words into a magical potion that would spirit away all of her daughter's disappointments as well as her own inevitable and unforgivable mistakes. Past, present, and future.

Julia, on the other hand, had always been very different from her sister. More like Mali, unable to give easily or to let her body soften and melt into her mother's embrace. Perhaps it's in our nature, Mali thinks now, eyeing the living room once again. Perhaps it's just unavoidable, the unsolved, messy things in our lives. Floating in her mind's eye, part of a recurring dream comes back to her. She remembers a cardboard box, filled with scrunched-up paper, and strange lettering stenciled all over the outside. Is she that box? She realizes her propensity to compartmentalize her life, build walls around herself. Breaking them down and reaching out has always been so much more difficult for her.

She imagines Michael's face, then the feel of her own against his chest and his arms tight around her body. Now she wishes he were already here with her. Oh well, she says aloud, as she grabs her wallet and her mother's keys and heads for the take-out place across the street, the one her mother used to frequent . . . Dammit, she says to herself as she presses the ground floor button in the elevator and feels the tears begin to smart in her eyes.

CHAPTER 17

December 6, 1988

My Sweet, when I think back to my twelfth birthday, I think of it as the separator in my childhood life: the *before* and the *after*. In the *before*, everything belonging there was wonderful; that is, *before* everything became so terrifying. In the *after,* although we were so happy and lucky to have garnered that coveted visa to England, I found myself in a constant state of confusion, on a roller coaster of mixed emotions. Yes, though our lives could move forward now, the past years—the good as well as the bad—had to be shuttered down, like blinds closed against the glaring light of our memories.

But these days, I find the need to open them wide, let the light back in.

We still lived in Berlin in July 1939. We'd had to leave our apartment in the Grunewald and move once again. This time to a *pension* on Meinekestrasse, while we waited for our final exit papers from the German government. We had two rooms in that boarding house and shared the bathroom and the tiny kitchen with another family.

All our belongings had been put into storage. I remember the day the moving van came, the rough-hewn wooden crates, like giant coffins, brought for our furniture. My father's beautiful rolltop desk, inherited from his father, the Persian rugs covering the wooden floors in our living room with fringes at the edges that my mother obsessed over keeping combed and straight. New artwork on the walls. My grandmother's Meissen china and silverware that she had passed down to my mother on her wedding day. Records and books and household items. Everything, except for a few of my father's favorites, had to go into storage. As soon as we knew the exact date of our departure from Berlin, my parents arranged to have the furniture shipped to New York, our ultimate destination. In New York, everything went back into storage again. But by the time Oma and Opa arrived in New York, ten years later, all our possessions had to be auctioned off to cover the shipping charges and the enormous storage fees.

To go back to the morning of my twelfth birthday. I'd woken at dawn and gone looking for gift-wrapped presents throughout the two small rooms of our temporary home in the boarding house on Meinekestrasse. I'd looked everywhere. Of course, I found nothing. I even went downstairs to look for birthday cards in the mailbox. I was disappointed again. But what had come was a very officious-looking envelope addressed to Opa. I went into my parents' room. I told Opa I wanted the English stamps when he was through with the letter. "English stamps?" Opa grabbed the envelope from me. He sat bolt upright, his straight, white hair sticking out in tufts all over his head. Oma sat up now too. The old bed creaked and groaned like an old man with arthritis as they moved around on it. And morning sunlight was sneaking in through the gap in the curtains. Suddenly, I heard yelps, screams, and laughter. The letter with the King George VI stamps on it was our entry permit into England. Mrs. Pick, an Englishwoman, had sponsored us. Apparently, as I found out afterward, she had sponsored many Jews. Two weeks later, we sailed for England. Just three weeks after that, Hitler invaded Poland, and England declared war on Germany.

Since Oma was a big believer in celebrations of all kinds, she couldn't let my twelfth birthday pass without giving me a present. After their excitement over the letter from Mrs. Pick in England had calmed a little, Oma produced a beautifully embroidered linen handkerchief, its four corners tied up with a blue satin ribbon. I undid the bow, and the handkerchief fell open to reveal a brooch. It was very special, she said. Her father, my grandfather, had given it to her for her twelfth birthday—just on the cusp of World War One. I tried so hard to look excited about the brooch, but as Oma said, laughing, my face was as transparent as a window and always betrayed my true feelings. She kissed me, hugged me, then fastened the horseshoe-shaped pin to my blouse. She said it had, and would continue, to bring me the best of good luck, as it always had for her. The golden brooch, inlaid with tiny seed pearls, had at each end of the horseshoe, a small, rectangular-shaped amethyst. If my grandfather had chosen the brooch for Oma, then it would be special for me too. After all, I adored my grandfather. I'll always remember him as a wonderful man, kind, generous, and very handsome. But he emigrated to America with his son, my uncle, in 1935 when I was eight, and I never saw him again. His was a strange and complicated story. I will try my best to tell it.

When my grandfather was a young man, he and his older brother visited the United States. They fell in love with the life here in America and became naturalized citizens. After a few years away, though, my grandfather—perhaps a little homesick, perhaps looking for a wife— decided to return to Germany to see his parents. On the way home, aboard the ocean liner, he befriended another young man. His name was Ernst Schreiber. Well, Ernst introduced him to his sister, Adele, who happened to be waiting for him on the dock at Bremerhaven. The romantic in me tells me it must've been love at first sight, because not long afterward they were married and Oma, the first of their three children, was born in 1902.

Now that my grandfather was a married man and living in Germany again, he needed to find a profession. But for him to work in Germany, he was required to renounce his American citizenship and reinstate his German one. He pleaded with my grandmother to leave everything behind, start afresh, and go away with him to his beloved America. She refused. It would be impossible, she'd said, to leave her family, her friends, her country. They settled in Dresden. He opened a marvelous food store on the Fressgasse.

I used to love to go there whenever we came to stay from Berlin. All kinds of salamis and hams hung from the ceiling. Vats of cucumber and tomato pickles stood by the counter along with wooden barrels of herring and onions soaking in their salty, vinegary brine. Huge burlap sacks of coffee beans surrounded the enormous grinder on the other side of the shop by the shelves of tinned goods. And of course, I loved the cakes, tarts, cookies, and breads. In between our visits to Dresden, my grandfather always sent us care packages, including *Teewurst* for me, my favorite.

Early in 1935, my grandmother died of breast cancer. By this time, the terrible persecution of the Jews in Germany had begun in earnest. My grandfather decided to uproot his only unmarried child and leave for America.

I'll never forget the day he came to our apartment in Berlin to say goodbye. After he'd kissed and hugged my parents and kissed them again, he turned to me and said, "Come Evichen, walk your old Opa to the corner." I threw on my coat and out we went. He took my hand and held it tightly in his. He began to speak. He told me I needed to be an especially good girl for my mother and father, to listen to everything they said. Then he became silent, and I remember looking up at him in anticipation of what he would say next. But there were no more words for me, only silent tears wetting his stubbly cheeks. We came to the corner. "Don't cry, Opa," I remember saying and reaching up to give him a hug and a pat. "Everything will be all right, you'll see." He laughed. He hugged me so tightly, I could hardly breathe. Then he let go of me and walked across the street. When he reached the other side, he turned back to wave. I never saw him again. But our last walk together is imprinted in my mind's eye for as long as I live.

My grandfather and my uncle moved to Detroit, where my uncle got a job with a distant relative. They lived together in an apartment and made a home for themselves there.

Still a very vital and good-looking man, at least that's what your Oma always said, he soon became involved with a woman in Detroit, a wealthy widow. Her married daughter, who was unable to have children of her own, wanted to adopt a young boy. She already had an adopted little girl. My grandfather suggested they look for a Jewish boy in Germany. To save even one life from Hitler's evil clutches would be a blessing. It was agreed. My grandfather wrote to Oma and Opa, asking them to look for such a boy.

While making the rounds at the Jewish orphanage in Berlin, Oma and Opa met a very handsome, talkative, six-year-old boy. A real charmer, Oma told me when I pestered her to describe him for me. I remember finding the whole idea of adoption most intriguing. To have a full-time, live-in playmate was beyond anything I could've ever imagined. Before the adoption could take place, though, he needed to be photographed and have recordings made of his voice. Everything was then sent to Detroit. Luckily, my grandfather's lady friend's daughter loved what she saw and heard. And Oma and Opa adopted him for her and brought him home to stay with us, until his visa and travel arrangements had been made. I adored him. His name was Horst. Although he was a little younger than me, we had such fun together. I considered him the brother I'd always longed for.

All of us participated in preparing him for the big, wide world of America. Oma and Opa found him an English tutor. We taught him table manners. And Oma took him clothes shopping for a whole new wardrobe. His visa arrived about six months later. Even though I knew that his future in America would be safe and secure—the absolute opposite of his life in Germany if he'd had to stay—I was heartbroken to see him go. He was the luckiest little boy, the chosen one from among the many others. And I felt so proud that my grandfather, my wonderful grandfather, had really saved his life.

I received only one letter from Horst in Detroit. It came shortly after he left us. He wrote how very happy he was with his new family. And that while he was writing to me, a man in white gloves stood behind him, ready to grant him any wish, within reason of course. He ended his letter by telling me I should hurry up and come to America too. He also mentioned that his adopted family changed his name from Horst to Philip. Opa had to explain to me that Horst was not an American name and that he'd have an easier time fitting in at school as Philip.

By the time my grandfather died—and I don't remember exactly when that was—he had already gone to live in New York with my aunt and uncle who'd just moved there from Dresden. We must have been in London by then. We lost complete touch with Horst and his new family.

I still often wonder about the boy. How he grew up. What he became. And if he remembers me and the few good months we had together in Berlin.

Little did I know then that the worst of our lives in Germany had yet to begin.

CHAPTER 18

October 26, 2014

Mali's cell phone rings again.

"Mom," Steffi whispers into the phone, as she always does when her children are sleeping. "What's going on? Are you okay? Dad says you're staying the night."

"I'm fine." Mali smiles to herself at her daughter's concern. "Really, I'm fine," she repeats in as reassuring a voice as she can manage. "Just a little tired, is all."

"You sure?"

"Positive. How about you? The kids?"

"A little out of sorts," Steffi says.

"I know. It's hard. Give them big hugs and kisses for me."

Mali watches another yellow petal fall to the table. There's quite a heap of them now.

"Have you heard from Julia?" Steffi says.

"Earlier. Why?"

"No reason. Just checking. She told me she'd call you after she got her kids to bed."

Julia was distant, keeping her sadness to herself the day of the funeral. And Mali hasn't had the chance to talk to her in the last day or two, except for the quick conversation they'd had concerning the business earlier that day.

A few years back she took Julia into her event planning business and re-named it, Feuer & Daughter. Lately Mali has had thoughts of slowing down, pursuing other interests, but unlike the tag line Julia wrote for their business— *We Plan for Every Event in Life*—Mali has no plan, has no clue as to what might even interest her. She's been so focused, working at her own business all these many years, she actually hasn't had the time for much of anything else, including, she's ashamed to admit, her own mother.

"Is Julia okay?" Mali asks.

"She's fine. She's just being Julia, if you get my drift."

"Yes." Mali knows just what Steffi means.

"I've been thinking. . .You know, what you said."

"What did I say?"

"That the kids should learn about the Holocaust."

"It's our family's history . . ."

"But I don't want them to worry it could happen again."

And Mali's not sure what to say to her daughter, believing it's neither as ancient history as Steffi would like to think, nor as remote a possibility to happen again as she would wish.

"I'm positive you'll do the right thing when you're ready for it," Mali says. "God knows it's a huge subject. Enormously complicated."

"Will you help me when the time is right?"

"Yes, of course, I will," Mali says, wondering when she became the expert on the subject. "I'll look for some children's books and we'll do it together."

"Great. Uh-oh, I hear Leila. She's not sleeping well these last couple of nights. Let me go and see what's up with her. Call me if you need me, okay?"

"Really, you don't have to worry about me. I'm fine."

"Dad should've gone with you . . ."

"No, no. There's nothing he can do for me right now. Honestly. Go take care of Leila. I'll speak to you later."

Mali puts her phone back on the table. She thinks of Julia, so strong now, and is reminded once again of the night she had attempted suicide. Mali is ashamed. She obviously hadn't done such a brilliant job of teaching the Holocaust to her own children. What crazy obligation had she and Michael felt, back then, to make Julia and Steffi understand? But to understand what? The seriousness of life? That even tiny moments of time couldn't be squandered away? Or mistakes made? No. They themselves weren't like that. What then? A certain gravity in living? That while they lived a stable and carefree life here in America, their grandparents and great-grandparents on both sides would have been in line for the gas chambers, had they not been lucky and well off enough to make it out of Europe in time.

There's a before and after in her own life, too; a hollowed-out line drawn through her past, a trough in the ground. She was twelve then. But hers was of her own making. Or was it? She takes her feet off the table, bends forward, picks up a handful of the dried, yellow rose petals, brings them to her nose. No scent. She drops them and watches how they float, weightless, to the papery heap piled on the low table.

One constant in her young life had never changed. It was her father's nonstop lecturing on the importance of education—the only thing, he always said, no one could ever take away from her. And his disappointment with each of her report cards telling him his daughter, the daydreamer, could do better, if only she'd apply herself.

Eventually, she did learn how to apply herself. Only not quite in the way her father had imagined it.

It had all begun in the middle of her second term at the Jewish grammar school when without notice, the French teacher left, and her replacement, Mrs. Gottlieb, came into their lives just as suddenly one rainy morning a few weeks later.

Mrs. Gottlieb was a tall, thin woman with eyes the color of dark chocolate and a complexion as pale and drab as the ill-fitting clothes on her body. She hardly looked at her class of twelve-year-old girls as she entered the room, but proceeded instead to the chalkboard, where she began to write her name in big block, capital letters. Then as though something had changed her mind, she paused in her writing and turned slightly toward the class. Fidgeting with the stick of chalk in her hand, she said in a strong foreign accent, "My name is Mrs. Gottlieb. I am your new French teacher." That said, she resumed her writing on the board. But just as she got to the last letter in her name, the chalk snapped. For a long moment she remained perfectly still with her shoulders stooped and her head bent toward the floor, almost as if she couldn't decide whether to pick up the bit of chalk at her feet or take a whole new stick out of the drawer in her desk.

Muffled noises—giggles, shuffling of feet, clearing of throats—began to ripple through the classroom. Mali remembers she'd felt embarrassed for this new teacher and jumped up from her seat. She didn't know why. Perhaps to retrieve the chalk, or just to set her back in motion. But as she started for the front of the classroom, Mrs. Gottlieb straightened herself out, turned toward Mali, her face even whiter than before, and told her, between clenched teeth, to go back to her seat. Mrs. Gottlieb's hands were shaking.

Shocked by her outburst, Mali didn't move.

"Don't you understand me?" Mrs. Gottlieb said, her voice gravelly and the blue ropey vein in her neck bulging under her pale skin.

The classroom became very quiet. Mali's cheeks burned. She felt everyone staring at her, waiting to see what she'd do next.

"If you spoke double Dutch to me, I'd understand you better," Mali blurted out, pleased with her quick-thinking retort.

Giggles burst out all over the room. Mrs. Gottlieb said no more. Instead, she stood very still by her unfinished name on the chalkboard and stared from one to the other of the girls, hopeful the beseeching look in her eyes would quiet everyone down.

It didn't.

After that first day, Mali and her friends began to play little tricks on Mrs. Gottlieb—hate notes scratched in hieroglyphic symbols of their newly created alphabet, or sunglasses worn in the classroom on dreary, rainy days.

Powerless as a dried leaf blowing in the wind, Mrs. Gottlieb would stand before them, her dark, watery eyes begging for their attention. There were times she'd yell, her face contorting as though in pain. But her pleading voice never reached as far as the back of the classroom.

Mali became obsessed with Mrs. Gottlieb.

Then, one day, while playing jacks on the gritty cloakroom floor and discussing the geometry test, they'd taken the period before, a brilliant idea came to Mali. She remembers feeling rather like a Yorkist lord out to murder the king, and as she detailed her plot to her friends, she grew more and more excited by it. In History class, her scheme had so absorbed her, she forgot that the king had fallen into Yorkist hands at the battle of St. Albans. And she'd missed a perfectly good throw when her turn came to bat in rounders.

It was pouring with rain the day of their exploit. The sound of it pelting down on the roof above them made it exceptionally hard to hear Mrs. Gottlieb conjugate the irregular verb *aller*.

She wrote the words on the board. "Can any of you tell me how else this verb is used?" She turned around to face the class.

Mali raised her hand. "I know," she said.

"Then please give the class your example."

"*Je vais vous tuer*," Mali said in triumph, encouraged now by the giggles coming from the rest of her cohorts.

At first Mrs. Gottlieb only stared at her. Then, in an even quieter voice than usual, she asked why Mali would want to kill her.

Still feeling brave and triumphant, Mali told her *tuer* was the first thing that had come to mind. Of course she hadn't meant it literally. Only as an example of how the verb *aller* can be used. Future form, right?

Mrs. Gottlieb didn't answer. Instead she told the class about another irregular verb. *Avoir*. A form of past tense. At the board once again, she wrote out the conjugation.

Mali coughed, and she and her friends jumped up from their seats and dashed toward the front of the classroom, the shiny, sharp tips of their compasses pointed in their teacher's direction. In the rush, the rubbish bin got accidentally kicked over. It landed on its side with a resounding, metallic bang. Crumpled-up paper and bits of chalk tumbled out. Stunned by the sudden clatter, everyone stopped dead, like statues in a game of Simon Says.

Mrs. Gottlieb's hands flew to cover her face and she fled the room, screaming.

Back at their desks, the girls settled into a strained silence. Ten minutes passed, then fifteen, then twenty. The bell rang. End of French class, time for Geography, and still no sign of Mrs. Gottlieb. Mali breathed a sigh of relief.

The school day ended in the usual way and as she walked home, her head bent against the drizzling rain, she defended herself in her imaginary courtroom, showing her prosecutor all angles of her innocence. Mostly, she'd said to herself—pushing open the back door to the kitchen, dropping her satchel to the floor, her raincoat to the nearest chair—it was Mrs. Gottlieb's fault. She should have been in control.

The next day was routine, except that everyone was particularly studious in French class. Mrs. Gottlieb picked up where she'd left off with the irregular verbs, as if nothing had happened. For a little while, Mali even thought she might have let the incident slide, let it be forgotten. But as the bell sounded and slightly above the din of desk lids slamming shut and chairs scraping back, she heard her say, "Amalia, please meet me in the teachers' room after school." Her heart thudded. It hadn't been forgotten, after all.

Mali ran up the three flights of stairs to the teachers' room and, finding the door ajar, gave a quick knock and walked in. Mrs. Gottlieb was standing at an open window, her back to Mali. Motioning her in, she told her to sit, but didn't move from her spot by the opened window. An eerie, death-like silence hovered in the air. Then quite suddenly, Mrs. Gottlieb seemed to have gained the courage to turn around to face Mali and began speaking in her quiet, strained, foreign voice.

"What you did to me yesterday was appalling." She stopped talking. Mali played with the pages of a book she held in her lap, never once looking up. "It wasn't a joke, you know, it was cruel. I don't understand why you would do such a thing. Do you?"

Mali lifted her shoulders in a shrug. She suddenly had no idea.

"I'm sure you weren't brought up to be hurtful, were you?"

Still focusing on the book in her lap, Mali shook her head.

"Maybe you think I'm not a good teacher," Mrs. Gottlieb went on. "But tell me, is that reason enough to hate me so much?"

"I . . . I don't . . ." Mali stammered, now completely lost.

Mrs. Gottlieb turned back to the window. And as she reached out for the latch to close it, the sleeve of her cardigan sneaked up her arm just enough to reveal a blue number eight tattooed into her pale skin. Mali stared at it, recognizing it to be the first in a string of digits indelibly scorched into her arm.

"I didn't teach in my old life," she said and, noticing her partially bared arm, quickly pulled down her sleeve to cover it. Too late, though. The grainy black and white images, Mali had seen before, flooded through her mind in horrifying detail.

"You see..." Mrs. Gottlieb said, "I worked as a translator for an import-export company in Berlin until the birth of my baby girl. It was the happiest time in my life."

She came away from the window and stood in front of Mali. Then, as she folded her arms across her chest, she said, "But my happiness was not to last."

She sighed. Uncrossed her arms. Held out her palms and looked at them, as if her child might still be there, and then resumed her walk, back and forth.

While Mrs. Gottlieb paced the small room, Mali watched her feet in the ugly brown lace-ups and wondered about her baby girl. She'd heard what they did to small children in those places. Her footsteps stopped. Mali glanced up to find her eyes, like fathomless black pools, staring hard at her.

Mrs. Gottlieb took a deep breath. "Dr. Grau helped many people in similar situations to me. Those of us whose whole families . . ."

She came to sit on a chair opposite Mali, crossed her thin legs, and pushed back the stray limp hairs that had fallen into her face as she sat.

"I don't have to tell you of all . . . the unspeakable . . ." she said, almost in a whisper. Bending forward just slightly, she reached out her hand, as if to touch Mali's knee, then quickly brought it back to her lap and straightened herself out.

"When I arrived here in this country," she continued, her voice almost back to normal now, "my first job was as a waitress at the Lyons Corner House at Marble Arch. You know it?"

Mali nodded.

"I had the breakfast shift. All morning long I ran back and forth between the kitchen and the dining room, serving up plates of eggs and bacon and pots of English tea. My back, my shoulders, my arms . . . everything ached. And my feet. A mass of blisters. But you know what? I loved that job. I loved that my body began to feel those ordinary aches and pains again. And you know what else?"

Mali shook her head.

"It got me out of bed every morning. I never had to think about it. I just did it. I had to."

Mrs. Gottlieb smiled for a moment. The smile changed her face, and for the first time, Mali found softness there, even beauty.

"So, when Dr. Grau gave me this opportunity here at the Hasmonean, I thought I could make a difference in the lives of young people like you, Amalia. I wanted to teach you—yes, French—but also how important learning is, how what you know can help you overcome all sorts of . . . well, I mean, learning makes you strong, makes you a mensch."

Mali envisioned her father's small, square-shaped hands open wide and raised toward his head. Then she heard his voice, the familiar-sounding, mispronounced words: "To have an education, to *learn,* I cannot tell this to you enough. Believe me, it's the one thing, the *only* thing, no one can ever take away from you." Then she saw the blue airmail letters that came every week from her mother, the return address in New York—a place that only resided in her imagination. And suddenly, she'd felt herself a stranger in a no-man's-land, belonging to no one, fitting in nowhere.

Without warning, as if she'd just reached her limit and had perhaps said too much, Mrs. Gottlieb stood up, and with a wave of her hand, excused Mali from the room. As she reached for the knob to open the door, Mali turned back.

"I'm so sorry," she said. "I didn't know."

But her words found no voice; only her breath hit the air. And Mrs. Gottlieb hadn't noticed her gesture. Her back was already to Mali. She'd reclaimed her place by the window, looking out at the street below, in that same eerie, death-like silence as before.

● ● ●

Now that Mali is totally distracted from her mother's letters, she decides she needs another coffee break and something sweet to eat. In the kitchen, she fills the kettle, puts it on the stove. The giant chocolate chip cookie she couldn't resist when she bought dinner at the market across the street, sits waiting for her on the countertop. A well-deserved treat, she tells herself, and laughs. While she waits for the water to boil, she leans against the door jamb and surveys her mother's living room again, and all these things she'll need to pack. There's an African carving of a tall, skinny woman with bended knees, pointy breasts, and droopy ears. Mali crosses the room to get a better look at her. She touches the top of the carved head, the tips of her fingers tracing the patterns of hair zigzagged into the wood. What will she do with her, and with the little statues of Buddha? Or the hand-woven carpets from Turkey, their colors bright on the parquet floors, and the many hangings and paintings that leave very little white space on the walls? Mali even recognizes one of her own, painted when she was twenty and madly in love with the artist's life. Or was it just the boyfriend she was crazy for at the time?

How will she sort through all these things? Where will she begin? She and her mother had talked so often about this eventuality, but always in the abstract. I'll come into the city, Mali would promise, and we'll go through everything in your apartment. Now she wonders why her grandmother's glass ashtray was so special, or for that matter, the wrought-iron candlestick. She wishes she knew. But time had run out before she'd had the opportunity to find out her mother's reasons. Or even to imagine this day, today, and the train ride into Manhattan without her mother at the other end of the line to meet her.

Lights shine out of the windows in the apartment buildings across the way. Mali imagines people home from work now, as she makes her way around the living room, to turn on the rest of the many little table lamps here in her mother's apartment, though none giving off enough light.

In the bedroom closet, she finds a pair of grey sweats folded neatly on the shelf above the rail of hanging clothes. Reaching for them, and as they come tumbling down, she catches the unmistakable scent that was her mother. She nuzzles her face into the soft material and recalls one of her mother's birthdays a few years back when, as always, Mali came into the city to meet her for lunch. And, as always, had procrastinated about a present until it was too late. The perfect gift never seemed to materialize. In the end, she would make do with a bunch of flowers bought at a Korean grocery on her way uptown from Grand Central and fight for the check at lunch. On this one birthday, though, Mali had wanted to give her mother a real present, something she truly wished for.

They'd wandered arm in arm through Bloomingdale's, looking for ideas. "Ridiculous," her mother kept saying. "That you're here spending the day with me is present enough." But then, she ended up admitting she could use a new bottle of the Givenchy perfume she had recently discovered. Amarige. Mali bought her the largest size bottle and felt somewhat vindicated for all the times she'd come almost empty-handed.

Comfortable now in her mother's sweats, the scent of Amarige envelopes her in an ethereal embrace. And her feet are warming up in an old pair of white cotton socks she's found buried at the bottom of one of her mother's drawers.

Back on the couch, she closes her eyes for a moment and wonders whatever became of Mrs. Gottlieb. If she knew that the student, she'd once been so angry with, was still thinking about her, some fifty or so years later, Mali's sure that she would smile and be very happy she had achieved what she'd hoped for. At the very least, she had touched this one child, had taught her what it meant to be a mensch.

She opens her eyes, brings her eyeglasses back down from the top of her head and picks up her mother's pages again.

CHAPTER 19

May 13, 2014

My Darling, along with my own stories, I've been going over bits of Vikram Seth's memoir again. I'm at the part where his German Jewish great-aunt and his Indian great-uncle have come to London from Berlin. His great-uncle has set up his dental practice inside their house in Hendon. I know the street they lived on. I can visualize those semi-detached houses and the park across the road with its expanse of green lawn. Now I'm re-reading the letters, the frantic pleas for help from their family and friends still trapped in Berlin. Seth's great-aunt and great-uncle were powerless to do anything from their new home in London. They grew more and more horrified as the tone of the letters quickly plummeted into a resigned defeat. Then, without notice, they stopped coming altogether, their absence screaming even louder than their pleas for help.

Still evacuated, still apart from my parents, I remember being at Bloomsbury Technical School in Letchworth the day I first heard of the camps at Auschwitz-Birkenau on the radio. For days and days, I walked around in a stupor. I didn't know how to tell myself what to feel. Then my thoughts turned to Marion, Lily, and Wolfe. Is that where they had ended up? I couldn't imagine it. Even now I can't. I mean I just can't imagine. All I could think of back then was how lucky we'd been. And still now, I'm so grateful luck has played its part in our lives.

Will there be another Holocaust? Will Israel be wiped clean of every one of her Jews? I worry. But, like your father, what can I, as a woman by herself, do about any of this anyway? I can only bear witness to my own Holocaust and watch from afar how that sliver of madness, like a tripwire in all of our hearts, endlessly changes us, and the way we live in the world.

I've gathered up the larger of the two piles of papers from my dining table and gone out to the incinerator, feeding the stack, bit by bit, into the chute, listening as the papers bounce off the sides and drop to the bottom. What a relief to have this done. Slowly but surely, I will empty my life of everything except what's truly necessary.

I have just found the beginning of a letter I wrote to you. I don't remember when I'd written it or even what had prompted me to write it. Strangers? A gap? What was I talking about? Did we argue? I hate when we argue. It always makes me feel so unsure of myself. Especially when I can sense you stiffen up as I come toward you to give you a kiss. It's as though a layer of protective armor sprouts up all around you. You're like an armadillo, just as impenetrable. I'm leaving the unfinished letter for you. I can't remember why I wrote it. Perhaps you will. And if you can't, well, that'll be okay too. Sometimes it's just best to let things go.

CHAPTER 20

October 26, 2014

Her mother's phone rings. Mali's tempted to let it ring, but then remembers it might be Philip calling. So she puts aside her mother's pages and runs for it, rescuing the phone from its cradle before her mother's recorded voice has a chance to kick in, and the caller an excuse to hang up again.

"Is this Eva?" a man's voice asks.

"No," she says, and for a long, strange moment there's only a silence punctuated by a faint static in the phone line. "I'm her daughter, Mali."

"Ah," he says. "This is Philip Schwartz. Is your mother available?"

"I'm so glad you called. I've been looking for your phone number to get back to you. I need to tell you something . . ."

"You know who I am?" he says, an upbeat tone in his voice.

"Yes. And I need to tell you that my mother . . ."

"She told you who I am?" he says again, this time with a hint of impatience in his voice.

"No, not exactly, but I'm so sorry . . ."

"Sorry?"

"She died last week." Those words, the first time she's uttered them, sound so odd to her. Unreal. Untruthful.

"Oh, no. I'm terribly sorry. My deepest condolences to you. I'm shocked. I don't know what to say. It must have been sudden."

"Yes, and no."

"Yes, and no? I can't believe it. My editor, Rachel, told me she'd had a lengthy conversation with your mother only a couple of weeks ago. She said she sounded absolutely fine."

Those words—*absolutely fine*—remind Mali of an interview she'd once seen on TV. The man being interviewed, a financial analyst, had written a book about corporate downturns and how to track the exact moment a spike begins its downward turn. He'd said the idea for the book came to him after his wife had been diagnosed with terminal cancer. One day, not long before her diagnosis, they'd gone out mountain hiking. In better shape than he was, she'd made it further up the mountain. The image of her ahead of him, full of energy and laughter, kept coming back to him afterward. The cancer was obviously already in her body that day, the spike on its downward turn by then. But had there been any warning signals at the exact moment it began its plunge? He believed there must have been some indication at the tipping point.

But what good were warning signals, Mali thinks, if the thing being warned against is totally unrecognizable—its outcome a slippery, evil truth, a warped journey through a darkness, as incognito as any common cloak-and-dagger villain.

"Well, at least you know now that she survived Hitler and the war. And like you, ended up here in the States, though quite a bit later in her life than you in yours."

"Can you tell me how . . . I mean . . . how she died?" Philip says.

"To be honest, we're not one hundred percent sure. A few years ago, the doctor found a spot on her lung. She kind of freaked. It was how my Oma, I mean, her mother, had died . . ."

"Ah, Luzie. I have such fond memories of her too. Forgive me, please continue."

"There's not much more to tell. My mother's way of dealing with unwelcome news was to ignore it. Whatever happens, happens. She was more afraid of ending up a chronic invalid, unable to live her life the way she wanted."

"I can understand that perfectly."

"Anyway, a few months ago, she had to visit her doctor because she was out of sleeping pills and the pharmacy refused to renew her prescription. The doctor insisted on a chest X-ray. Long story short, the spot had grown."

"Oh, my goodness," he says. "It's so strange for me to think of her this way. The only image I have of your mother, of course, is of a young girl, a child, really. I think she was only around eight or nine when I knew her."

"To be honest, I'm having quite a tough time believing it myself. I expect her to walk in at any moment, see my feet up on the table, and yell at me to get them off."

Philip laughs. It's a sweet laugh.

"What an ironic twist of fate," he says. "To find someone after more than a lifetime and simultaneously lose her, all in the blink of an eye."

"But what serendipity to have found each other in the first place."

Their conversation lulls for a moment, and she thinks of the time when Michael, flipping through TV channels, had settled on a National Geographic Special on Arctic exploration. Mali, indifferent to the Arctic, decided to read her book instead. But then there was something she heard in the upper-crust English voices on the TV that made her look up at the screen. A woman and a man were being interviewed. To her astonishment, she realized she knew them both.

The woman had been at boarding school with Mali. They were in their teens then and best friends. The man, her husband, had been her friend's childhood sweetheart. Mali remembers that he was quite a bit older than they were and that he'd smuggle miniature bottles of gin, along with packs of cigarettes, into school for them. All prohibited of course. As was the coveted transistor radio they would sneak up to the roof above the art studio, where in secret and after 'lights out,' they drank and smoked and listened to the latest pop songs on Radio Luxembourg, while shivering with the cold and the terrifying prospect of being caught.

And here were these ghosts from her past, alive and well, and as grownups on TV. He'd written a book about his explorations. She was his helpmate, keeping the home fires burning midway up the mountain, while he pressed on to the top.

Mali had contacted his publisher for his email address, then written to him. While she waited for his response, she imagined their correspondence. How many years had it been since she'd left England? Thirty? Thirty-five? His reply came quite promptly. Of course, he remembered Mali. And her friend? Too late, he'd written. She was in a coma, riddled with cancer, and waiting to die.

"Yes," Mali says into the phone now. "Life's full of those ironic twists of fate, isn't it? But if it's any consolation, my mother spoke of you often. In fact, she always said how she adored you, the little boy who came to stay. The baby brother she never had."

"That's so nice," he says. "For me, those few extraordinary months living with your mother and grandparents . . ."

"It's definitely too bad you never got to meet each other again," Mali interrupts him, still thinking of those ironic twists of fate. "It would've been incredible."

"We came so close, too. I'd really love to know more about her. Do you have time? I mean, I don't want to impose."

"No imposition, of course," she says. "But where do I even begin?"

Mali's mind turns blank, suddenly a foggy hole. How will she describe her mother to this stranger? She glances over at her mother's pages of writing, imagining that the words could magically lift themselves off the paper, like butterflies, to fill her empty head with the answers he's looking for.

"Are you sure now's a convenient time?"

Her mother's world time clock, a birthday present from Mali and Michael one year, sits on the edge of the bookshelf. It's eight-thirty.

"Yes, I'm sorry. I'm just . . . I don't know . . . a little at a loss, I guess. But first, tell me about her conversation with your editor."

"She never told you she spoke with Rachel?"

"No. This is the first I'm hearing of it. I can't figure out why I never knew. What did Rachel have to say?"

"That she sounded charming."

"Exactly what everyone always says."

Mali stands up and looks down at York Avenue. A police car with its lights swirling and sirens blaring, zooms past. Then the rumble of a fire truck.

"Please, I'd love to know more." he says.

"Okay, I'll do my best. So, to begin with," Mali says, turning back to the living room. "My mother was stunning, striking in fact. People were naturally drawn to her."

"She was a beautiful child, no question," Philip says. "I can remember strangers coming up to your grandmother to tell her so. Of course, she never looked Jewish."

"Funny you should say that. Apparently, a woman from their neighborhood in Berlin approached my grandmother in the greengrocer's one day to ask if she'd let my mother join their youth group. They were planning a rally in the coming weeks, a parade in Berlin for the Führer. She was sure my mother would have a grand time. My grandmother was so taken aback, so uncharacteristically shaken up, she blathered an excuse to the woman, grabbed my mother's hand, and ran from the shop before she even bought the few meager vegetables allotted to her as a Jew."

"But looks alone don't get you through life. Surely there was more to her than that."

"Yes, of course. I think she had a gift, a knack, maybe even a talent . . . I don't know how else to describe it . . . for the way she would take an interest in you. Even if only for the moment. And whomever she met never forgot her."

Mali paces the living room. What else could she tell him about her?

"Do you remember Schani, the dog?" she says.

"My God, yes. How could I forget? Your mother adored her dog."

"She always said that having him helped her through her roughest times in Berlin. Here in New York, she couldn't let a dog pass her in the street without stopping to pet it."

"She never got another?"

"No. She didn't want to be tied down. Next to dogs, traveling was her passion."

"Traveling? Where did she go?"

"Where didn't she? South America, Asia, India, Africa, Europe naturally, Russia, the Middle East. She has countless albums filled with the photographs of her world travels. Come to think of it, there are more pictures here in her apartment of strangers and far-off places than of the people in her own family."

Mali wanders into her mother's bedroom now. She goes around turning on all the lights.

"Lucky she could afford it," Philip says.

"She scrimped and saved and cut corners wherever she could. I think she was very brave. You can add bravery to her list of attributes. And strength. After her husband, David, died, she needed to find her independence. And the traveling helped. It was so good for her."

"Her husband, not your father?"

"Oh, boy!" Mali says, walking around her mother's bedroom. "Where do I start with that? The abbreviated version is that when my mother and grandparents escaped from Berlin in 1939, they went to London. My mother met my father, who was also a refugee. They married and later divorced. In the meanwhile, my grandparents had come to New York. My mother followed, as I eventually did, too, but years later."

"A lot of moving around," he says.

"For sure."

Mali sits on her mother's unmade bed, the phone still tight to her ear. She looks through a small drawer in the night table. Tucked inside, she finds her mother's Baum & Mercier gold watch, a thick gold ring inlaid with lapis, and a short, dainty gold chain, an *E* for Eva, dangling from it. She recognizes the watch and the ring, but not the chain. Mali wonders who had given it to her. She lays the phone on the bed for a moment, while she puts the watch on her left wrist and the ring on her right middle finger. Noticing a collection of long, beaded necklaces dangling from the closet's doorknob, she gets up. The glass beads are quite beautiful, like miniature marbles. She takes them off the doorknob to get a closer look, and hangs them, one by one, around her neck. Then she picks up the phone again and, turning off the lights, leaves her mother's bedroom.

"Are you still there?" Mali hears Philip say.

"Yes, yes. I'm still here, just a little distracted and disoriented."

"I thought I lost you there for a moment," he says.

"I'm sorry for being such a flake. I'm not usually this bad."

"Don't worry, I understand," he says. "We can always talk on another day."

"I'm fine, really I am. Besides, we still have things to talk about, things I want to ask you too," she says.

"Okay. Ask away."

"So, according to my mother's friend, Elizabeth, you practice immigration law. Your book recounts your experiences with immigration in general, as well as your own personal ones. Did she get it right?"

"More or less. I do still have my practice, but I'm mostly retired now. And my book does cover many kinds of experiences with immigration. You know, I've been on a book tour around the country these last few weeks and I must say, I've learned a lot. It's so interesting to talk to the people who come to my readings. Very gratifying. Especially when I can turn a person's mind around, make them see my point of view. People are much more open than I expected."

"That's so interesting. I would've thought the exact opposite."

"You see," he says, his tone a little more formal. "I always begin my readings with me, the small child in a Jewish orphanage in Berlin. Then I go on to read about my extreme good luck at having been adopted by your grandparents who, and I make a point of telling the audience this, were adopting me for their family in the US. Afterward, I read portions from cases I've worked on, the men, women, and children I've helped. The life-threatening situations they have escaped from. I try to show . . ."

"Then you believe in open immigration?"

"That's a little too broad, I'd have to say. Rather, I'm trying to help work out new policies that are generous and helpful. Ultimately, I believe there are just two main reasons why people pick up and leave their homes to come here. First, because they're running away from devastation, political or weather-related, in their own country, and second, which doesn't preclude the first, they want to better themselves."

"You're an optimist of the first degree," Mali says. "What about the terrorists who come and want to do us harm?"

"Unavoidable," he says. "But—and here's the big but—there are and always have been more immigrants who made something of their lives, gave back in one way or another to their adopted country, than became wanted criminals. My book has statistics. So, yes, it's always a gamble, but a worthwhile one, I believe. Besides, I have a theory to explain all of this."

"Tell me," Mali says.

"You don't want to get me started."

"Why not?"

"Because I'll chew your ear off and bore you to tears." Philip laughs his sweet laugh again.

"Try me," Mali says, holding one of the necklaces with the colorful glass beads up to the light.

"So here's the thing," he says. "I think this country's schizophrenic when it comes to her immigration policy. We love and take such pride in our heritage, our history of the Wild West, the caravans of people traveling thousands of miles across the country and the Statue of Liberty, her beacon, welcoming the huddled masses who came to thrive. But what's happened in the last, say seventy, eighty years?"

Philip clicks his tongue, as if to punctuate his thoughts, then continues: "I can't help going back to the Holocaust. Did you know, for instance, that America only let in around thirteen hundred Jews without a sponsor, of all the thousands and thousands fleeing Hitler's Europe during World War Two?"

"I remember seeing a documentary on TV a few years back. Weren't they sent to a camp somewhere upstate, around Ithaca, New York?"

"Yes, yes that's the one."

"My mother was in complete disbelief and disgust after coming home from her first cross-country road trip. So much vast, unused space in this country, she'd said. America could have saved hundreds of thousands of Jews. She never became a US citizen. She said that since England took her in, England was her savior. So her loyalties lay with England."

"That's quite funny."

"But what about you?" Mali says. "Tell me about your life. You were, what, six when you came here?"

"Yes, and one hell of a lucky kid, let me tell you. But I'm going to digress a little. I hope you don't mind. Do you know what collision theory is?"

"Sort of, I guess." Mali lies flat on her back on her mother's thick Turkish carpet in the living room and closes her eyes.

"It's the theory that molecules need to collide in a certain way, with a certain amount of energy, to form a new product. Do you understand?"

"I think so."

"So, I believe life itself began in a collision," he says. "And that collision continually reproduces itself in certain patterns and repeats those patterns over and over in a myriad of diverse ways."

"Like . . . ?"

"Oh, I'd say, for instance, something as palpable, as beautiful, as diverse, as a mountain range, or a spider's web, a piece of art or music, or as obtuse and difficult as the way we humans behave."

"Everything stemming from a collision?"

"Or several of them, yes. The collision in my case happened when your grandmother . . . this is one of the things I can remember so clearly from that time, and what most probably got me started on my theory to begin with."

"So my grandmother sparked your grand theory?"

"Yes, absolutely. Here's what happened. You see, she caught my eye and winked at me from across the dreary orphanage classroom, and finding her wink funny, I laughed back."

"I can see how your laughter would've charmed her."

"But do you see that if I hadn't reacted, if I hadn't laughed, there'd have been no collision, and without a doubt I'd have been passed over and . . . God knows . . . ended up in line for the gas chambers."

"What a strange and terrifying thought."

"Indeed. But my point is you can apply my theory to immigration as well. I strongly believe that the mixing up and melding of dissimilar cultures and societies is a good thing. It will make us stronger human beings. Ultimately, we might even have more peace in the world."

"What a truly phenomenal . . . fantastic idea," Mali says a little too loudly, as she opens her eyes, sits up. "And I seriously question it could ever happen."

"Why do you say that?"

"We humans are way too hard-wired for war. We're a tribal lot. Our sole interest is in our own kind, and consequently, what we'll take up arms for. Naturally, some will stick their necks out, but . . ."

"A little cynical, perhaps?"

"Maybe. But look at what the world has gone through and persists in going through, time and time again. I mean, just take World War One, for instance. How could they have even imagined doing it all so soon again? After such a terrible, terrible war. I'm sorry but I really don't think world peace is ever possible. It's sort of like our idea of heaven—unattainable, but we pray and struggle for it anyway."

Philip laughs again.

"I'm sorry," she says. "Did I come on too strong? I hope I didn't offend you. I didn't mean to."

"Don't worry. I shouldn't have got you started on my collision theory."

"But you never do know . . ."

"Let's talk about your grandparents instead," he says.

"Before we go there, I do have a question, though."

"Shoot away."

"I hope you don't mind my asking, but did you ever find out what happened to your biological parents? How you ended up in an orphanage?"

"I tried going through the archives, but never found anything," he says. "Of course, I didn't know my parents' names. The orphanage gave me mine and then it was changed again when I came to America. But I have a very silly notion . . ."

He stops talking for a few moments.

"What is it?"

"You sure you want to hear another of my crazy theories?"

"Why not? I promise to be better behaved this time."

"Well, I believe my biological parents were taken away from me by political action," he says. "Somehow, I can't accept that my mother gave birth to me out of wedlock and, too ashamed or without the wherewithal to keep me, dumped me on the orphanage steps."

"Is that what they told you?"

"Yes, but I just don't believe I lived in the orphanage from birth. Snatches from another place come into my consciousness every so often. Almost dreamlike. The flash of a kitchen table, the view from an open window looking out onto a garden, a big bed with a fluffy white duvet, and then the sound of a woman's voice crying."

"Your mother?"

"Yes, I most certainly believe it was my mother crying. I think my parents were rounded up one night, brought to Gestapo headquarters, and imprisoned there. No one heard from them again. Unfortunately, I realize, this scenario wasn't unusual."

"How were you saved then?"

"In my theory, or fantasy, if you will, a kind and brave neighbor saw what had happened and came into the apartment to rescue me. She'd have brought me to the Jewish orphanage."

"How old do you think you were?"

"A year, maybe."

"Wow!"

"As you can see, I've experienced lots of collisions in my life."

"I can understand how you believe in this for yourself. I can even accept the theory as you have presented it to me. But you'll never get me to agree that your collision theory could eventually lead to world peace."

"That's okay," he says. "We can agree to disagree. By the way, to change the subject, do you know if your mother ever received the yellow roses I sent?"

"Ah! So, you're the one. The secret admirer."

"I am," he says, and chuckles.

"They're still here. Dried up and falling off their stems, but still here. I'm sure they were beautiful when you sent them."

"I'm glad to hear it. But I do still want to hear about your grandparents. You said they got out of Germany and went to England first."

"Yes, in August '39. They were safe from the Nazis, but after the English declared war on Germany, they arrested my grandfather, sent him to the Isle of Man and held him there for around a year, I think, as a friendly enemy alien. When the Blitz began, a mass evacuation of London's school-age children sent them to foster homes all through the countryside. That's where my mother spent the war. And my poor grandmother had to dodge the falling bombs over London all by herself. In 1949, my grandparents received their visa at long last and left London for New York. And that's basically the story."

Mali feels herself drifting.

"Well, I shouldn't keep you," he says. "I'm sure you have plenty of things to do. Perhaps we can talk again another time. I'd love for you to read my book and tell me what you think, even if you disagree with all my theories."

But will they ever really speak again? she wonders.

"I'm going to look for your book now. It must be in the apartment somewhere. And if not, I'll go out and buy a copy."

"Perfect," he says. "It was lovely to talk to you. And again, I'm so sorry for your loss. She was a great kid, and by all accounts, it sounds like she grew up to be a great woman."

"Yes, she absolutely did."

Mali puts the phone back in its cradle. She's sure this conversation wasn't one he'd anticipated. She feels badly for him somehow. She wonders if perhaps his renewed connection with her mother—even though only in thought and memory rather than in the flesh—turned something upside-down inside him, as though a bright light had suddenly been switched on, shining to illuminate the threads, the links, long buried in his life.

CHAPTER 21

December 11, 1988

I'm in the hospital cafeteria. Only one other table is occupied among the sea of neatly lined-up empty tables and chairs. A middle-aged man and woman sit opposite each other, their heads bent forward, deep in conversation. They occupy the table to my left by the window. I'm facing the door, always expecting to see one of David's nurses coming in to look for me. A Styrofoam cup filled with black coffee steams on the table. Next to it, my pen and paper. I've torn out blank pages from my notebook, so I won't have to carry the whole, bulky thing with me as I make my daily trek to and from the hospital. I put my hands around the cup to warm them, then take a sip. I've given up caring about sleeping at night. I live in a timeless world right now; it shifts and changes as predictably and unreliably as the weather.

CHAPTER 22

October 26, 2014

Michael calls. "Hi," he says, his voice upbeat. "How're you doing?"

"Not sure." She gets up and comes to a standstill at the wall of photos in the hallway outside her mother's bedroom. "I just had the longest conversation with Philip, you know the guy who was the six-year-old kid my grandparents adopted from an orphanage in Berlin."

"How'd it go?"

"Good. He's interesting, and full of theories."

"On what?"

"Oh, immigration and collision."

"Sounds heavy," he says.

"You can say that again. I'm exhausted. And I still want to finish my mother's stories before I fall asleep."

"Are they interesting, at least?"

"As a matter of fact, very."

Mali looks up at a photo on the wall of herself with Julia as a baby. In the picture, she looks like a child herself. Her long, curly hair is piled messily on top of her head. She is smiling into the camera, her tiny daughter fast asleep in her arms.

"Except," Mali says, her eyes still on the photo. "I found this half-baked, unfinished, cryptic note among my mother's letters. There's no date so I have no way to know when this was, or even what might have caused her to write it. She herself couldn't remember and wrote if I can't figure it out not to worry, but just to let it all go."

"What's it say?"

"I'll read it to you, it's short. *After you and Michael dropped me off at home this evening, which was very nice of you to do and for which I thank you both—the dinner at Petaluma was especially good—I must admit I felt very unsettled . . .*"

"Unsettled? What a strange word."

"Yes." Mali reads on: "*Unsettled is maybe even too mild a word. It was as though my memory, my whole inner being had suddenly been picked up and shaken about so violently that all the old stuff, long buried on the bottom, rose to the top.*"

"Rather melodramatic," Michael says.

"But listen to this: *So here I am, writing this down because in all that old stuff, I couldn't find you. There's a gap I can't bridge. We are like strangers, you and I.*"

"Strangers? Now that is bizarre. And you have no idea when this was?"

"No, I told you. I was hoping you might remember."

Still mesmerized by the photograph on the wall of her young self with Julia, Mali realizes something important had happened to her that warm, sunny afternoon in May. Before Michael had called to her to look up into the camera, she'd been gazing at her new baby—studying her little hands and feet, her heart-shaped face with the perfectly-formed mouth, her closed eyes and enviably long lashes—when a sudden overwhelming sense of mothering, of almost painful love stabbed at her heart. It was at this precise moment, a freeze-frame shot in her mind, that she realized her utter failure to comprehend how her mother could've left her in London all those years ago.

"I can't even remember the last time we went to Petaluma for dinner," says Michael. "Can you?"

"No, me neither. Funny that Elizabeth was going there for dinner tonight."

Mali wanders away from the wall of photographs and comes back to the window in the living room. The river and the city lights twinkle in the clear, starless night.

"To be honest," she says, "I feel as though I'm living in an alternate universe. All these old stories and photos and people showing up. It's really kind of weird. Anyway, Elizabeth told me my mother had found Philip, you know, the adopted boy, after she'd read about him in the *Times*."

"The *Times*?"

"Yes. He wrote a memoir and the *Times* interviewed him."

"Interesting. He must be quite important. Or his book . . ."

"But such bad luck that they missed each other. Don't you think?"

"Mm . . . I guess," he says.

"But why would she have kept it a secret from me?"

"Your mother had strange ways of doing things."

"Like what, for instance?"

"Like leaving you that crazy letter you just read to me, for starters."

"Yes, it is very bizarre, I'll grant you that. A mystery. Oh well. Never mind. So, you'll be here first thing tomorrow morning?"

"Bright and early." He mumbles a quick *I love you,* makes that funny sound as if he's kissing the phone, and hangs up.

CHAPTER 23

December 13, 1988

In yesterday's paper, I read an article dealing with how we perceive our future selves, or rather how we can't see, and don't imagine, that in the future we will have changed, as we've changed from the past to the present. The writer claimed we don't think of ourselves as changing. But I don't think we can see ourselves in the past either. We only see our past selves from our present perspective. I'm sure of it. Memory is so elastic, so unreliable, so full of imagination—such a bad copy of the original.

· · ·

As you know, when the Blitz began in September 1940, I was evacuated from London to the countryside with roughly a million and a half other children. Opa, still away from us and still considered a friendly enemy alien, had been imprisoned in the Isle of Man since the beginning of the war. Life for Oma had become even more difficult with both of us gone now. I could only go back to visit her one weekend a month. I lived for those weekends. I didn't like my foster family. They never fed me enough and the house was never warm. So I was always starving and cold.

Your Oma found a job at the Czech Club, which was in a big, old house in West Hampstead, not far from where we lived. She had to brew pots of tea and do the washing up, things she'd never had to do in her previous life. Sometimes, she'd be called on to fill in as a fourth in a bridge game, the highlight of her day. If Oma minded her job, she never let on—at least not to me. She always seemed in good spirits when I saw her. I don't know how she did it.

A safe haven of sorts, the Czech Club had become *the* place in wartime London for the Jewish refugees fleeing Nazi Europe. Every day new refugees arrived. Those who'd come earlier anxiously grilled the later arrivals for any possible news of their families still in Europe. The club was a very noisy place. Always in an uproar over something or another. You can imagine how many different languages we spoke. Everyone trying their best to understand everyone else. Sheer madness. A favorite gathering place was the long, narrow front passageway where notices, such as job postings or rooms and flats to let, covered the walls on both sides. But it was the hundreds of snapshots that took up the greatest space on those walls—mothers, fathers, brothers, sisters, grandmothers, grandfathers, cousins, aunts, uncles, and friends—all with the same heading: *Have you seen Bertha or Louis or Fred or Wolfe? If so, please ring up Helga or Ruthie or Sam or Heinrich.* Most of the time, if there were news, it was never good.

Something else we refugees shared back then was financial ruin. The Germans had extorted everything from us in exchange for our exit permits. They wanted to make sure we were completely broken in every sense of the word.

This was where I met your father for the first time. On furlough from school, as I used to call it, I kept Oma company at the club. I had nothing much to do there. Occasionally, a boy or girl my own age would show up and we'd play a game of table tennis. Otherwise, I'd be stuck in the kitchen, trying hard to concentrate on the English spelling and grammar workbooks spread out on the large wooden table before me, but succeeding, more often than not, on fanciful daydreams. The day I met your father, Oma had been called on to be a fourth at bridge. Relieved from my books for a while, I found a chair in the corner of the card room. Lost in thought and only half-watching the goings on around me, I didn't notice at first when a short, dark, handsome stranger plopped himself down on the chair next to mine.

"My name is Hirschel," he said, tapping my knee to get my full attention.

"I'm Eva."

"Tell me, when did you get here?" He crossed his legs and lit up a cigarette.

Always the first question anyone ever asked of each other on a first meeting here, it was the *when* that revealed the difficulty, the pain, the sorrow, and even the magnitude of the journey undertaken, to land in England in relative safety from the Nazi killing machine decimating the European Jews.

"August, last year," I said. "Just three weeks before the war started. But I'm only visiting my mother for the weekend. I've been evacuated to Bedford, where I live now, where I go to school. When did you come?"

"A few weeks ago. Can't you tell by how badly I speak English?"

"Not so badly," I lied. "Where did you come from?"

"Antwerp. And you?"

"Berlin," I said, and thought, how far away the city I grew up in, seemed to me at that moment. Those memories of my life in Germany, floating away bit by bit, were like sheets melting off an ice floe. What would I remember of it after all of this ended?

"It's a regular mixing pot here, isn't it?" he said, taking in the room around them.

"Yes. And the less people understand each other, the louder it gets. Have you noticed?"

"As though shouting at each other will make up for it." He laughed and moved his chair around to face me.

"Are we shouting?" I said and laughed too.

"I just want to look at you when we talk." He smiled and tapped my knee again.

"Did you have a sponsor to help you get here?" I said, suddenly conscious of my usual slumped posture and uncombed hair.

"No. My mother was the one who pushed us to get out."

"Lucky." I sat up as straight as I could and crossed one leg over the other, trying to look more sophisticated and older than my thirteen years.

"Yes, very," he said, raising up his hands and making a funny kind of chortling sound in his throat. Then he continued, "My mother instructed my father, my brother, and me to layer as many of our clothes on our bodies as possible. We each had to pack our knapsacks to over-flowing. You should've seen us, a family of Michelin tire people."

He stopped talking, took a drag on his cigarette and stared at his hands now resting in his lap.

"And you just picked up and left?"

"What choice was there?" He looked up into my face now.

"I suppose," I said as I raked my fingers through my hair, twirling it out of my face and behind my ears.

"We walked to the coast of France and from there, a boat to Southampton. Originally, we'd planned to go to Calais first. A little less than two hundred kilometers away. But . . ."

"But?"

"The Germans got there first."

"Weren't you scared to walk?" As I bent forward toward him, I caught my mother's curious eye from the card table. Ignoring her, I smoothed out my grey pleated skirt and leaned back again in my chair.

"Yes, of course. Terrified, more like. The roads, you can't imagine, packed with all sorts of people, everyone trying to escape. Nights, when the bombing began, were the most frightening. We didn't always have shelter. You just never knew . . ."

A cheer came from the card table. Someone had won. We both looked up and over at the players. Your father laughed.

"That's my mother over there," I said. "The one who's smoking and giving us the sly looks. She's wondering who you are."

"Then I must introduce myself and tell her what a beautiful daughter she has."

I felt my whole body go hot and red. "But go on," I said, trying to recover. "Tell me more of your story."

"Sounds so impossible, doesn't it?"

"It does, but so do all the stories I've heard here."

"Well, we got as far as Dunkirk. Bombs were dropping everywhere. It was impossible to keep going. As I said, the Germans had already marched into Calais."

"So, what did you do?"

"We found a small apartment building and hid under the staircase in the hallway. I'll never forget it. The staircase was beautiful. A spiral. You know, like when you peel an apple in one go?"

I nodded.

"It circled up to the most amazing roof I'd ever seen. All glass. As you can imagine, our eyes never left it for the whole night. We only breathed again when daylight came, and we could see the bombers turn back. The sudden quiet was so eerie, though, let me tell you."

"Then how did you get from Dunkirk to London?"

"More luck," he said. "More great luck. A Polish freighter at the docks agreed to take us. We zigzagged the English Channel for five days, dodging German bombs and torpedoes before we were finally able to dock at Southampton."

He stopped talking, took another drag on his cigarette.

"Go on," I said. "What happened next?"

"On the night we arrived, we slept on cots in the Southampton cinema. The Red Cross provided blankets and food."

"Lucky."

"Very, very lucky." He sighed as he stubbed out his cigarette in the ashtray.

"How long did you stay in Southampton?" I reached out to stroke his arm with the tips of my fingers.

"Only that first night. The following day we took the train to London."

"And here you are."

"Yes," he said and smiled. "Here I am, one more refugee at the Czech Club, hoping to survive the Blitz and start my life over. What about you?"

By the end of our conversation that day, I had fallen madly in love with him. He became my hero, my knight in shining armor. Whenever we spent time together, sharing our hopes and dreams, all the craziness we lived through seemed a little less frightening.

Shortly after we met, your father went to work in a diamond factory, and learned how to cut the rough stones. A wrong cut could devalue the gem, he explained to me. But brilliantly cut facets, he said, an impish grin on his face, would make it sparkle and shine as nothing you'd ever seen in your life. It would also increase its value, as well as the value of the cutter. Did I understand all that? It didn't matter to me then. Only later did I care, when, like the business itself, much of what he did seemed shrouded in mystery and silence.

• • • •

So what had gone wrong with our marriage?—you might be asking. What had I been looking for that I thought I was missing?—you might also be wondering. I'm not sure I'll be able to answer that, even for myself. Perhaps I felt alienated from my friends once we moved into our new house, located further from the center of London. I had no access to a car, though of course, I could have always taken the bus. But soon the feelings of neglect, loneliness, and boredom began to seep into my being. Insidiously at first. And before long, those feelings filled me up. I became numb, dead inside. Had I grown so used to living on the edge—worry, fear, and anxiety always there, sharpening my senses to their brightest—that I couldn't bear the quiet, the sameness, the tedious dullness of everyday peacetime living? And your father? A clichéd story perhaps. Working hard, traveling. Somehow, I got left behind. He never told me about his work. He considered me too young, too inexperienced in life to participate in his. If I ever began a conversation, I ended up feeling like a spoiled brat who couldn't appreciate everything he'd been doing for me, and for you.

Then, one evening, while we were getting ready for a party and as he zipped up the back of my dress, I decided to begin the conversation.

"Hirschel," I said to the blank wall. "I need to be doing more. I'm bored with my life. Let me get a job."

"Job?" he said, barely able to spit out the word, as he spun me around to face him. "What can you do?" he went on. "Sell in a shop? Be a bloody shop girl?"

"Yes, why not?"

"What will people think?" His eyes glassy, the expression in them hard. I shrugged my shoulders.

"They'll think I don't make enough to support you, that's what. Impossible," he shouted, and stormed out of our bedroom.

End of conversation.

We kept silent in the car and arrived at the party still bristling from his angry words. I remember I'd felt inconsequential and trapped in a life I didn't know how to extricate myself from.

Although you never asked, I always knew you'd been curious about the man I had the affair with. He wasn't a handsome man, but he was charming. I met him at the party that night. Booze flowed. Big bands played on the phonograph. Most of us were young refugees bent on putting our pasts behind us, starting afresh. A determined lot. I remember someone had put on an old-time, slow, smoochy song. Something like *I'll Be Seeing You.* Standing by the living room door at the time and feeling sorry for myself, I watched a couple grind to the music in the center of the small, smoky room. In a corner, four people sat around a card table, a bridge game just beginning. As I drank up the last of the Scotch in my glass, a friend of your father's, a man I barely knew, came over, took the glass out of my hand, and led me to the middle of the room to dance. He wasn't the best dancer, but he held me tight, and oddly enough, I felt safe with him. As if he could read my mind, he seemed to sense how I felt deep inside, where those feelings of hurt and unhappiness lay. His breath was on my ear and his hands pressed into the small of my back, drawing my body into his. A sudden involuntary current of excitement rippled through me. Perhaps I'd had too much to drink. My cheeks burned. When the slow dance ended, I tried pulling away from him. But he held onto me. Then another slow song rang out. I tried pulling away from him again. I knew I should. But then it was useless, my limbs felt weak. And he began to whisper words of flattery into my ear—words I realized I'd been craving, like a drunkard's addiction to the bottle, for way too long. All evening we danced. After the party, we said goodnight. I thought that would be the end of it.

But a couple of weeks later, I ran into him at Frohwein's. Embarrassed, we laughed at the ridiculousness of bumping into one another at the butcher's, of all places, though each secretly believed Providence had brought us together once more. We went next door for a coffee. That was the beginning. The end wasn't very far off. A colleague of your father's spotted us, arm in arm, on the Golders Green Road. How stupid could I have been?

I think I expected your father to be jealous. And that his jealousy would make him want me more, give me what I so desperately needed, a life that would breathe and make me feel alive again. But, as you well know, the exact opposite happened. He closed up like a clam and sent me packing. I'd behaved like a stupid and careless woman, I'll grant you that. Thoughtless too. And I've been paying for it with a terrible guilt that has lived inside me ever since.

•   •   •   •

All these memories have brought me back to when you were a little girl and I still lived with you and your father in London.

Perhaps you'll remember that before we had the house on Finchley Lane, we lived in a two-bedroom, ground floor flat in Moreland Court, a

Tudor-looking block with a huge back garden behind it, a garden just like the *Hinterhof* in the center of the square-shaped apartment building in Berlin, where, in happier days, my parents and I had lived. Aside from its spaciousness, I think it was the garden that sold me on the flat in London.

Anyway, at lunchtime every day, I'd pick you up from nursery school on the Wellgarth Road in Golders Green, bring you home and feed you tomato soup, your favorite, and a grilled cheese sandwich. Then one day you came into the kitchen and told me you wanted to change your name to Susan. You must've been around three. When I said I couldn't change it, you threw yourself down onto the blue mottled linoleum floor and had a temper tantrum. I tried to explain that you had a very special name. But to you, the specialness didn't matter one bit. You continued to lie on the floor, flailing your arms and legs and screaming your head off. I was powerless to calm you. Eventually, you fell asleep on the floor, your breathing labored through a stuffy nose, your cheeks going in and out, as you sucked noisily on your thumb, your closed eyelids fluttering every so often, like the wings on a butterfly.

I'd tried to explain that you had been named after your father's grandmother, Amalia. She must have been a remarkable woman. Very stern-looking. Maybe you've seen a picture of her. I seem to recall at least one among the messy jumble of old photographs your grandfather kept in the drawers of his old desk. The short-cut version of her story goes something like this: Her husband, Schlomo, left her in Krakow, Poland, where they lived, and went in search of a better life in Cologne, Germany. Most probably he left in the early nineteen-tens. Amalia took back her maiden name, finished raising her six children alone, and continued to work every day in her store, selling fabrics to the peasant women who sewed the material into shawls. After her son, your grandfather, came back from the war—World War One, that is—he went into the silk business. He did quite well for himself. But when the markets crashed in 1929, he lost his business and, seeing no future for himself in Krakow, decided to move his young family to Antwerp, Belgium. There, he joined his cousins in a family business of diamond dealers. Your father had just turned eleven when they left Krakow in 1930.

So you see, your name is the bridge to a past that will never come back. Amalia died in 1942. I must admit I have often wondered—had she died of old age? Or was she one among the frightened thousands picked up one cold and rainy night and brought in an overloaded truck to nearby Auschwitz? I never did find out.

Your father's family always remained dead silent on the topic.

CHAPTER 24

October 26, 2014

Six lines of empty space on the page; as if they stand for dead silence; or as if her mother had reached this point and needed to take a deep breath before continuing. Mali looks away from the pages in her lap. How impossible to think that all of this existed only one generation ago. Mali remembers her father's story of escape from Antwerp, and how his telling of it made her see, and understand how vulnerable, how random, how dependent she was—for her wellbeing, even for her life—on the particular moment in history she was born into.

This realization came to her on a day in late May when she was fourteen and at boarding school in the south of England. She pictures her dorm room, the sun's rays pushing through the open window and, like a large, sleeping tabby cat, settling into a warm, bright patch on her bed. She was reading a letter from her father—usual with its scrawled, misspelled words on the thick, white imprinted letter paper, but very unusual with its hint of sentimentality.

We had not a penny to our name, he'd written, and she can still bring back the sound of his voice, his foreign accent. We had to leave everything behind. But I will never forget my first night in England. How kind and generous the English were to us. I am so very proud and immensely grateful to be a British subject.

And she sees his smile.

She'd read and reread his letter, feeling alternately happy and sad for him. It was the twenty-one years that had struck her as unfathomable. That here she was, the next generation, sitting cozy and warm in this patch of sunlight aglow on her bed, in the dorm room of an English boarding school. He could have never dreamed up this, his daughter's reality, on his first night in the Southampton cinema, where he, his brother, and their parents, slept on cots under blankets borrowed from the Red Cross to keep warm.

He'd caught up.

Leaning forward, Mali absent-mindedly scoops up a handful of the yellow rose petals heaped on the coffee table by her feet. But how difficult it must have been for him at the beginning. He'd had to learn a new language, adjust to unfamiliar ways, and then, throughout the rest of his life, be reminded, as soon as he opened his mouth to speak, that he was a foreigner, a refugee, a Jew from the Holocaust.

She remembers another time when her father's sentimentality got the better of him.

Once a year, and on her own, she'd go back to London to see him, usually in October when she could steal away for a few days, after Julia and Steffi had settled in a new school year, and before she was overtaken by winter's inertia. It was never easy leaving. She always felt torn. She remembers how Steffi would squeeze her hard, kiss her, over and over, barely able to let her go. How Julia's lips would only brush Mali's cheek, softly, like a starling's feather. And how Michael, dressed in only a shirt, with a mug of coffee steaming in his hand, would walk with her to the driveway, kiss her, say I love you, I'll miss you, then wait in the chilly, early morning darkness, as the limo started up, and backed out onto the street. She was leaving. But only for one week, she always had to remind herself over and over, swallowing hard to keep the tears from coming.

On the last day of one of her visits to London, Mali had accompanied her father to the passport office in the City. His renewed passport was waiting there for him to pick up. Why not have them send it by post? Out of the question, he said. They were sitting side by side in the tube. Suppose it got lost. Or suppose something was wrong with it, his name misspelled, for instance, or a date recorded incorrectly. No. Better to be present to correct any problems straightaway. Besides, he didn't want to have to wait another week or two for it to arrive by post. No, he said when she asked, he'd had no immediate plans to go abroad. But she must understand. To be without a passport for a moment longer than necessary . . . he shook his head. Impossible.

The familiar-looking Persil, Bovril, and Tetley Tea billboard ads plastered along the concave walls of the underground stations they passed, made Mali think back to the times her stepmother, Fleur, had taken her to Oxford Street to clothes-shop. First, they'd gone to Marks & Spencer's for underwear and pajamas, then to Selfridges or C&A for skirts and sweaters. Always on the chubby side, Mali hated shopping. Nothing ever looked good on her. And those ugly outfits Fleur had bought for her didn't help. She smiled at the memory, at the picture she had of her younger self.

Just loud enough to be heard over the clatter of wheels on the train tracks, her father began to speak about that long-ago time. So very unlike him, she'd thought. His usual mantra was that the past, as with the buried, was to remain in the past. But now he talked of suffering. How the children in divorce suffer the longest, suffer always. She wanted to tell him it didn't matter anymore. She couldn't, though. She just let him rattle on. Even though she didn't want to hear, and then imagine, how things might have turned out differently, how her life might have been, or who she might have become, had she remained in London with him.

After the passport office, they walked to Westminster Abbey. The weather that day had been so changeable. One minute, the sun shimmered brightly over the grey streets, turning everything to shiny silver. Then without warning, the skies turned dark with racing clouds and it poured. Luckily, her father had brought his big black umbrella with him.

They passed a busload of tourists, standing outside the Abbey, listening to their tour guide fill them in on a little English history. Mali would've been happy to stay and listen for a few minutes. Wasn't she a tourist now too? More groups crowded inside the Abbey, their voices from all different countries. To where had she pretended to belong?

She smiles now, as she remembers a childhood game she and her cousins used to play. They'd invented a language, to make everyone around them believe they were from somewhere else, some exotic, other place.

But what country, which place, does she really belong to? She never really knew.

Shortly after Mali and her father had come into the Abbey, a man's voice came over the PA system. Echoing through the vaulted, stone space of the church, he asked for a few moments of silence, while he recited the Lord's Prayer. Everyone around them stood in place, their heads bowed. In this country, there is no separation between church and state: between the church and the state's ancient and volatile history.

Released from their bowed heads and motionless positions, Mali and her father wandered through the side rooms filled with crypts. But, soon tiring of the musty air, the tragic ancient history explained on engraved plaques mounted to chiseled walls, they hurried through it all, their steps echoing on the worn, stone floors, shiny with centuries of footsteps gone before them. On their way out, they passed a cloistered courtyard. It looked so peaceful. Then her imagination took over, and she thought of the violent schemes and twisted plots that must've been conceived in these drafty corridors through the centuries.

At first, the weather held as they made their way along Whitehall, passing Downing Street and Horse Guards. But soon it began to drizzle. Her father put up his umbrella again, took her arm, put it through his, and they continued on to Trafalgar Square.

"So, tomorrow you're off," he said to her, as they waited in a sheltered stop for the number 113 bus. "It's back home to your husband and children."

She sensed an ever so slight twinge of regret surfacing with his words. But he laughed it off, put his arm around her shoulders, and squeezing her into him, kissed the top of her head. The bus came. She found a seat by the window and watched the scenery of her childhood pass by. Her father sat in silence beside her, his eyes fixed straight ahead, his fingers fiddling with the wooden handle of the closed umbrella he held upright between his knees.

She wondered what he was thinking. And if he'd ever thought back to the day they'd stood together on the platform at Victoria Station, waiting for the train to take her away to boarding school for the first time. She couldn't stop it, that day came roaring back to her; a giant wave engulfing her completely.

She'd stood alone with her father. Dusty shards of light filtered through the immense glass roof of the station. Steam hissed and billowed from the undercarriage of the waiting train, like foggy sheets on a clothesline. Further along the platform, porters pushed overflowing luggage carts. Girls of all ages shouted out to one another in excitement. They hugged and kissed, as if they hadn't seen each other for years. Their parents looked on from the sideline, placid expressions on their faces.

Her father turned her to face him. He put one hand on her shoulder and the other inside the pocket of his charcoal grey trousers, jingling his change, as impatient, it seemed, as she, for this to be over.

"You'll write," he said.

His curly, brown hair, shiny and wet-looking with brilliantine and slicked back from his high forehead, accentuated the intensity in his dark eyes.

"I'll want to know how you're getting along." He took his hand out of his pocket and placed it on her other shoulder, squaring her to him.

But Mali's attention was focused on the other girls waiting to board the train, trying to guess who, like her, was new this term and who, like her, stood with only one parent, while the other lived far away in America.

Her father smiled. He gently put his hand under her chin and lifted her face. He stroked her cheek and began to talk to her, the noise and bustle of the station rapidly fading away.

"Play it down," he said. "Don't become a leader. Don't give them *any* reason . . . any reason at all for them to get back at you." He took his hand away from her cheek and pointed it vaguely in the direction of the schoolgirls further up the platform and repeated with even more urgency in his voice: "Any reason at all for them to get back at you."

She listened and, as with the pocket money he gave her for *just in case*, she pocketed his words. Then she promptly forgot about them as she boarded the train for her new school in Eastbourne. That is, until one

Friday afternoon, a few weeks later, when those words came walloping back at her, in the middle of a biology class.

She and her new best friend—the one she'd seen on TV all those years later—had been in a fight. Perched on high stools at opposite ends of the science lab—a smelly, dank, prefabricated structure no larger than a single-car garage and tucked between the two large Victorian houses that made up their school—they were shouting at each other across the four lab benches that separated them. Finally, their teacher, a man with prematurely white hair and a permanently red face, told them to shut up and get back to work. Mali picked up her scalpel, but before she'd completely directed her thoughts back to the frog, stinky, stretched, and pinned to a wooden board in front of her, she mumbled loud enough for everyone to hear, but to no one in particular, "Oh, go to hell."

She heard a stool scrape the floor as it was pushed back.

"You can't say that," her friend said, her round cheeks red with indignation, her blue eyes glistening with hate. "You're a Jew."

In a flash, the entire history of the Jews, in all its atrocities, descended upon her. She felt ghostly ancestral fingers clutching at her, pulling her away, holding her back, protecting. But there was no escape.

Her father's words flew back at her then too, as though they'd been packed into a boomerang and slung far out into space, only to slam back into her at this unexpected moment. How could she have known, as she'd stood with him on the platform at Victoria Station, where the fine line had been drawn before she had transgressed it? Or even understood what his words of warning had really meant?

•   •   •   •   •

She turned back now to face her father in the bus. He continued to keep his eyes focused straight ahead of him, his fingers still toying with the wooden handle of the umbrella he held upright between his knees.

Afraid to blink, she looked away from him. What had come to her as she'd stared out through the bus window, grimy with London's greyness, were the airports and the train stations of her childhood—all those hellos fraught with expectations and all the goodbyes brave with barely held-back tears.

Suddenly, still looking out at the city of her childhood, she felt herself afloat, disconnected, as though that long-ago little girl, who'd searched and searched for the missing piece to put her broken world back together again, had never existed. She couldn't help it. She had to blink. And the tears fell.

CHAPTER 25

May 16, 2014

My darling, a day in June 1955 nags at my conscience like an insistent toddler pulling at its mother's hem. I pour out the contents of that day, as if dumping them from an open box, and spread the memories before me.

The bus ride back to Golders Green from town had been uneventful, I remember. I'd sat upstairs in the double-decker bus, watching snatches of everyday life go on below me: the traffic ebbing and flowing; pedestrians walking, their heads bent in determination; and the shops lit up, as if welcome beacons in the uncertainties of the day. But I'd felt invisible, sitting up there, detached from the world, and passing, it seemed, from my own familiar life into another's. I was on my way back from a lunch date with your uncle Willy. Lunch that had sat untouched in front of me, as he listed the rumors he'd heard of my affair. Why, he had demanded to know. I sat there, across from him, dumb, as though only my shell, my body, dressed in my best navy-blue suit, was all that still existed.

After I got off the bus, I decided a walk along the Golders Green Road would do me good. Since you weren't due back from school for another couple of hours, I figured I'd catch the next bus further down the road at the stop outside Woolworth's. I needed the air to breathe and the time to think.

I looked in at shop windows, hoping for a distraction. Instead, a blurry, watery version of myself mirrored back at me, as the sun played hide and seek with the clouds. Willy never let on who had told him about the affair.

And as I stood outside Franck's, my face pressed up against the window, to get a better view of the Playtex girdles and bras, the flannel pajamas, silk dressing gowns, and the lacy negligees, I realized I hadn't even summoned up the courage to ask.

That evening at home, dinner dishes washed and dried, and you busy with your bath, I went up to my bedroom. The lacy black negligee I'd fantasized over and finally bought at Franck's lay on the bed. While I undressed, I tried to remember your father, the way he used to be, before distractions of business and other life situations interfered and stole his time away from me, stripping me of my self-assurance as a woman. Had there been an exact moment when our love for each other reversed itself?—I wondered, as I pulled the lacy negligee over my head. Or had it been a slow and steady transformation, sneaking up on us stealthily, as if it were some wild and vicious animal eyeing its prey? The black, silky material clung to my body. How did it get reduced to this, after ten years of marriage, to my standing alone in our bedroom in this sheer covering? Who was I really trying to seduce?

I sat at my dressing table to brush my hair, but instead found myself staring deep into my eyes in search of answers that eluded me. Then I stood at the full-length mirror. I reminded myself of a film star from the nineteen thirties, long and willowy and terribly feminine. Pleased with my mirror's reflection, I went downstairs.

Flickering black-and-white images flashed across the television's small screen. Serious, dull voices of the newscasters droned on about disaster. Was the end of the world just around the corner? I stood in the doorway to the lounge and watched your father watch the news. He took everything so seriously, as though whatever had happened that day, had happened to him. Did he care that much for humanity? Or was it solely out of fear of another war, another Hitler, that he studied world events with such intensity? What did he think he could learn from the news? History has this uncanny way of repeating itself, especially for the Jews. And what could your father, a man alone, do about it anyway?

He turned to face me. I couldn't see his eyes; the light was playing funny tricks. I could only see my own reflection thrown back at me from his eyeglasses. In that instant, the image in the mirror upstairs of the irresistible, willowy, feminine film star from the nineteen thirties completely vanished, and in her stead, stood a frightened girl, the goose bumps on her arms, the betrayer of her fantasy.

"I've heard all about your affair," he said, his voice sounding twisted and ugly. He turned back to the TV in time to see angry Egyptians—mouths hollowed, fists raised—on the march in the streets of Cairo. History ready to explode over the Suez Canal.

"Can't we please make another go of this, Hirschel?"

But before he had a chance to say anything, I asked if he'd like a cup of tea. I thought this would give us both a little more time to sort things out. I really didn't want his answer that quickly. I needed time to come up with a new idea, in case . . . Of what, I don't think I even knew.

I left him with the Sinai desert, the mobilizing Israeli soldiers and their tanks, and went into the kitchen.

I filled the kettle with more water than I needed and lit the burner. I watched as the blue flame shot up from around the gas ring, then as it flattened with the resistance of the kettle on top of it. A few biscuits might be a good idea, I thought, and went over to the larder to see what there was. Macaroons. Perfect. I opened the tin, took a small plate from the cupboard, and filled it with the biscuits. Now there was nothing left for me to do but wait for the water to boil. I wiped away the few water drops from the chrome sink. It always looked so nice when it shone. Then I aligned the glass salt and pepper shakers in the center of the wooden kitchen table, like black and white toy soldiers at attention. Next, I checked the dirt in the two potted plants on the windowsill above the sink. They were fine. I remembered I had just watered them yesterday. The kettle began to whistle. My heart raced. Too much hinged on these next few minutes. In one way, I wanted them to fly by, get his decision and move forward. But I was also terrified. I measured the tea, poured the boiling water into the pot, and cut a lemon, each in slow motion. What would I do without this evening ritual? Better not to think of it. Instead, I concentrated on arranging the two cups and saucers, the dish with the slice of lemon, the teapot, the strainer, and the plate of macaroons on a tray. An offering, I'd whispered to myself, as I looked around the kitchen just once more before flipping off the light switch and leaving the darkened room behind me.

As you well know, my love, my stupid efforts on that June evening in 1955 failed miserably. They backfired and then stuck to me like long shadows at the end of the day, the two suitcases half packed on my side of the bed, the proof.

Your father had brought them down from on top of the cupboard later that night in an enraged silence. He'd slammed them on the bed and said, "I want you out. I can never live with you again."

I said nothing back. I only cried and wrapped my arms tightly around myself, nursing my failure like an incurable disease. I don't remember how we got through the weekend. Only that he and I never talked. A smothering silence enveloped the house.

And here I was, on Monday, packing up to leave and feeling as though, all along, I'd only been a guest in this house, with an open-ended departure date that had just become firmly scheduled.

The top drawer to my dressing table overflowed with old black-and-white photographs. I'd meant to put them in an album one rainy afternoon. God knows, there had been enough rainy afternoons over the years, and still the pictures, those unreliable recorders of my life, remained a Hodge-Podge in the drawer. I began to pull them out one by one, looking at the laughing faces, the poses, the clothes, the friends we no longer knew, the places we no longer visited. We were just a group of refugees back then, all of us from Europe, each with a different, but similar story to tell, or most often, to forget.

I remember how I loved those summer Sunday afternoons when we'd descend en masse to the beautifully manicured gardens of the Selsdon Park Hotel in Surrey. We'd sit on the grass—the green-and-orange-striped canvas and wood-framed deckchairs, planted in a semi-circle facing the pale English sun—talking and laughing and watching you, our small children, alternately play peacefully with each other one moment, then squabble and cry over the few toys you had, the next. Sometimes we'd even take summer holidays together in rented cottages in Sandbanks or Bournemouth. We laughed a lot back then. Giddy, I think, from the knowledge of what might have been, if not for the very precious commodity of luck we each seemed to have had, hiding in the linings of our pockets, as magical and surreal as the potions of gold dust sprinkled throughout the fairytales we read aloud to you, our children, at bedtime.

Those were happy days. We had escaped Hitler's Europe and survived the Blitz. We had lived the war years on the very edge of life, at every moment of every day. And we had grown up too quickly, always afraid of missing out on something or another if we didn't do whatever it was, right then and there. For me, I think that something was marriage.

I dumped the stack of photographs into one of my suitcases. From the cupboard, I pulled my clothes off their hangers and threw them onto the bed. I grabbed another drawer from the chest and, holding it upside down, let its contents spill out. I stared at the empty drawer on the floor beside me—an empty husk waiting to be buried. A posed picture of my parents and me, taken shortly after our arrival in England, had escaped the batch and floated face up to the floor.

Everything to do with the picture came right back to me: the circumstances, the place, the very late lunch afterward, and the passport photo taken just beforehand. Like now, I had two packed suitcases. It was September 1940. An evacuation boat, the SS City of Benares, with room for ninety children, was to depart for the US and Canada. The notice in the newspaper promised that the children would be saved from the ravages of war. The boat was to sail them across the neutral expanse of the Atlantic Ocean to safety. The only catch, the children needed their own passports. How ridiculous, Opa had said when we found out at the last minute. Why must children have passports at a time such as this?

At first, everything had seemed simple enough. Directed to a door halfway along the wide hallway in the passport office, we entered a packed room. An officious-looking man in a navy-blue uniform greeted us. It will be a long wait, he warned. Opa told him about the ship. The man waved his arm at the room. So are all these children, he said. After a while, my mother and I found two wooden straight-back chairs to sit on, while Opa paced, his temper rising, his patience lost. The big clock on the wall marked off the seconds, the minutes, the hours and still we waited, as though caught in some meaningless, timeless web.

As the hours ticked by and the crowded room thinned out a bit, the boat with its cargo of children pulled away from the dock. They were on their way to safety, and I didn't even have my passport.

Sometime the next evening we heard the news on the radio. A German U-boat, the announcer said, had torpedoed the ship with the evacuated children aboard. Their ages ranged from five to fifteen. It sank immediately. Of the ninety children, seven had survived. By a stroke of dumb luck, I'd been saved. While my parents celebrated, I thought of those children, of myself, who might have been among them, terrified by the noise, the fire, the water. Then I imagined the charred bodies floating on the vast, deep, unforgiving ocean. It took me many months not to think about them anymore.

The familiar thud of your book-laden satchel dropping to the kitchen floor sounded as I snapped shut my last suitcase. I ran downstairs.

"I need to leave for a while," I said, coming into the kitchen. "Opa is ill and in the hospital in New York. I have to go and see him."

You didn't say anything. You were in the larder looking for the biscuit tin.

"A taxi's coming to fetch me in a short while," I said.

"So you're leaving today?" You turned from the larder and came toward me.

"Yes, in around an hour or so."

I stroked your hair, pushed a few strands of it out of your eyes, and wound it behind your ear.

As you ate, we didn't talk. I asked how your day at school was, but only got monosyllabic answers from you.

After your tea, you said you were going up to your room to change out of your school uniform. I drank another cup of coffee, smoked another cigarette. Perhaps the reality, the gravity of the situation hadn't penetrated yet because, hard as I tried to imagine this as the last time in my own kitchen, drinking my last cup of coffee, while sitting here for the last time with you, I couldn't grasp it. I couldn't quite fathom that beyond this day there wouldn't be a future, comfortable in its familiarity, for me to face.

I checked the time. The taxi would be here at any moment. I put on my sequined beret, adjusted it to its proper angle at the mirror. As I was about to re-redden my lips, I caught your reflection behind me on the stairs. Still in your school uniform, you seemed so small and vulnerable, suddenly, so sad. I turned and went to you. I took your hands and pulled you up toward me.

"I'll be back before you've even realized I've gone. You'll see," I said, wishing, hoping I spoke the truth. "Don't cry. Be my big brave girl. You'll need to take care of things while I'm away. Please don't cry. We'll write to each other."

The taxi hooted outside. I let you go, walked to the front door, opened it, signaled for the driver to wait a moment, then came back to where you stood. I hugged you, kissed you, and held you at arm's length for a few moments to study, to memorize, the shape and color of your eyes, the texture of your hair, the rosiness in your cheeks, the little nose, and the shape of your face. Then I picked up my two suitcases and walked out through the open front door, my stomach in aching knots, my legs wobbly, my eyes filled with tears. When would I see you again?—the only thing I could think about as I walked down the steep drive and into the waiting taxi. When would I see you again?

You most probably won't remember that day, will you? You were so young.

CHAPTER 26

October 26, 2014

There's a sudden scraping in the ceiling above, sounding like a chair is being pushed back from the dinner table. Mali is startled at first, unused to the noises of apartment living. She stretches her arms up high until she feels the muscles in her back come alive. Then she stands, snatches the eyeglasses off her face, and once again paces the living room. And remembers. Of course she remembers. How could she not?

She was eight on that long-ago Friday night, when she'd sat at the table on the overstuffed upholstered Queen Anne dining chair, one foot locked beneath her bottom, the other dangling close to the carpeted floor. Her mother sat across from her, her father, between them, at the head. She remembers the crystal chandelier, the countless shapes and facets of cut-glass glistening in the light. Footsteps across the room upstairs made the chandelier appear to dance and tremble. Mali could imagine it falling one day and the fragments of glass lying formless and lifeless, like her father's unpolished diamonds, on the shined surface of the dining room table.

Mali watched her mother, tall, dark-haired, and beautiful, serve her father, next her, and lastly herself from gold-rimmed Limoges serving dishes. She always waited for her mother to begin eating before she even lifted her own fork. But suddenly, on this evening, she felt her chest constrict into a tight knot. She couldn't eat. She looked up at the reflections of light and found herself fighting back tears of indignation, intimidation, as she realized for the first time, her own special vulnerability.

"They think they can snuff us out just like that," her father said, banging a closed fist on the table, while pointing with the other at the two flickering Shabbat candles in their silver holders.

Her mother sighed and continued to eat in silence.

There was much talk about the Suez at the time—talk Mali didn't understand except for isolated phrases and words, which hung in her head like a collection of oddities at a jumble sale. She listened to the newscasters who reported more trouble for Israel. They said that the British and the French had begun their invasion of the Suez Canal, that the Englishman in the street was not happy. Headlines in the London papers were unfavorable toward Israel. Mali couldn't understand why Egypt wanted to destroy the Jews, why the world wanted to snuff them out like unwanted flames. Or why her very existence depended upon, and intertwined with, the future of a country so many miles away, and even younger than herself. Her father said Israel must survive for the sake of all the Jews living in every other country of the world.

Those were days when Mali took her father's words as law and believed in what he believed. She hadn't yet learned how to doubt.

Eyes wide, she had listened to stories of war and displacement and had conjured up in her mind pictures of people, their tears so real she could taste the salt, and of their broken-down, bombed-out houses, the char-burned carcasses stretching upward in ghostly memorials to the open sky.

She would often dream of one she'd seen in Hampstead. It was a grand old home, sheared in half like a doll's house, with its insides bared to the street, its pink flowered wallpaper barely visible under the soot-covered walls of a bedroom. In the dream, she lies in her make-believe bed and listens for the sounds of marching boots drawing closer and closer. Then, a sharp rap at the door. Outside, Gothic arches shoot up in the air, and tumble back down, stone by stone, in a mass of destruction. Next, her mother is running away. Mali is caught by soldiers. Back at their headquarters, she's made to sit at a large, shiny wooden table. A crystal chandelier with countless shapes of cut-glass glimmer in the light and tinkle with the vibration of an explosion. It sounds almost musical. Watch out, a guard warns. And as she looks up, the chandelier comes plunging towards her . . .

Startled awake by her dream, Mali would sit up and look around her own darkened bedroom until the familiar objects became more real than the dream and the explosions inside her head had stopped.

Yes, she wishes she could tell her mother now. Of course, she remembers.

"Then don't talk politics to me," her mother had finally said to her father, waving her fork in the air, her voice becoming shriller with each word. "I've lived enough of it to last me the rest of my life. No more."

Her father shrugged. He set his knife and fork on his plate and left the table.

Her mother looked up, a surprised expression on her face, as though Mali hadn't existed before this very moment. Then she caught another look she'd never seen before. She thought it was fear.

"Go start your bath," her mother said. "I'll be up in a few minutes."

Upstairs, in the pink bathroom with the large bath and sink and the shower stall used only to store mops, sponges, and Ajax, Mali secretly practiced her singing routines. She saw her name formed out of brightly lit bulbs on the marquees of theatres around the world. Here in this bathroom she dared to dream. When she grew up, she resolved, she would be famous.

She put the plug in the drain, started the water, and watched the flow from the taps for a few moments. Then she turned to view herself in the mirror. She made faces at herself to see if she could catch the changing expression in her grey eyes. She laughed. Her eyes disappeared in the folds of her face. All she could see were two shiny, crescent-shaped slits, no expression. She didn't like how she looked when she laughed. She hated the way her eyes curled up and her mouth and teeth took over her face. Now she became serious. She liked that better. Some days the reflection in the mirror showed her pretty, other times not. She hadn't decided, couldn't tell, which days were the true ones.

She turned back to the slow-running water and, dropping her yellow flannel into the bath, watched it unfurl and sink to the bottom. She began to undress but realized she had forgotten her pajamas and dressing gown in her bedroom. She wrapped the large bath towel around her half-naked body and left the warmth of the pink bathroom to fetch them. She was sure to close the door behind her so as not to let in the cool air from the hall. As she passed the stairs, her parents' strained voices rose up to her in muffled tones. She couldn't make out what they were saying.

She tiptoed down a few steps, careful to avoid the creaky bits, and sat shivering on the landing.

Her father was shouting at her mother. She could catch his words and phrases now, the bitter fragments of his anger.

"Don't tell me you love that child . . . you care nothing . . ."

Mali had never heard him talk this way. It was as if those words, pushed up from a strange, foreign place, had twisted his voice. They hung on the landing with her, like dirty grey smoke signals. Her teeth began to chatter noisily with the uncontrollable shaking inside her cold and half-naked body.

"You're dead for me, and you're dead for her," she heard her father roar.

Her mother sobbed. Mali pulled her knees close to her chest, folded her arms tightly around them, and rocked on the last few notches of her spine. She couldn't stop the shaking. She bent her head down and dug her knees so hard into her eye sockets, she began to see stars of quickly changing colors: reds, yellows, whites, blues. She lifted her head, rested her chin on her knees.

She heard her mother, but only her voice, not her words. She wanted to dash downstairs, throw her arms around her, tell her how sorry she was for not always changing out of her school uniform when she got home. Sorry she hadn't sat closer to the table and eaten over her plate, so that the drop of bright yellow yolk from her soft-boiled egg wouldn't have dribbled from her spoon and landed in her lap, dirtying her grey, woolen school skirt. Sorry for being angry when she wasn't home to help her with her math homework. Sorry she hated those Saturday mornings at the Aida Foster School for Tap and Ballet. Sorry for being a crybaby, for being clumsy, fat, ugly. So sorry for being the daughter she was. But she was too scared.

Then she remembered the running water. She ran back, turned off the taps, let the towel fall off her, and stepped into the bath, sinking her body into the warmth of the water. Fame and lit bulbs vanished as she stared at the dark frosted window. How dull it was at night, how black. She closed her eyes against it. Pink fantasies rolled before her like ribbon from a spool. She tried to concentrate on flamingoes, pink flowered wallpaper, strawberry ice cream, party dresses, carnations. Sweat beaded up on her upper lip and her forehead.

The next day, Saturday, in the car with her father, she wanted so much to ask him what he'd meant when he said the night before that her mother didn't love her. But as he drove, he kept his eyes focused directly on the road ahead, as though changing his line of vision would cause the car to veer off the road and into an imaginary ditch. Something forbidding about him made her too afraid. Their silence filled the space around them in the car as thick as fog.

They were on their way to her grandparents. With her forehead pressed against the cool, smooth side window, she watched giant cotton-woolly clouds, in shades of white and gray, fly through the blueness of the sky. Traffic jam at the Heath . . . cars stopped . . . glimpses of toy sailboats racing across the man-made pond by the road . . . children queuing up for pony rides . . . or gathering around for a Punch and Judy show. Traffic moving again—no art shows on the wide pavements today—and they ride down the narrow, winding, hilly road to the High Street.

He parked the car outside her grandparents' block of flats on the Wedderburn Road. "Come, let's go in and have our tea," he said, as though to reward her for the silence she'd allowed him on the way over. He draped his arm over her shoulder as they walked to the ground-floor flat. It felt heavy, oppressive, just like those too many unspoken words between them.

The next day, Sunday, she was back in the car with him. Errands first, then lunch. They went to Sam's Deli for frankfurters and bought rye bread at Grodzinski's.

"We'll go for a little drive before heading home," he said.

She thought he might talk to her, tell her the truth, untangle her confusion.

Instead, he drove around London's northwest suburban streets, stopping every so often at a house with a For Sale sign outside it. He asked her opinion of the houses. Invariably, they were bigger than theirs and on more prestigious streets.

"Are we going to buy it?" she asked him as they got out of the car to have a better look at one.

"Of course not," he said. "It's much too expensive."

"Then why are we looking at it?"

"Because it interests me," he snapped back.

She followed him around outside the empty house and peered in at the same windows he did.

The fenced back garden was big and overgrown. The unmowed grass almost reached the wood swing that hung from a large chestnut tree. Children once lived here. Why had they moved away? She studied the fieldstone house, the uncurtained windows, the panes crisscrossed with so many mullions, and tried to guess which room had belonged to them, which to their parents. Had their father slept alone on a couch in his study too?

"Come," he said. "Let's go home for lunch."

She had to run to catch up to him. He was already on the driveway, walking toward the street where the car was parked.

On the way home, they sat side by side again in the Daimler, silence once more enveloping them. Mali looked over at him. His mouth, set tight, thin-lipped, and pale. Laugh lines—leftovers from another time—creased his cheeks from his nose to his mouth and spread out from his eyes to his temples. His silence made her feel so odd inside, so strange and disappointed, as if it were her birthday and no one had remembered.

On Monday, she sat on the next to bottom step on the stairs, watching her mother at the front hall mirror. Her back was toward Mali. Two suitcases stood by the wide-open front door. The beige carpeting felt scratchy on the back of Mali's bare legs. She looked at her shoes. Licked her finger and rubbed at the scuff marks on the toes. The brown leather darkened for a few seconds, and when it lightened, she tried once more with another finger, but gave up when it lightened again. She rested her elbows on her knees and held her head in her hands. This Monday it didn't seem to matter that she was still in her school skirt. The old pair of woolly trousers she was supposed to have changed into, as soon as she got home, remained draped over the desk chair in her room upstairs.

"You'll see," her mother said, looking at her through the mirror. "I'll be back in no time flat." Mali watched her adjust the sequined beret to the perfect angle on her head. Next, shaping her mouth into an O, she reddened her lips.

A sudden, cool draft whirled around Mali. She shivered and wrapped her arms around herself. A car's impatient horn began to hoot outside . . . once, twice. It was the taxi her mother had been waiting for. At the open door, she held up her hand. A moment, she mouthed across the short expanse of their front garden. Just one moment. She came over to Mali and pulled her up and into her. Her mother's body felt warm. Moving her hands up and down Mali's back, her mother stroked her, just as she would when they hugged before she tucked her in at night. Mali buried her face in the folds of her silky blouse and circled her arms around her waist. Her mother pulled back, bent to Mali's height, and stared into her face for a long few seconds, and then quickly straightened and turned from her. She put on the navy jacket that matched her narrow skirt, picked up her two suitcases, and without another word, walked out through the open front door.

Mali watched her go down the driveway.

"Is it true?" she said, her eyes never leaving her mother as she gave the driver her suitcases and stepped into the taxi.

Mali stood and watched and waited.

But her mother never turned back to look at her, not even once.

"Is it true?" This time yelling at the top of her lungs, as the taxi started up. "Is it true you don't love me?"

CHAPTER 27

May 16, 2014

The very first time he allowed me to see you after the day he sent me packing from the house on Finchley Lane, came in the last weeks of that summer in 1955.

When Oma and Opa heard of my expulsion, they insisted I come at once to live with them in New York. Oma, especially, worried that a beautiful, young woman adrift in a big city like London would invariably get herself into trouble. I tried arguing with her. But she only threw my transgressions back in my face. Her worries and her exasperation, showing through the words she wrote to me on the translucent, onion-skin letter paper, were hardly unfounded. And I could see her face, as she wrote all this to me from their new home in Flushing, Queens—her blue eyes staring flat and unblinking and her lips, a straight, narrow line. What about Mali? I'd written back. How am I to leave her? One thing at a time, she'd answered. First you must have a home to call your own. Then we'll figure out a way for Mali to follow you. I told her I needed the summer before I could leave. I'd thought I could convince your father to take me back. Sounds so archaic, doesn't it? Take me back. As if I were a pawn in a chess game. Oma finally gave in to my wishes, but with many stipulations on how to behave as a single young woman, all spelled out in another long letter. So I stayed in London for the summer. I don't think you ever knew; your father kept me from seeing you.

My girlfriend, Lotte, took me in. Do you remember her? She kept me afloat and sane in those last months in London. She owned a small dress shop at Swiss Cottage, up the road from John Barnes, the department store where I used to buy my linens. Lotte was a marvelous woman with the energy of a horse, if that's the right expression, and the most generous person I knew then. She suggested I come to work in the store. It would help keep my mind off things. I thrilled at the idea. My job was mainly to keep the shop tidy. I cleared the dressing rooms, put the tried-on dresses back on hangers, then returned them to their rightful places on the racks along the walls. Occasionally, I'd be asked for my opinion on a dress. I learned all about truthful diplomacy that summer. And Lotte was right. I loved being there. The work stopped me from feeling sorry for myself and made getting out of bed in the mornings so much easier. I was very happy with the money I earned and especially pleased I could spend it as I wished.

And finally, in my new role as independent woman, I summoned up the courage to call your father and invite him out for a drink. He accepted, and we arranged to meet at a pub the following Monday.

When I arrived, I found your father pacing the pavement, like a caged lion. Perhaps, I thought, he was suffering from a case of the jitters. I could have well understood that. After all, we hadn't seen each other since June when he'd ordered me to leave. Or maybe, as my imagination began to run away with me, forcing me to slow down my own pace, he was working out a way for me to stay, rehearsing the right words to convince me of it. And what would I say in response? What would I do? Leave anyway? Stay? Blame myself for all that had gone wrong with us? I remember how my thoughts, like butterflies inside my head, flitted all over the place. As I walked toward him, I began to pray he'd forgive me, take me back, even if only for you, our child's sake. But by the time I reached him, was held at arm's length, looked over, and kissed on both cheeks, I sensed a new arrogance to him. It must've been in the perfection of his charcoal-grey suit, his starched white shirt, and the Hermès tie. Obviously, his thoughts about me, about us, had not changed in these last months. And I felt a fool—as we walked into the darkened pub, found a table near the bar, and ordered drinks—for all my hopes and wishes.

As we sat across from one another, the marble tabletop cold to the touch between us, I couldn't help but wonder if there hadn't been some facet of our story that could have altered the outcome, transformed our thinking, and kept us together. We had been so in love in the beginning.

I must admit my surprise on that drizzly summer day at the pub that your father never once asked me how I'd been managing these last few weeks. He only inquired in between stilted fragments of conversation that dealt mainly with you, as to my departure for New York. Suddenly, I wasn't even sure why I'd wanted to meet him in the first place. I felt more and more intimidated, the longer we sat. My attention began to drift away from him. Bits and pieces of a conversation at the bar between the bartender and a complaining pensioner seeped into my consciousness. The dreary late afternoon light filtering in through the window made me nervous about the time—I didn't know why. I wanted so much to get up and walk out. But there was you. And so I sat tight.

"We're going away on holiday next week," he said, checking the bill for our drinks.

"Oh! Where to?"

"Klosters, Switzerland. My mother's coming with me to help with Mali. I've rented a flat in a chalet. It'll be good for all of us."

"All of us?"

"You know what I mean," he said.

"I don't. I truly don't know what you mean. And when were you going to tell me you were taking her away?"

Coins clinked in his hand as he counted out loose change for the tip.

"Well?" I said.

"Well what?" He stood.

"When were you going to tell me?"

"Don't worry your pretty little head about it," he said cutting me off. "Now you know."

"But . . ."

"It's not as though we're going to the ends of the earth, for Christ's sake. It's only Switzerland. What's all the fuss for?"

He came around the table to help me with my coat. I was speechless and furious.

We walked out of the darkened, dreary pub and into an even gloomier afternoon. He kissed me on both cheeks again and said he would telephone with their address in Klosters, and by the way, why didn't I consider visiting for a couple of days?

It didn't take me long to decide. The following morning, I made the arrangements through a travel agency to fly to Zurich and from there to take the train to Klosters. I found a reasonably priced hotel in the village across the street from the train station.

No sooner had I arrived than your father left for London, apparently with urgent business to attend to. I was upset at first. I guess I'd misunderstood his intentions. It wasn't meant as an invitation to talk. Rather, I think, he never imagined I'd show up.

But you were excited to see me.

We had two glorious days together. Mornings we walked up and down the well-worn mountain footpaths, where long grass grew wild and clusters of purple and yellow flowers bloomed everywhere around us. High above, the mountain peaks showed white with snow. Puffy clouds raced by in blue skies. And wherever we were, we heard the sound of cows grazing, their heavy bells clinking and clanking as they moved. In the afternoons, we went to the village swimming pool. You had just learned the breaststroke and were so proud to show me. Your friend, who lived on the ground floor of the chalet, came with us. You girls splashed around, while I sat on the side, watching, and thinking. A few days from now, I'd be thousands of miles away. How often would I be able to come back from New York to visit you? When would your father let go of his anger for long enough to allow you to vacation with me in New York?

On my last morning in Klosters, I woke early, packed and, instead of going for breakfast right away, I took a walk up to the chalet. I figured I'd pick you up and we'd have our last walk down the mountain together, have breakfast in the village, and afterward you could see me off at the train station. I wondered if your father and I would cross paths—I leaving, he returning—like two small ships in a starless and lonely night.

The sun shone that morning, as if it were a giant flashlight sweeping its brightness over the mountain tops. The fir trees seemed to be an even deeper green than usual and the air, cool and thin. For those few minutes, as I walked up the steep road, I felt practically at peace with myself, almost happy, as if I'd suddenly been given the courage and resolve to tackle anything the world would twirl my way. But as the chalet came into view, my insides began to tighten.

When you came to the door, still in your pajamas, you looked surprised to see me, not happy as I'd hoped. We had said our goodbyes the night before—you weren't expecting me. Nevertheless, I hadn't thought there'd be anything in the way of our seeing each other once again, or any reason why you wouldn't want to.

"Hurry up, go change," I said. "We're going for breakfast in the village."

You lingered at the door. You fidgeted.

"What's the matter?" I asked.

You looked at your feet, the words in answer to be coaxed from them.

Finally, you said, "I was going to play with Katya, you know my friend from downstairs."

"She'll understand."

But you didn't move.

I stood in that open doorway for a few more moments and when I realized you weren't coming with me, I bent to kiss your cheek, and without another word, left.

I hardly noticed the walk back to my hotel. I kept my head bowed to hide my tears from the people passing me in the street. What had I expected? I was leaving you. Again.

At the hotel, I had breakfast in the dining room at a corner table set for one. Afterward, I went up to my room, gathered my bags, checked out, and walked to the train station. I looked for you, hoping you'd changed your mind and would meet me here. The train pulled into the station without any sign of you. I found myself a seat in an empty compartment. The guard's whistle blew, the doors closed, and I was on my way back to Zurich, then London, and finally on to New York—this time, a long journey of planned connections into an unknown future.

CHAPTER 28

October 26, 2014

Neatening up the pile of her mother's letters she'd put on the couch next to her, Mali leans forward, interlaces her fingers, and straightens her arms out in a stretch above her head. If only she'd known her mother was never coming home again. If only she'd known the faraway place she was going to. If only . . . *if only,* she shouts now at the collection of things she's brought to the low table. She views the tarnished silver tea set, the stack of Holocaust books her mother had been reading in secret, and now this confetti of dried, yellow petals falling everywhere, touching everything; so like the memories of childhood, Mali thinks.

The disappointment in her mother's face and voice that morning in Klosters, stayed with her for a long time. After her mother had left her standing at the door to their apartment in the chalet, she went to get dressed, have breakfast, and go downstairs to find her friend Katya. She rang the bell to their apartment. No answer. She pushed the bell again. Still nothing. She had even put her ear to the closed door. Silence. Mali couldn't understand. The day before, they'd made plans after swimming, to play again today. Mali had hung over the banister, shook her head from side to side, her wet hair spraying all the way to the first floor, where her new friend giggled uncontrollably as she tried to catch the water droplets. Now, she felt betrayed. She'd given up this last time to be with her mother. Tears of frustration and anger welled up in her eyes. She turned from her friend's door and ran from the chalet. She ran past a herd of cows, past mothers carrying aluminum cans of the fresh unhomogenized milk she hated and refused to drink. She ran down the steep mountain road toward the village, passing kind people on the way who stopped to ask her: *Was ist los, Kleines Mädchen?*

And prayed it wasn't going to be too late. Please, don't let the train leave the station without me, she remembers bellowing at the ground beneath her feet. She'd felt a dread-filled guilt, the kind that knocks your heart from your chest to your throat and prickles your cheeks with heat. The kind that couldn't be undone. How could she have chosen a silly, unreliable friend over her mother?

By the time Mali had arrived at the station, out of breath and shaky, she was too late. The tracks were bare, the platform empty, and her mother—traveling away from her now—was gone. At that very moment, as she stood on the empty platform, trying to catch her breath, with tears rolling down her cheeks, and hardly noticing the majesty of the snow-capped mountains all around her, Mali could have never even imagined that missing her mother was to become the huge hole in her life. Forever.

CHAPTER 29

May 18, 2014

I've just now remembered a story your Oma once told me, or rather reminded me of, a few years ago. I don't know how I could've forgotten about it. Blocked from my consciousness, most probably.

It was shortly after the war. Your father and I were already married by then, and Oma and Opa were still living in London. Your father and your uncle Willy very generously decided to set Oma and Opa up in business. It was a distributorship of electrical wires and such. Something like a hardware store for electricians.

Every afternoon, Oma would take the dog—another white poodle, this one called Bella—and go to the shop to help out Opa. One day, Opa gave Oma money from the till. I'm sure it must have been to pay for her bus fare. How much could he have possibly given her? A few shillings? When your father found out, he was so angry, he took back the business from them.

Left with nothing and no means of support, Oma and Opa decided it was time to leave England and join the rest of their families in New York. We didn't even take them to the train station the day they left. We had to say our goodbyes the night before. Oma thought your father regretted his decision. She said he cried for a moment when he kissed her goodbye.

I can't help thinking how differently things might have turned out if your father hadn't sent them packing. It seems your father had a penchant for banishing people from his life when things got too rough for him.

After Oma and Opa came to New York, they opened a cleaning store in Flushing. And when I first arrived here, I worked with them in their store for a while. I also tried my hand at modeling. I did get a couple of jobs with a hat manufacturer in Manhattan. But I never made enough money to sustain myself. And Oma was anxious to see me settled again. In other words, married off. A divorced woman was not commonplace in those days, let alone a young one with a child across the Atlantic. My only chance at a second marriage was to find a divorced man. Which, as you know, I did.

I found those early days in New York both destabilizing and exhilarating. Destabilizing because I didn't have you or your father with me, and my days felt surreal, that sense of loss always tugging at my empty side. But I loved New York. The newness of it. The freedom of it. The old European, straitlaced customs didn't exist here, and if they did, they didn't matter as much. It wasn't a strike against you, or your man, if you went out to work.

To make extra money I took a Saturday job at Gimbels, the one on Broadway at Thirty-Second Street. Do you remember it? I worked in the hat department. Since I'd learned how to model hats, management thought it would be an added plus for the customers to see the hats modeled for them while they shopped. I enjoyed my work there, even though I was exhausted by the end of the day. And my feet. Not one pair of shoes fit comfortably enough. I did begin to make new friends, but since I believed my stay here only temporary, a sort of extended hiatus until things got sorted out with your father, I wouldn't allow myself to feel settled or get close to anyone. It would be like giving in, or giving up.

I lost weight those first few months. My period even disappeared. Opa and Oma worried. And the only thing I ever wanted was to return to London to resume my old life with you and your father. Hating my unhappiness, Opa decided he'd try to mend my broken marriage for me.

He wrote to your father. He'd fly to London if your father agreed to talk, which he did. At first my spirits lifted. But then I remembered our last meeting in London. Where had that gotten me? Maybe this would be different, though. Two men talking.

Opa arrived in London early in the morning, after flying through the night, and took a taxi to meet your father at his office in Hatton Garden.

I've taken a little liberty here with my imagination, although I do remember Opa telling us, in as much detail as he could remember, about his visit.

When Opa arrived, your father was sitting at his desk, a loupe to his eye, an uncut diamond held up to the light between his forefinger and thumb. Opa's letter sat close to the edge of the desk, as if your father had just pushed it aside after reading it again. Assortments of small stones were strewn across the green blotter. They looked amazingly like the ordinary pebbles you might find in the street, Opa told us.

Your father came around the desk and shook Opa's hand. He motioned for him to sit and offered him a cup of tea. He called out for his secretary to put on the kettle. Then, back on his side of the desk, he scooped up the stones with a little shovel-like utensil and poured them into tissue-paper pouches.

"How's business?" Opa said, as your father sat back down at his side of the desk.

"Not too bad, thank God. And you? How's everything in New York? Your . . . what's it called . . .? Cleaner store?"

"Yes, believe it or not, our cleaning store is giving us a living. Eva's working with us now as well."

"How is she? And Luzie?"

"Well, truthfully, Luzie and I are very worried about Eva."

"Why? Is she ill?"

"Not exactly ill, but she's lost weight and . . . well . . . the reason I've come . . ."

"I know, you want me to let everything go back into the shambles it was when she left." Grabbing the pouches off his desk, he stood and walked behind Opa's chair to the opened safe. With the pouches safely inside, he slammed the heavy door shut. Coming back around to his desk, he added, "It won't work, Robert, this reconciliation thing. It won't work."

"Haven't you punished her enough?"

Just then, his secretary came into the office, holding a tray with two cups of tea, a milk pitcher, a sugar bowl, and a plate of chocolate Digestives. She put the tray down by your father and left the room.

"It can't be helped," your father said, pushing one of the teacups in front of Opa and offering him milk, sugar, and the biscuits. "I can't change what's done."

"You're so quick with your answer, Hirschel. And so stubborn. I'm only asking you to think it over. Yes, I agree, she was a silly girl . . . but hardly grown up . . . you married a child, don't forget. And children, just like us grownups, make mistakes."

"I can't . . ."

"You mean you won't."

"No. I can't. I can't forget what she did, and I can't forgive her for it either."

"Even for the sake of your child? Don't you think she needs her mother?"

"Ach! Like a hole in the head."

I could so easily imagine your father at his desk, stirring in the sugar, the spoon clinking against the inside of his cup, the tea sloshing over the rim.

"Eva is no mother," your father ranted. "She never cared more than this . . ." And to show that his words, spoken out loud, weren't enough, he picked up a corner of the blue airmail letter Opa had sent, and flicked the thinness of it between his thumb and index finger, then let it drop back to the green blotter on his desk.

"Hirschel . . . Hirschel . . ."

"She was only interested in shopping and . . . carrying on with . . ." He took a swallow of his tea, put his cup down and added, "Look, it's just no good."

"I'm begging you, Hirschel, to think a little more . . ."

"I have," he said.

"But the burden of bringing up a child on your own . . ."

"It's all under control. I hired a governess, as you've most probably heard, a woman from Australia—a widow, very nice, very proper. She takes care of Mali and the house. Yes, things are very much under control."

"But this woman can't replace her mother."

"Of course not. I never said she would."

"And don't you think she misses her mother?" Opa said.

"Yes, but it can't be helped."

"Eva misses Mali. And believe it or not, she misses you too."

"She'll find another man."

"How can you be so . . .? Have you found another woman? Is that it? What was her name, Sonia?"

"For Chrissakes, Robert! If you're referring to the woman, I had a little snog with at a party, then let me tell you nothing happened. Besides, it's not the same."

"Not the same? How do you figure that? Did you ever wonder, for even one moment, how Eva might've felt when you walked out of a strange bedroom wiping another woman's lipstick off your mouth?"

"We were at a party. It was different."

"Different for you, you mean."

"Ach! Robert. Have you never . . .?"

"Never."

The men stopped talking. They drank their tea. Opa looked around the small, stark office. No pictures on the white walls. No photographs on his desk. The only window in the room faced other windows in the building opposite. He said later that it struck him how very impermanent and impersonal it felt.

"Look," Opa said to your father. "Nothing is ever that one-sided. You must recognize there were things you did, and didn't do, to push her away, to make her look elsewhere. I'm not a fool, you know, and I wouldn't have come all this way, if I'd thought for one minute she was the only one to blame."

"Robert, it's over. And so is this discussion. Are you ready to come home with me now to see Mali?"

Opa leaned forward in his chair. He told us how he'd spread his hands wide on your father's desk, to plant himself there, or perhaps for the strength to say, "I want to take Mali back to New York with me."

"What?" your father said. "Over my dead body." His teeth clenched tight. "Never, never, never. Mali stays here with me. End of discussion. Subject closed."

"She needs her mother," Opa said, folding his arms at his chest.

"Not that mother, she doesn't. And if you're scraping by with your cleaning store, how do you expect to take care of her, educate her? What an absurd idea! Come on, let's get out of here before I change my mind about taking you home with me."

Opa said later that all he could think of on their way back to Finchley Lane was how he wished he'd stood his ground at the start, put his foot down and prohibited me from marrying your father in the first place. Had he taken the painless way out back then? Had I pressured him too much? He couldn't help feeling responsible for the mess we were in now. And here he was, ten years later, trying to mend my marriage, as if I were a child and had brought him the severed limbs of a broken doll to put back together.

But then, as soon as the door to the house on Finchley Lane opened and he saw you standing before him, he told us that all his feelings of anger, defeat, and pessimism melted away in an instant. He'd fallen in love with the sweetest and most beautiful girl he could ever have hoped to call his granddaughter.

Do you remember his visit? The Snow White and Cinderella records I helped him pick out for you? He hadn't seen you in quite a few years, and although you were obviously much older, he insisted he would've recognized you anywhere. Your face hadn't changed a bit, he said. You were still so beautiful.

CHAPTER 30

October 26, 2014

Outside her mother's bedroom, Mali stares at the white wall jam-packed with framed photographs. Up high on the wall, is a formal black and white of Mali, a child of nine, in school uniform, and her Opa, a man in his sixties with thick, large, magnifying eyeglasses in a tortoiseshell frame looking too big for his narrow, bony face. They both smile for the camera. It was a special day.

Mali slides to the floor, wraps her arms around her legs and, resting her chin on her knees, stares up at the two faces to reconstruct her Opa's first visit to see her on that foggy November day. She remembers being nervous to meet him. She had searched through the shirt box of old photographs at the bottom of the airing cupboard, but only found a few of him as a young man. She had tried to keep that young face in her mind. But, standing before the open door of their house on Finchley Lane that afternoon, her hair freshly brushed for the occasion, she found, instead, a white-haired gentleman in a black and grey tweed overcoat, a white paper bag clutched in his hand and a wide smile curving up in an almost perfect semicircle toward his eyes. The white paper bag contained two records: Snow White and Cinderella. Even now, she can summon up those smooth-sounding American voices on the recordings. What magic they'd held for her in those days.

Mali's father took her Opa's coat and ushered him into the lounge. Under his tweed coat, he wore a grey wool suit, baggy and out of style, a collared white shirt, but no tie. How impeccable her father had looked in contrast, so starched and untouchable, much the way the conversation between the three of them was going. Opa smiled at her. He lit a cigarette. She watched the smoke from his Camel billow around him each time he exhaled. Her father asked him a few questions: how the weather was in New York at this time of year, if New York got fog like London. Then, after a few more moments of silence, her Opa turned to Mali and said he hoped she would enjoy the records he'd brought. He loved fairy tales and music himself. Mali assured him they were the perfect gifts, and they lapsed into an awkward silence once again, her Opa puffing away while drumming his fingers on the arm of the upholstered chair, not in an impatient way, but in a rhythm so distinct, she was sure music had to be playing inside his head. After a few more minutes of polite conversation, her father told her to hurry up and put on her coat. She and her Opa were going out.

The glass and wrought iron front door closed behind them. They walked down the steep drive to the cold foggy street in silence. Almost night now, the street took on both an eerie and magical quality, as if a painted stage set to a Dickens story. Chimney pots smoked like huddled old men puffing away on giant-sized pipes. Lights were turned on, illuminating rooms in the houses they passed.

Mali loved to fantasize about the families inside; how they would gather around their white-clothed dining tables at teatime and listen to their favorite programs on the BBC, while warming to the bright, blue-and-orange fires roaring beneath ornate, marble mantelpieces, crowded with silver-framed, family portraits.

As they reached the shops at the top of the road, the streetlamps had turned fuzzier in the thickening fog. The cars drove very slowly, their headlights giving off an almost touchable cone of light, obscuring rather than showing the road ahead. They were on a mission, her Opa said. He wanted to get her a special gift to mark their day together, something she would always remember him by. She took him to Josephson's, the stationer. Since her Saturday morning ritual was to come here and browse—examining the pens, the sketching paper, and the notebooks— she thought she'd have no trouble picking out that special present. Only now, nothing seemed quite right, or important enough. They walked up and down the jammed aisles of the little shop, bending to inspect the glass cases, then craning their necks, Mali on tiptoes, to see high up, what surprises the top shelves might hold. All the while, her Opa talked to her in his gravelly voice, his foreign accent the testament to the life they should have had, and the one they now lived.

But what she'd really wanted to know that day was why she could never banish the image of her mother at the front hall mirror—the red lipstick at her mouth, the sequined beret askew on her head, the two packed suitcases by her side, and the taxi, waiting to take her away. Perhaps it was those memories that clogged her mind. So many of her questions lay buried inside her. She'd tried building the sentences in her head, formulating the words, one by one. In the end, though, her courage had blown away from her, taking flight like a dried-up leaf in the wind.

Just then, Mr. Josephson returned from the storeroom behind his shop with a beautiful set of Caran d'Ache paints. When your mother was your age, she loved to paint as well, her Opa told her. The tin's cover had a picture of a Swiss chalet. Bordered by evergreens, it sat on the edge of a shimmering blue lake and was surrounded by snow-laden mountains. This reminds me of places I've been to in my youth, her Opa said, admiring the picture on the tin. Mali opened it. The paints were evenly arranged in little squares: eight to a row, eight rows to the box. Four shades of green, two whites, and a whole row of reds, oranges, and purples. Mali can still remember how smooth, soft, and perfect they'd felt on her fingertips.

By the time they left Josephson's, a paper bag clutched in her hand with the paint box packed inside it, the fog had thickened even more. Mali worried about their walk home. Her Opa didn't seem to mind though. He pulled up the collar to his coat, shoved his ungloved hands into his pockets and led her across the street to Behrens, the photographer. Her Opa introduced himself. They spoke German for a few minutes. Then Mr. Behrens led them into his studio at the back of his shop. They sat on tall stools for the camera. In between takes, her Opa explained to her that Mr. Behrens had been a photographer in the war and had captured many fascinating pictures. When she got older, she must come back, take a good look at them, and burn them into the plate of her memory so that she would never forget—no matter the difficulties she might face in the future—how incredibly lucky their family had been.

What else had gone through her mind that day? And on other days, a few years later, when she was trying to fit in at boarding school? Had she ever thought of why one half of her family came to be living in America? Had she thought it out beyond the divorce? Had she realized how her relatives had been on a collision course with the history of the world? How, like meteorites, they'd been tossed out of their sphere, had crashed through space, and had landed as shattered fragments in whatever corner of the world was brave enough to accept them.

She never did get back to see Mr. Behrens's photographs. For a long time, the idea frightened her. Then when she had finally plucked up the nerve to go, she found the store closed, and in its place, a beauty salon. She never learned what had become of Mr. Behrens or his photographs.

CHAPTER 31

May 18, 2014

Well, My Sweet Girl, the other night I found myself engrossed in a TV show. Its subject: the way certain mammals give birth and how they care for their newborns. I was fascinated, I must admit. And that reminded me. Did I ever tell you the story of your birth? When I think back on it now, I enjoy a good laugh at myself. I was such an immature nineteen-year-old, so awfully naïve. My obstetrician had told me you were due mid-April. The sixteenth, to be precise. I took his word as law and believed I would deliver you on precisely that day. The day came. I waited for signs. There were none. My elderly neighbor recommended I drink a whole bottle of castor oil. To ease the delivery, she'd said. I did just as she suggested. Then checked myself into the small maternity nursing home on Shoot-Up Hill. The nurses took one look at me and said, "Your baby's not ready." And they sent me home, disappointed, and embarrassed. I waited and waited. I thought you'd never come.

Until one beautiful, sunny day toward the end of May, with the lilacs and rhododendrons in full bloom, I began to experience the long-awaited-for labor pains. With my overnight bag still packed and waiting from the last go-round, I returned to the nursing home. But instead of checking in— the day too glorious to be inside—I strolled out to the back garden where, among the flowering purple and red bushes, I found a deckchair, turned it to face the sun, and carefully lowered myself into it. I sat back, closed my eyes, and pointed my chin up into the rays of brightness. The warmth, an

JACQUIE HERZ

elixir. Every so often I'd feel my insides contract. But I wasn't ready; not ready this time, to give up my day in the sun. Then, quite suddenly, my contractions became stronger and more frequent. You, my child, were all set. Too bad if I wasn't. I hoisted myself up from the low-slung deckchair and waddled up the stairs to the back door of the nursing home. This time the nurses took one look at me and said, "What in heaven's name were you waiting for, ducky? Your baby's head is crowning."

They delivered you—ugly, scrawny, wrinkled, red-faced, and screaming. The doctor arrived after you were born. He said the afterbirth was so much more important than the birth. What did I know? I almost had you, while sitting in a deckchair, glorying in the sunshine, for God's sake.

CHAPTER 32

October 26, 2014

Mali wonders at her own reluctance to be born. Perhaps she'd had some magical foresight. Now it's her turn to laugh at herself. She remembers her mother telling her how huge she'd become when pregnant with her, and how disappointed to deliver such a tiny, scrawny baby. But by the end of the conversation, she'd always say, "You certainly made up for it." And she had. Mali has a baby picture of herself. Her father's holding her. He's laughing. Her fat face looks directly into the camera, a contented smile crinkling-up her eyes into shiny almond-shaped sparkles. Her life was good then, happy. She feels that to be true, deep inside herself. Only later did her world get turned inside out and upside down.

But where was her father in this story of her birth? Was he bent over his diamonds, pincers in one hand, a jeweler's loupe held up to his eye in the other? Were the seeds of separation already planted? Why wasn't he pacing the hall outside the delivery room, the way husbands did in the movies, chain-smoking with anxiety and worry?

Her father. A picture of his face, closed and unsmiling, settles into her mind's eye now. Then, herself, at eight, nine, ten, or eleven—it didn't matter the age—the scenarios always held the same nagging images.

· · · · ·

Shortly after she and her father had come back from their summer holiday in Klosters, Mali discovered a bunch of old black-and-white photos abandoned in one of the drawers in her father's desk. Starved for clues that would help her understand her mother's abandonment of her and her father's distant behavior, she studied each feature of her mother's face, of her father's, of her own, to look for similarities, differences. But in those glossy-coated mementos, she only saw their smiles, as they had once held and loved her. In her baby photographs, she thought she'd even looked pretty.

But by the time she was nine, the reflection in the dressing table mirror was ugly. Tears rolled down her cheeks. Her father stood behind her. Consoling. He pleaded with her not to believe what she saw in the mirror. He said it was a distortion, this crippled view of herself. She couldn't believe him. Only what the reflection showed: the truth.

She'd wanted so much to go and live with her mother in America.

Just as he'd done so many times before, he turned her around to face him, then took her hand and brought her into the lounge downstairs. He closed the door behind them and sat her down on the brocade-covered couch. Although the window was behind her, she could still picture their small, square back garden with the rhododendrons and lilacs in bloom, the pansies waving their smiley purple and yellow faces, the pink roses climbing up the side of the garage.

Her father asked her again what this nonsense was all about, this longing to live with her mother in America. Wasn't she happy with him, here in London? Didn't she love him? Mali couldn't say. She counted the sculpted lines in the beige wallpaper instead. Her mind had become as blank and dark as the unlit television screen, a gaping black hole staring stupidly out at the room. Every one of her carefully planned-out arguments gone, voided by his eyes staring at her, shiny with hurt and impatience. She thought of her bedroom, a refuge, where she could dream of an easier relationship with him, where her body could move freely, smoothly, not disjointed, and clumsy. In her room, her imagined words, expressed for the moment, were neither fraught with past meanings and hidden messages nor shrouded in fear of their consequence. She pictured her desk by the large, curtained bay window and each one of the things she treasured on it: the green blotter littered with words and sketches, the Caran d'Ache paint box from her grandfather, the dip pens from Woolworth's, the fountain pens and ink bottles from Josephson's, and the large, colored photograph of her mother.

In the photograph, it's summertime. Her mother looks very serious and beautiful. The sky is movie-color-blue, and in the background behind her mother is a low white building with windows, thick as the bottoms of Coke bottles. Mali always wondered about the building. What lay behind it? Next to it? Around it? What New York was really like?

She wanted so much to go—a refrain, like the chorus to a pop song that repeats and repeats in her brain and won't let go.

Slouched next to her father on the brocade-covered couch, Mali superimposed an image she'd harbored of a blossoming lilac tree in the back garden onto the blank television screen. She concentrated on the tiny petals, so radiant and delicate against the blackness. Tears began to gather in her eyes. Willed not to spill. Afraid to blink. Her eyes stung. The roof of her mouth ached. Then the pressure gave way, and they began to fall, the tiny lilac petals washing away from her mind's eye. Her father stretched out his left leg, reached into his pocket, pulled out a freshly ironed handkerchief, passed it to her.

"Why don't you go upstairs and wash your face," he told her, giving her knee a reassuring pat. "You'll feel much better, I promise you."

He got up off the couch, sighed with the effort, and bent to kiss her forehead.

She watched him walk away from her. He looked back as he opened the door and smiled. But through that smile she saw an image of herself—immobilized on the couch, round-shouldered; brown curly hair, tousled; eyes, red and swollen; a crumpled handkerchief, twisting in her hands—as a relic, a faded ribboned-medal from a long-ago night she'd never been able to let go of.

After her mother was gone, her father hired Viola—a middle-aged housekeeper in tweed skirts, woolen twinsets from Marks & Spencer, and clunky, brown lace-ups, shined and sensible on her quick-stepping feet—to take care of her. She'd come with excellent qualifications, the best references. He was impressed. Wisps of over-permed, light-brown hair framed her pale, freckled face. Mali remembers her eyes, a piercing blue, and her magenta-colored lips, drawn into a thin straight line.

She taught Mali how to eat like a real English lady. Her father would laugh about this, his words of pride coated in his heavy refugee accent. She's very good for you, he'd say to Mali, in the same way he might have told her to drink up her milk or eat her spinach, whenever she complained Viola was too strict.

How could Mali have guessed at the frightening fury that would spill out of her? The resentment for her everyday job of caretaking, her hatred for the visiting mother with her presents and promises, seducing the child into loving her. And afterward, after the mother had gone away again and the holiday was but a faint memory and the day-to-day job of life had settled back in, it was she, Viola, who was left to deal with the torment of Mali's yearning.

Not long afterward, Fleur, her father's new wife, entered her life. Mali remembers Fleur's disdain of everything American. No matter what Mali's mother brought for her, it was neither the perfect fit, nor what even suited her. Poor Fleur. Generosity was not her strong suit. Though Mali can understand her better now. Her jealousy, those feelings not so different from Viola's, got in her way. All the grunt work of raising Mali fell to her and all the glory, the gratitude, went to Mali's mother. On the other hand, Mali wonders why, if she had agreed to marry her father with a child in tow, she couldn't have been more of an adult, better able to cope. She must have known, to a degree, what she was getting into. Though Mali has to admit, she was not an easy child. Moody and stubborn. Maybe Fleur hadn't noticed at first. Maybe her father, so eager to remarry, had painted too rosy a picture for her.

Mali was ten when they married in Paris. She hadn't been invited to the wedding and was upset. Did they imagine they could be young, frivolous, and childless, even for that brief time? When they came home from their honeymoon, Viola was let go. Mali was happy for that.

She thinks Fleur must have tried her best at the beginning too, not only with a new stepdaughter, but also with her new husband's pain. Had he shared every intimate detail of his divorce with her? Mali expects so. It hadn't been easy for him; he'd have explained to Fleur. And Mali is sure that it wasn't. The visits from her mother were especially hard on him. She knew he couldn't stand the interruption, the disruption of it all, the excitement, the upheaval. It was always the same whenever her mother came. Mali's tears and pleading. His attempts to console her. It took days after her mother left for Mali to settle back down again.

While dreading so much disturbance to his life, can she blame him for keeping her mother's pending visits a secret until the very last possible moment?

•   •   •   •

Mali remembers one of her mother's visits to London. She must have been around eleven or twelve at the time.

Perched on a stool at the kitchen counter, she was eating her breakfast of buttered toast and milky coffee. As usual, she had been listening for the letterbox in the bottom of their front door—for the metal lid slamming shut and for the faint flutter of envelopes dropping, one by one, to the beige, carpeted floor. She was always on the lookout for the ones made of blue paper, so thin and light, they weighed no more than the air they traveled through to cross the Atlantic. She knew airmailed letters took three days to fly from her mother's apartment in New York to her house in London. She also knew, by this time, when to expect one.

So it had surprised her that among the usual assortment of brown-enveloped bills, she saw the familiar blue airmail letter. Her mother's rounded script marked the pre-lined address form, but it was her father's name written on the row above, instead of hers. She shuffled the envelopes around and stood them on the shelf under the mirror, the blue one barely visible between two larger brown ones. The letter could have meant only one thing. Her mother must be coming to London to visit her. She skipped back to the kitchen, swallowed the remains of her breakfast standing up, shouted goodbye to no one in particular, picked up her satchel, and headed out through the back door to school.

After dinner that evening, she sat on the couch, her eyes glued to the TV, but hardly able to take anything in.

"Bedtime," her father announced with a clap of his hands as *Emergency Ward 10*, her favorite TV program, came to an end. "Don't dillydally," he added. "It's a school night."

She got up slowly, went to him and kissed his cheek, rough with stubble.

"Goodnight," she said, hovering over him as she tried to think of a reason to delay going up to bed. Maybe he'd forgotten about the letter. If she lingered a little longer perhaps her lingering would jog his memory.

"Bedtime," he repeated. "Come on, Mali, why is this always so difficult?" He uncrossed his legs.

If she asked him if he'd seen her mother's letter, he'd accuse her of sneaking around behind his back.

"I need five shillings," she said. "We have an outing to Hatfield House on Friday."

"Again?" He stretched out his right leg and reached into his pocket. But he only had a sixpence, two three-penny bits, and a penny. "I think you have more outings than you have school," he said, laughing. "See if I have more change upstairs on my desk."

"Thank you," she said.

She pretended to be a tightrope walker. Putting one foot directly in front of the other, and as slowly as she possibly could without losing her balance, she went to kiss Fleur goodnight too. She left the lounge, closing the door behind her, and waited there for a moment. Maybe he'd remember he had something to tell her and call her back in. But the only sounds she heard were coming from the TV. She climbed the stairs.

She went through the motions of getting ready for bed. She shivered in the toilet, a small, narrow, echoing room with a little window high up on the back wall that was always open, no matter the weather. Next, in the pink bathroom, she washed her hands and face and brushed her teeth. On the way back to her room, she passed the open door to her father's bedroom. She went in to look for the five shillings she needed for her school outing. She picked up two half-crowns and was ready to leave when she noticed the blue airmail letter crushed in the wastepaper basket. She picked it up, smoothed it out.

Dear Hirschel, she read. *I hope this letter finds you well. After searching and almost giving up, I finally found a reasonably priced roundtrip flight to London. I will be arriving early on the morning of the 9th and leaving again the following Thursday evening. Best wishes to Fleur. Eva.*

Mali had guessed right. She balled up the letter, threw it back into the wastepaper basket, and tiptoed out of the room. Why hadn't he told her she was coming? Maybe he would tell her tomorrow.

But he said nothing to her the following day either. Nor the days that followed. When, without a word, he sent her off to bed on the evening of the eighth, she felt sure she'd either imagined the letter or her mother had changed her mind. Or worse, she thought, maybe something terrible had happened to her.

The next morning, a quick, loud knock on her bedroom door woke her with a start. Her father came into her room. Still in his pajamas and dressing gown, his hair sticking up at the back of his head, where he'd slept on it badly, he stood at the foot of her bed.

"Hurry up," he said. "Get dressed. Your mother is coming today. She'll be picking you up from school this afternoon."

He then turned on his heels and left her room, his opened silk dressing gown billowing and flapping noiselessly behind him.

The letter was real after all. She had begun to think of it as a blue figment of her imagination. Or gone crazy with wishing so hard, the longing for her mother had materialized into a thing of flesh and blood, as if she were a magician performing miracles with smoke and mirrors. Why had he waited until now to tell her?

She got out of bed. Chose her favorite white blouse to wear with her school uniform. And took extra care with her short brown hair, wetting her unruly bangs and brushing them flat to her forehead.

She has always needed to look perfect for her mother, she muses now. . .

CHAPTER 33

May 20, 2014

Do you remember, my darling, when we'd talked about Oma dying and Opa's denial of it? I only bring this up to let you know that David and I have no secrets from each other.

On the other hand, I sense that our relationship, yours, and mine, is often on very tenuous ground. I'm never quite sure how we'll be from one time to the next. If I try bringing up the past, you tell me everything is fine and there's no need to go over the whole story again, no need to continue feeling guilty. But it's not so simple. It's the part of my life that keeps coming back to me. And it's not only guilt I feel, but anger as well. Anger at myself, at my own stupidity and my weakness, and at your father and his. You'll never know how I plotted and schemed over the years to get you back. Still today, you have an edge, an anger deep inside that seems all too ready to bubble up and boil over. I find myself going back to see if I can set the record straight. But because my recollections crisscross over so many timelines, I never find a straight path to the past. I suppose it's true for everyone, but I imagine my roads back are more convoluted than most.

My visits to London to see you were always difficult, awkward, and tense. On the Golders Green Road, for instance, a muddle of memories would overtake my thoughts. Lily & Skinner was where we'd come to buy you shoes. Remember the foot-measuring machine, the green-colored X-ray that showed the bones in your feet like skeletons? I preferred going to Dolcis for mine; they were more fashion conscious there. Jaeger, a beautiful women's clothing store, was where I'd go to look at the smart suits and coats, most of which I couldn't afford. And of course, there was Franck's, the lingerie shop, reminding me of the bitterest of my memories.

By my third visit back to London to see you—I had been gone for four years then—I was determined to make up for our lost time. I had a plan.

• • • • •

It was springtime and the weather unusually mild for early May in London. By now, you were almost twelve. We had spent a fun afternoon at Battersea Park and were on the way back to Golders Green—I had borrowed Lotte's Mini—to grab a bite at Kardomah's Café before getting you home. We were silent in the car. I was distracted by my plan, going over and over it in my head, to make sure I had every aspect of it covered. There could be no mistakes. But until that very moment, I hadn't thought of the possibility you might turn me down. Then what? I concentrated on the bold white line painted on the road, separating my lane from the oncoming traffic. In that case, my scheming would have been for nothing, and life would go on as it has these last four years. I would continue to be a yearly visitor in your life.

Seated at a table by the window in Kardomah's, our order for dessert taken, I looked around at the other tables, now filling up with chattering housewives on a break from their daily routines. I must confess, I hadn't missed this London life.

I was so wrapped up in my thoughts, I didn't hear you at first.

"Why can't I come and live with you?" you asked again, louder this time.

Was my scheme mapped out on my forehead for you to read? My mouth felt very dry all of a sudden. I took a sip of coffee, lit up a Player's, and as I let out the smoke, I said, "I'm going to tell you something you will have to promise to keep top secret. You can't breathe a word of this to anyone. Do you swear?"

"I swear." You sat up a little straighter in your chair, your eyes bright with expectation.

"I have a plan," I said. And right or wrong, I couldn't stop the rush of words about to tumble out of my mouth.

The waitress arrived at our table, a dessert in each hand.

You eyed your mille-feuille, then poked your finger into the escaping bits of crème from in between the layers of pastry. You looked up at me, licking your fingers, and waited for me to continue.

"My plan," I said, leaning in toward you, measuring my words to give each one equal weight, and still thinking, in the back of my mind, that I was crazy to be telling you all this before I was one hundred percent sure it would work.

"Yes?" you said, impatience in your voice. You picked up your fork and dug it into the cake, the hard icing crumbling on your plate.

"My plan . . ." I said, holding my breath. "My plan," I said again, now crossing my fingers under the table, "is to . . . kidnap you." The Swiss Roll in front of me was drowning in a pool of custard. I couldn't eat. I stubbed out my cigarette.

But the look on your face made me laugh. I wished I'd had a camera.

You bolted straight up in your chair, as if you'd just been pinched. "Like in the films?"

"What do you think? Am I totally crazy?"

"No. No. I'd do anything to come and live with you. Anything."

"There's one hitch, though," I said. "I will have to wait to hear from my lawyer first. We must be sure your father can't have you on a return flight back to London the minute you land in New York."

A frown of worry rumpled your forehead.

"And there's one last thing," I said. "If everything's a go, you will have to find your passport."

"When will you know?" The frown on your forehead intensified.

"Tomorrow. He'll call me tomorrow."

"Not 'til tomorrow?"

"I shouldn't have told you. I'm getting your hopes up and . . ."

"No, no. It's okay."

"You sure?"

"Yes," you said, "I promise." And you began to dissect the layers of your mille-feuille, spooning out the crème to eat first.

I turned my attention back to the people around us, having their tea. Nothing too much seemed to have changed in this country since the war.

The women still dressed in pleated tweed skirts and woolen twin sets. I sipped my coffee. You were still preoccupied with your dessert.

"What will happen if I can't find my passport?" you said, scraping the last of the crème from your plate onto your fork.

"Don't worry, we'll figure out what to do. I'm a champion figure outer. I bet you didn't know that about me, huh?"

You laughed, took a sip of your tea, and we went over the plan again. You were to walk to school as usual and I'd pick you up along the way. I'd be in Lotte's Mini. You would've already told your father and Fleur you were going to a friend's after school, which would give us more hours before you'd be missed.

Luckily, you didn't ask me again how or where to look for your passport. I had no idea what I'd have told you.

"Hurry and finish your tea," I said, suddenly feeling very foolish. "They'll be expecting you at home soon."

Home . . . I hadn't been back to Finchley Lane in more than a year.

In the car, we talked about how much pocket money you'd get, the school you'd be going to, your new bedroom in New York.

When we arrived at the house, I remember how surprised I'd been, to see it still look so much the same from the outside. Neither the red of the bricks nor the roundness of the lacy-curtained bay windows gave anything away of the change that had taken place within it.

You opened the car door and leaned over to kiss me goodbye.

You retrieved your brown leather satchel from the back seat and, without a word, left me and walked up the drive to the front door of the house. A few seconds later, I saw the frosted-glass and wrought-iron door open. I held my breath. Would he wave? Should I get out of the car and shout, "Hello, how are you?" from across the still-empty flower beds in the front garden. Would he ask me in for a drink? But then, before I could even formulate my next thought, I heard the click of the door shutting and saw, through the wavy opaque glass, the fuzzy gray silhouette of a man bending toward the shadowy image of his daughter's face in a kiss.

Shaking my head, as if to rid myself of all those old memories, I looked over at the red-brick house on Finchley Lane one more time, then released the Mini's hand brake, clicked on the right-turn indicator, and merged the car into traffic.

A telegram waited for me at my hotel. I took the yellow envelope from the desk clerk and walked slowly up the two flights of stairs to my room. I already knew what the pasted words on the yellow sheet would be. The lawyer could've sent me a blank page, saved the dollars spent on the words. I put the oversized key in the lock and opened the door to the little room. I dropped my bag to the floor next to the night table, took off my shoes, sat on the edge of the bed, and stared at the sealed yellow envelope. Why today? Couldn't I have had just one more day of illusion? I thought of the two silhouettes behind the closed glass door and, all at once, felt my cheeks go hot. I was jealous.

Then I remembered what else had happened at the party that changed my life, and yours.

While I was dancing, I wasn't paying any attention to where your father was, or who he was with until, out of the corner of my eye, I saw the bedroom door open and our friend Sonia walk out. Her hair was tousled, her makeup smudged, and her clothes rumpled. I kept my eye on the door to see who would follow her. A few moments later, pulling out the handkerchief from his pocket, your father strode from the bedroom, a little smile curling his mouth and rubbing at the bright red lipstick Sonia had deposited there.

Why hadn't I thrown this back in your father's face, you're probably wondering. I don't know the answer. Perhaps I was too scared and stupid. Why was it always okay for the man to stray, to experiment?

The yellow envelope sat on my lap, still sealed. I already knew its message but prayed for it to be different anyway. I took a deep breath, ripped it open. Through my tears, I stared at the three little printed words. Sick of it all, I ripped the telegram into tiny shreds and flung the pieces across the room. For a long time, I sat on that strange bed and watched London's evening sky outside the window turn darker and darker until finally, I could see nothing at all.

CHAPTER 34

October 26, 2014

Mali remembers she had wanted to turn back and wave to her mother in the Mini that day, but the front door to her house had opened too quickly, and as though the very atmosphere outside was suffocating, her father had pulled her in, slamming shut the opaque glass and wrought iron door behind her.

He kissed her hello, asked without interest how her day had been, and retraced his steps back to the lounge. *Rawhide* had just begun on TV. She dropped her satchel by the stairs, followed him into the lounge and kissed Fleur, who was sitting curled up in her chair, her legs folded beneath her, a French paperback in her lap.

Without looking up, she said, "Are you hungry?"

Mali said she wasn't, and crossed the room to the couch, immediately becoming engrossed in *Rawhide.* She loved to watch Clint Eastwood squint his eyes against the brightness of those same vast American Plains he surveyed each week.

"Do you have homework?" her father said, as the credits rolled.

She couldn't remember but stood anyway. She kissed them both goodnight and left the lounge.

Up in her room, she unbuckled her satchel and took out the small, shiny, black box her mother had brought for her. Nestled on a square of cotton wool was her new charm bracelet. Tiny golden replicas of the Empire State Building, the Statue of Liberty, the Brooklyn Bridge, dangled from the chain. Mali tried to fasten the bracelet onto her wrist but couldn't catch both ends for long enough to clasp it. She could run downstairs to see if Fleur would help, but then she thought of her passport. She lay across her bed, held the bracelet high above her face, and examined each of the gold charms, as she mapped out how to get from her bed to her father's desk, how to avoid all the creaky parts on the landing. In her mind, she counted the steps from her room to theirs. She held her breath. Her heart pumped. She felt it pounding in her throat, in her mouth, in her head.

The phone rang. She jumped, as though she were already guilty. Her father called for her to pick up. She ran into their bedroom, not worrying now about the creaky parts on the landing and lifted the receiver.

"My plan won't work," she heard her mother say. "I can lose all my rights to see you. I could go to jail."

At first, Mali felt relief at not having to rummage through her father's desk drawers in search of her passport. But then, there came a crashing sense of hopelessness and the feeling that nothing would ever be right again. She'd grown so used, in these last few hours, to the idea of living with her mother in New York, the thought of staying here in London with her father suddenly became abhorrent, unbearable. Her mother kept talking, apologizing.

"I should have never told you any of this," she said.

Hearing the tears in her mother's voice, Mali felt sorry for her.

"I'll think of more ideas, I promise you. He'll have to give in," she said. "Yes, in the end, he'll have to give in," she said again after a little pause. "You'll see."

"Yes, in the end," Mali echoed her mother's words, then told her she needed to go. She still had a ton of homework to do.

"I love you," her mother said.

"I love you too," Mali repeated, and put down the receiver.

She remained sitting on her father's side of the bed for a while. She stared at the phone, hoping it might still deliver a different message. And then she wished she could've willed her body into a cloud of smoke so the feelings inside her, of guilt and betrayal toward one parent or the other, would just evaporate into the icy blue of the sky.

•　　•　　•

Sitting on the yellow couch in her mother's Manhattan apartment, the blue blanket wrapped around her, she can't seem to get her memories of Finchley Lane out of her head.

The red-brick house. The rumble of the 143 bus outside her bedroom window. Lorries and cars zooming along the dual carriageway of the North Circular Road at the bottom of her street, just a few houses away from hers. And in the opposite direction and up the hill, the sweets shop, where she'd buy banana split toffee bars for the Saturday afternoon, old-time Hollywood movies she used to watch on the small-screened black and white TV.

· · · · ·

In those days when she was twelve, Mali had a best friend, Ruthie. Sometimes, they walked to school together. Ruthie would rattle on about her family—brother, sisters, and mother and father—as they made their way through the suburban side streets of red-roofed houses, lacy-curtained bay windows, and pretty flower beds in small front gardens, all very different from hers. Mali had wished for something she could say about her own family. Not that she didn't want to. Rather, it was that she just didn't know how—as though the words inside her head spoke to her in a foreign language, and she hadn't learned enough of them yet to convey what she meant. It didn't matter. There was comfort in listening to Ruthie and knowing her world had not changed the way Mali's had.

They used to pass an old stone church on their way to and from school. It loomed up large on their horizon, the Gothic spirals like spears to the heavens, as if the congregants' words of prayer weren't lofty enough. Mali had often dreamed of stepping inside that sacred fortress, to breathe in its ancient air and rest within its cool, chiseled walls.

But she never did.

As the last bell sounded for the end of each school day and while the other kids ran for the door, Mali would stay behind, purposefully slow in putting her books together. She tried to extend those last minutes, to stretch them way out, as if they were bits of elastic, so that she could cling to her only hope, safeguard her greatest wish for as long as possible. When she finally did reach the door, her throat dry and knees shaking, she could never be sure she'd actually make it down the stairs, through the gate, and into the arms of her waiting mother. She'd scrunch up her eyes for a second, cross her fingers, then push open the door and look for her among the others on the pavement outside.

She always knew from the very first moment at the top of the stairs. She knew that if she were there, she'd be standing apart from the crowd of waiting mothers so Mali couldn't, wouldn't miss her. Mali would look anyway, a second, then a third time before bolting down the concrete steps, pushing open the little wooden gate, and running, as fast as her legs would take her, up the road and toward the old stone church.

As she ran, she tried hard to conjure up her pink fantasies—flamingoes, pink flowered wallpaper, strawberry ice cream, party dresses, carnations—and to roll them before her mind's eye, like ribbon from a spool. She tried to stop the tears from coming. But the only image rolling before her was the one of herself, sitting on the second step from the bottom, watching her mother's O-shaped mouth at the front hall mirror, the shiny sequined beret, the new navy-blue suit she'd bought for Rosh Hashanah, and the two large suitcases filled to brimming, beside her.

I'll be back, she'd said, before you've even realized I've gone.

But the sharp words, the bitter fragments of her father's fury from that Friday night, still echoed loudly in Mali's head.

Then, as she came to the old stone church, Mali strove to recapture each movement, each word and phrase, laying them out in her mind as if photographs to be examined. Her struggling mind became fixed and sleepy, as though trapped in a marshy bog, searching, and sinking. Again and again. What was the piece she had missed that would explain why her mother hadn't come back?

She wished she could tell Ruthie.

Or find the right words to tell her friend how she'd lie in bed at night and listen for the sounds of marching boots on the red-tiled path below her bedroom window. Then hold her breath for the inevitable smashing of the glass and wrought-iron front door. Or describe for her those airless foggy nights, when she passed by the old stone church in her dreams, the tips of her fingers feeling for the imperfect, uneven blocks of granite, locked one on top of the other into rough, cold walls. Just as she became locked, one memory on top of another, into this place and time that frightened her.

Run, the voice in her dreams would command. She tried. *Run faster*. Her short legs pumped hard. She could hear the smack of her feet against the pavement, like waves slapping the beach on an incoming tide. The scenery wouldn't change though. *Keep going*, the voice yelled out. But as she opened her mouth to shout back, only the sound of silence greeted the pearly, grey air.

So, instead, Mali told Ruthie about her visit to the queen.

It had begun on Coronation Day. Mali was six. She and her family, seated around the tiny black and white television set in the lounge, watched the princess ride in her golden carriage from Buckingham Palace to Westminster Abbey. As she waved from her carriage to the cheering crowds in the street, Mali wondered if she'd felt the weight of all that history, the spirits of the old kings and queens before her. In the Abbey, with her royal cape trailing yards behind her, she'd walked slowly toward the throne that was destined to be hers for life. When the Archbishop of Canterbury placed the crown on the queen's head, Mali thought she noticed her body diminish, fold in on itself under its burden.

And she couldn't shake this image of her, weighted down like a bird grounded from flight. Perhaps, too, came the realization that a real person of flesh, blood, and bones lay under all that royal finery. That even she, the queen, could not escape the effects of the heaviness put upon her.

On the morning after the coronation, Mali had sat outside on the red-tiled steps by the front door and composed a letter to the queen. *I'm sorry the crown weighed so much*, she'd written. *I hope it wasn't too heavy.*

An answer to her letter came back a few weeks later. The queen's secretary thanked Mali for her concern and invited her to wait outside the palace gates one Friday afternoon at four o'clock, when the queen would be returning home.

But Mali didn't tell Ruthie that she'd dreamt she'd visited the palace. In her dream, the queen saw her from the royal black Daimler with the Union Jack, the standard-bearer from all those centuries ago, flying at the tip of its bonnet. The queen stopped the car, rolled down her window, and invited Mali to tea at the palace. Afterward, the queen's chauffeur drove her home in the royal sedan. As they pulled up to her house, her father came rushing out to greet them. In his thick European accent, he thanked the queen's chauffeur for driving her home. Mali stood on the pavement outside their red-brick house. And willed her dream to stop.

She told Ruthie that thousands of people had waited outside the palace gates with her on that grey, wintry Friday afternoon. Thousands. Had they all received the same letter? The queen was late. Damp coldness crept into the soles of her shoes. She shivered. She could only see the backs of the people standing around her, nothing more. Then all at once, a hushed excitement spread through the crowd. Craning her neck and jumping up and down, she only just caught a glimpse of a hand waving regally from within the Daimler, as it sped past and disappeared through the open gates and into the courtyard at Buckingham Palace.

It didn't matter, she'd said to Ruthie, who seemed more disappointed than Mali. Those were not her dreams, she explained, not her history. After all, she was only a visitor in this royal country, a child born of refugee parents, living in a borrowed culture, like a renter in someone else's home—the furniture, the pictures always there to remind her that none of it ever really belonged to her.

CHAPTER 35

September 10, 2014

You and I had arranged to meet for lunch at the French restaurant on Sixty-Second Street we both like. It was one of those glorious fall days when the cloudless sky is the brilliant opaque blue of Wedgewood, and the sun shines with the last of its summer warmth. I'd decided to walk all the way, first going west on Seventy-Second, then heading south on Lexington, window shopping and daydreaming as I went.

There's so much I want and need to say to you, Mali, my darling. But somehow when we sit face to face, every thought, every idea, seems to spin away from me and land in the black hole of my brain. Then, as I try to pull out this thought or that, I see—or is it in my imagination?—a certain look in your eyes. Is it accusatory? Or just plain impatience with me, now that I'm an old woman?

I travel backward into that jumbled place inside my head anyway and wonder how I can explain the twenty-seven-year-old I was when I was forced to leave London. Do I even know that young woman anymore? That child in a woman's body, who'd needed so much love and attention. And that man? Her husband? Your father? How he had become so stingy, not in the usual money-giving way, but of his self, both physically and emotionally. Everything felt too heavy, too serious with him, as though he'd coiled himself up so tightly within his core that if he dared to let go, even a tiny bit, his whole being would unravel into a messy, tangled heap, like string loosened from its ball. He'd become someone I didn't recognize.

And I began to feel as neglected as those empty flower beds that bordered the front garden of our house on Finchley Lane. Somewhere along the way, I realized, I'd lost the man I'd so loved and adored.

You must admit, though, I always tried my best, through all those years, to look at his side of things, present a fair picture to you, which is more than I can say he'd ever done for me. The times I'd sat in Lotte's car outside the house on Finchley Lane, waiting for you to come out. Or dropping you off and watching you amble up the driveway, making funny faces at me before the front door opened and you were sucked in, as though by the very house itself. Never once did your father acknowledge my presence, never once a wave from the door or an invitation in for a drink. After all, we did still share the well-being of our child.

No, I'm wrong. We didn't share. He made all the decisions for you. I became as voiceless, as silent, as the dead mother he pretended me to be. Had he threatened me? Yes. Many times. He even had your pediatrician deem me an unfit mother for the court. And I believe he and Willy paid off my divorce lawyer. I was defenseless, and always afraid he'd come up with one reason or another to bar me from seeing you altogether.

Which is why I had to give up my plan to kidnap you from London. I couldn't take the risk. My lawyer told me later that your father would have had the authorities on the plane as soon as it landed in New York, and you would've been whisked off and put back on the next flight to London in the blink of an eye. And me? What would've happened to me? The lawyer just shook his head. I shudder now, just thinking about it. I'd had such high hopes. Truly, I had.

For months, obsessed over my plan, I thought up every possible angle, every detail. Then I began to imagine you in my everyday life. Walking along the street, the tug of your arm in mine, your chatter about friends and school, or the party you'd been invited to, and the dress you saw in Mimi's shop window you absolutely had to have. I thought of the sightseeing trips we'd take around New York, a walk in Central Park, a riverboat cruise around Manhattan, an elevator ride to the top of the Empire State Building. Then I'd introduce you to the places and people in our neighborhood, and to the family and friends you'd never met. I had everything worked out. Or so I thought.

But all my hopes shattered when I got back to my hotel after our afternoon at Kardomah's in Golders Green and found the telegram waiting for me. Loud and clear the words printed on the yellow cablegram read *DON'T DO IT.* Those words stabbed, like shards of shattered glass.

After I rang from my hotel room to tell you that my plan wouldn't work, I lay down on the horrible, sagging, single bed stinking of stale cigarette smoke, and cried my eyes out.

By the time I got to the restaurant where we had arranged to meet for lunch, I felt worn out. Too many memories in my head. Too many aches and pains in my body. The hostess showed me to a table in the far corner. I sat facing the door. You arrived a few minutes later. You looked beat. Out of breath. You'd had to run, you said, to meet me on time.

You bent to kiss me, first on one cheek then the other, and settled into the chair across the table from me. You unfolded your napkin and retrieved your eyeglasses from your bag. Not such a young chicken anymore either, I thought, as I watched you scrunch up your eyes to scan the menu. But now I sensed something new in you, something I hadn't noticed before. Suddenly, you seemed so very far away from me. But perhaps, I told myself, this is the way between mothers and daughters; the early intimacy pushed away, banished, just as surely as the sun drops below the horizon and darkness envelops us. And then I wonder if your children ever really do belong to you? I'd always believed so. As unquestionably as the genes that color their eyes or shape their noses. That's what I'd thought the day you got off the plane at Idlewild. You were mine, and you had finally come home to me.

After we had given our lunch order and dispensed with the usual questions and small talk about Michael, the girls, your work, and my health, my mind began to drift, and I found myself going back again to when you first arrived in New York. I was tempted to ask if you remembered the day too. I didn't, though. I didn't want it to lead to the questions I've asked you a million times before: Were you ever sorry you came to live with me? Did I do the right thing in fighting to get you here? I imagined you'd smile at the questions, look down at the table for a moment, then re-arrange your knife and fork, as though the new arrangement could help you with your thoughts. Next, I envisioned you'd cross your arms, perch your elbows on the edge of the table, lean toward me, and say, as you have so many times in the past, "You know, my life would've been quite different, had I stayed in London."

The waitress brought us bread and butter and each a glass of Chablis. After our Caesars arrived, you picked up your knife and fork, lifted the three anchovy strips lying in a triangle on top of the Romaine lettuce, and dropped them onto my plate. You didn't have to ask.

Tell me, I wanted so desperately to say to you, How do I explain this dragged-down feeling of responsibility I've carried inside me all these years? I changed the course of my life, and as a result, yours as well.

Penny for my thoughts? you said and sipped your wine. I seemed to be a million miles away.

I then explained how I'd been thinking of that July afternoon in 1963 when you first arrived. Remember it? Remember the heat of the day, the air so dense you could barely breathe, and the sun blazing like a torch through the murky sky? It must've been in the nineties. I worried you'd take one step off the plane and never want to take another.

I'd worried for nothing, you said, and laughed, because I hadn't known yet that you, a sun worshipper, loved the heat. What else do I remember about that day? you asked.

What else? A dream come true for me. I'd waited so long for you that the day itself, when it finally did arrive, seemed to take on giant proportions all of its own. The hours and minutes slowing to a kind of timelessness.

I must confess that for weeks before you'd arrived, I'd spent forever looking for a new outfit to wear for the day. I finally found a pair of white pedal pushers at Alexander's—remember Alexander's?—and a cotton sleeveless shirt to match, black and white checkered. I even found a perfect pair of sandals. Everything had to be just right. I wanted to give you the best possible first impression.

At the airport, I paced the windy observation deck, watched dozens of planes take off and land, my nerves churning inside me and sweat glistening my face, as I tried my best to ignore what the hot and humid air—closing in on me, suffocating and heavy—was doing to me and my brand-new outfit.

And then my heart . . . oh my God . . . it wouldn't stop its wild dance inside my chest. Here I was, finally, after eight long years, waiting for your Pan Am flight to land. I could hardly believe it.

But, you wondered, hadn't I thought beforehand what it'd be like to live with you, a sixteen-year-old teenager? Especially since I didn't even really know you.

Didn't know you? My daughter, my own flesh and blood? What else did I need to know? Besides, I'd fixed up your room, given you your own television set and three or four LPs for the old record player in the big wooden box I'd painted bright red for you.

You shook your head, as though to negate everything I said.

But truly, you reminded me, hadn't we been on such separate paths, you, and me? What you'd wanted, you said, what you were desperate for, now that you lived here with me, was to settle down and be immersed in your new life. You wanted to conform, not be the little English girl with the accent everybody loved to listen to. How could I not have understood?

Indeed, I think now, as I write to you. How could I not have remembered wanting to fit in? Or wanting to feel in charge of my own life? You remember, I was only just twelve in 1939 when we fled Germany. War broke out shortly after we arrived in England. Then, Opa, detained as a friendly enemy alien, had been shipped off to the Isle of Man, leaving poor Oma and me alone in our flat in London. And when the bombs began to fall, I got shipped off, too, in a mass evacuation of schoolchildren and was sent to a foster home in the countryside. Here was an opportunity, I'd thought then, to grow, to be somebody. But my ideas were thwarted almost immediately when I realized that a refugee girl, especially a Jewish one, was considered a second-class citizen. Instead of the photography class I'd wanted to take one term, they forced me into homemaking and sewing. I hated those classes. In sewing, I spent most of the class twisting and twirling broken-off threads and rolling them between my spit-licked fingers to guide them through the eye of the needle. Then I'd try following the McCall's pattern, hating both the outmoded shape of the blouse and the design and color of the fabric I'd had no say in choosing. And cooking? Still not my favorite.

Many parallels govern our lives—yours, and mine—I realize. But sitting across from you at lunch that day, I had no answer for you except to say I'd had certain built-in expectations for our mother-daughter relationship, mostly based on making up for lost time.

The waitress came to clear the empty salad plates from our table. We took a last swallow from our wine glasses and ordered cappuccinos and an apple tart to share for dessert.

Lost time, you insisted, could never be made up.

Maybe that's true, I said, a terrible feeling of sadness washing over me.

And as though we'd reached a dead end, we stopped talking and let our memories recede into the bare whiteness of the cleared tabletop.

I absolutely need you to understand that, ultimately, it would never have worked out between your father and me. This is what I want to say to you now. Eventually, he and I would've separated. Oma and Opa had it right in the first place. It was the war, they'd said. It was infatuation, puppy love. The want of a settled life, of happiness.

But then, I often wonder, had it been my neediness that caused it all to fall apart? A stolen childhood, after all, feels like a house with no foundation. What did I understand of consequences, of a life that could become irreparably undone and need cutting off, like the frayed ends of a broken thread, too scrappy, even, for spit? I didn't fully understand myself back then. Only after all the thinking and brooding I've done recently, the quilting of the bits and pieces, the gathering of the disparate colors and patterns, can I finally begin to see my life as one.

Over coffee, our conversation came back to the present. You filled me in on how Julia's and Steffi's kids were faring at school, how their extracurricular activities were taking up too much of their time. Then we talked some more about Michael, the business. Life certainly seems much more complicated now than in my day. With defined roles gone, the sky's the limit. I would've loved that. But then I wonder . . . if things had been different, if I'd been born into today's generation, would I have had it in me to run a business, write a book, be a movie star, be educated enough to be anything I wanted?

After lunch I walked a little of the way back to Grand Central with you. We kissed each other goodbye at the corner of Fifty-Seventh and Lex. I kept watch on your slight frame, while you crossed the wide street until, swallowed up into the crowd, you had completely disappeared from my sight. As I turned away, a sudden ancient fear I might never see you again took tight hold of my heart.

I rummaged through my bag for my Walkman. I untangled the wires to the earbuds, put one in each ear and pressed the play button to Haydn's Piano Concerto in D. Then I began my walk home, concentrating on the music to shake off the fears and ghosts tumbling inside my head.

CHAPTER 36

October 26, 2014

No! No! Mali says, her voice loud in the stillness of her mother's apartment as she re-reads her mother's questioning insecurities. She had always known that once the decision was made, she could never go back to living with her father in London, even though he'd assured her before she left— as they'd sat side by side, two nervous Nellies, waiting for her flight to New York to be called—it wouldn't be the same as losing face. No . . . she wished she could tell her mother now. She'd fought too long for that moment as well. It would have felt like a betrayal. A failure.

To distract herself from her father's words that day, she'd concentrated her thoughts on the rows of bright orange seats, tethered together in straight lines across the airport lounge, and imagined them as obedient children, joined at the waist, cheery and inseparable.

After all, her father had gone on to say as he brought his arm around her, it was only all about her happiness. He squeezed her into him and kissed her cheek. She put her head on his shoulder. Stretching out his left leg, he reached into his trouser pocket, exactly the way he'd done so many times before, and handed her his freshly ironed handkerchief for the tears streaming down her cheeks.

She still has his handkerchief. Washed, ironed, and tucked away in a little wooden box of mementos.

•   •   •   •   •

She had kissed her mother goodbye, first on one cheek then the other, on that beautiful autumn day when they'd met for lunch at the little French café on Lexington and talked about her first day in New York. She recalls them standing for a few minutes in silence at the corner of Fifty-Seventh Street and Lexington, as though reluctant to let each other go. Then, shivering with a sudden gust of wind, she had turned from her mother and, falling into step with the crowd around her, crossed the wide, two-way street and continued to head downtown.

She'd never known how her mother had felt while waiting for her at Idlewild that first time. She remembers more than anything else the thrill of finally arriving at the place she'd only dreamed of for what had seemed like her whole life.

An unexpected feeling of breathlessness had hijacked her the moment she'd stepped off the plane in New York and into the ninety-degree, muggy heat of the late afternoon in July. Her body smashed through a wall of air thicker and heavier than she'd ever felt. But in the time it took to descend the metal staircase, walk the few steps across the tarmac to the terminal— her best navy-blue dress, damp and badly rumpled, clammy stockings held up by a garter belt tight to her waist, and her swollen feet in the pointy two-inch heels she and Fleur had bought together to match her dress— she'd fallen in love. After she had collected her suitcase, gone through customs, and had her British passport stamped and the alien number of her brand-new green card checked against columns and columns of others printed in a very fat book, she followed the exit signs.

Suddenly, magically, the frosted glass doors of the International Arrivals building swung open and, still in the dream she'd fantasized about a million times before, she saw her mother. She saw her standing in exactly the way Mali had always imagined she would—a little apart from the waiting crowd so that Mali couldn't, wouldn't, miss her.

The enormous, white Chrysler New Yorker convertible, her mother and David came to pick her up in, looked so beautifully, typically

American. As she'd sat in the back seat with the hot, humid air whooshing in her face and the unfamiliar scenery rushing by in an unfocused blur, the sudden newness of it all, the uncertainty, made her feel her freedom from the past, like a dizzy exhilaration.

And here, at long last, was the dark-colored brick six-story apartment building, which for most of the past eight years had only resided in her imagination and on the address lines of the blue airmail letters she had posted to her mother every week. Fire escapes zigzagged along the exterior walls of the older building. Just as they did in *West Side Story*. The living room, located at the center of the apartment, with the other rooms off to the left and the right of it, hardly ever got used, she'd found out later. It remained closed off, a wrought iron gate placed at the entrance, as if to ward off any untidy intruders.

The following morning, a Sunday, her inner clock still on London time, she'd woken up very early. Kneeling on her new bed, she'd looked out of her wood-shuttered bedroom window, beyond the fire escape and through the leafy branches of the beech tree—so close she could almost touch them—to Gus's, the corner luncheonette across the street. How still the air was in the hazy, Technicolor cerulean sky. How quiet the street, lined on both sides with the Chryslers, Fords, and Dodges, she'd only seen in the movies, and reminding her more of giant sea creatures, with their fins and spiky tails, than vehicles of the road.

So this was America, she had giggled to herself. America, the place she had been daydreaming about, longing for, with an ache as tangible and heavy as the trunk packed with all her possessions and due to arrive from London a few weeks later.

But what had she expected of her new life once she had settled into her new home here? This, the question she now asks herself, as she puts her mother's unread pages on the table next to the rose petals. Not so many more to read, she notes. And, tired of sitting, she stands and stretches her arms high above her head, then rubs her tired eyes.

What had made her leave behind everything familiar in her life for this foreign land? What magical lasso had her mother used to rope her in? Surely not just the dolls and the dresses. Those dresses meant for thinner bodies than hers, with their stiff petticoats billowing out under wide poodle skirts and long, wide sashes tied into big bows at the back.

No. In the end it was her own doing. On a day in the South of France. A day out of their summer holiday. A day her father and Fleur would never forgive her for. The day he'd found the letter. The day that inexorably changed the trajectory of her life forever.

•   •   •   •   •

A movie reel is spinning in her mind's eye, and she sees herself standing by a sandy towel in the shade of a green-, white-, and red-striped Cinzano beach umbrella. Her body, cool under her bathing suit, is still damp from her last swim. A straw boater perches on her frizzy, wire-haired head. Screwing up her eyes against the sunlight, she looks out over the Mediterranean, a sea spread smooth and blue before her.

She watches her father and Fleur, her stepmother, walk toward the water, away from her, arm in arm, heads bent, deep in conversation. She lies down on the towel, turns over on her stomach, props herself up on her elbows, and opens her new Agatha Christie. English books, mostly second-hand Penguins, are in limited supply here, in L'Aiguebelle, a tiny village near Le Lavandou on the French Riviera. She tries to get into her book, but without success. Something gnaws at her. She turns back around, sits up, and sees her father and stepmother at the water's edge, waves of the incoming tide swirling back and forth at their feet. Arms still looped around each other, their oiled bodies glisten in the warming sun. She slams her book shut and stands. The sand is hot and soft on her feet, but as she wriggles her toes around, she finds a cool solid dampness below the surface heat. She yanks up the towel, sending a shiny spray of tiny crystalline granules into the breeze, and runs toward the water's edge to tell her father that she's going back to her room.

On the stone steps leading up to the hotel from the beach, she bumps into her new friend, Jonathan. So *very* English, her father has said about him, as though he belongs on a separate planet. Perhaps he does. Mali watches him and his parents at mealtimes. They talk and laugh a lot.

Jonathan, three years older than Mali, attends boarding school somewhere in Sussex. She only has cruel images of boarding schools from reading *Tom Brown's Schooldays*. He assures her his school is nothing like that. In fact, he says, he loves being away from home.

Does she want to go to the bookshop with him now? he asks. Perhaps new books have come in. She agrees, even though she's only just begun hers, and won't need a new one for a few days. They walk along the road in silence, Mali's towel wrapped around her like a sarong. Her flip-flops slap against her heels. Her inner thighs rub together. It's hot under the early afternoon sun.

They wander around the one-room shop, relieved to be out of the heat. Mali speaks French well enough to ask the lady in charge if anything new has come in, but she doesn't. She prefers instead, to poke at the rows of used books lying neatly, spine up, on old wooden trestle tables, set out in rows along the middle of the room. She thinks she might find a surprise that way. Now she follows Jonathan from table to table. Every so often he picks up a book, opens the front cover, reads the first paragraph, then puts it back. He doesn't enjoy murder mysteries, especially Agatha Christie's. Too predictable, he says. She reads them for just that reason. He shrugs— she's only a girl after all—and continues to look through the titles. His favorites are science fiction and historical novels about war. Mali says war and divorce are taboo subjects in her household. He looks at her, and she realizes she's said more than she intended. No one here knows that her stepmother is not her real mother. Her father hates when she blabs, as he puts it, about the divorce. It's nobody else's business, he always says. Mali doesn't understand why it's so important to keep the truth from strangers. He's never given her reasons. Perhaps she never asked.

Finding nothing new in the bookshop and bored of wandering around the small room, they leave. The sun is even hotter now. Mali knows she ought to go back to her room to change out of her damp bathing suit, but she doesn't want to be apart from Jonathan, at least not yet. They walk slowly on the dusty road toward the main part of the hotel. Mali wants to hear more about boarding school. He asks her about war and divorce. Just as they pass the hotel's Annex, she sees her father pacing the balcony outside her room. When he catches sight of her, he shouts for her to come up to him. She leaves Jonathan and the warmth of the sun, and climbs the stairs to her room slowly, in no hurry to learn what she has done wrong.

The door to her room is wide open. Her father sits on the wooden upright chair he has moved from the desk and placed facing the bed. She stands at the threshold, the nerves inside her body bristling, as though from a million tiny thorns. "Come in and sit down," he says, pointing to the area of the bed directly opposite him. Blue sheets of letter paper are clutched in his hand. At first, she doesn't understand, doesn't notice that the pages are filled with her own handwriting. Then her chest tightens as she realizes what they are. She can't look at him. She stares at her bare legs, concentrating on the brown mole in the middle of her right thigh. Her body sinks into the too-soft mattress. She crosses her arms and hunches up her shoulders. She knows his eyes are fixed on her, but she can't look up to meet them.

"For God's sake," he says. "Sit up straight."

She lifts her chest and uncrosses her arms, sliding her hands under her thighs for leverage. She looks up for a moment, long enough to see his eyes, bloodshot, glassy, and hard.

"I came in here to ask you if you wanted to go into town with us," he says. "And what do I find? Not you, where you said you'd be, but this . . . this . . ."

He waves the sheets of blue letter paper in the air. Then flings them at her.

"Read," he says, his voice straining. "Read this to me. I want to hear every word loud and clear."

Mali gathers up the blue sheets of paper, puts them in order, and begins:

"*My Dearest, Darling Mummy,*

How are you? We're on holiday in the South of France now. It's been hot and I'm so tanned from being at the beach and floating in the sea on top of my Lilo. I got sunstroke, but I'm better now . . ."

She stops reading. Her tears are hot behind her eyes, her cheeks burn, and her stomach turns queasy.

"Go on," he says, the ropey vein in his neck throbbing, punctuating his words. "I want to hear you read all of it."

"*This holiday has been horrible,*" she reads. "*He doesn't love me anymore . . .*"

"I didn't say you could stop," he says, his voice rising still more.

Mali shuffles the papers, crosses her legs, and hunches up her shoulders again, as if she can bury her ears in them. She clears her throat and begins to read as quickly as she can: "*They leave me in charge of all their beach stuff, piled on a towel under the umbrella, while they go off for walks. I'm like their servant. I hate them. I want to come and live with you . . .*"

She stops reading. She's crying. Her words, spoken out loud, sound hateful, not the way they'd looked to her when she first wrote them. She begins to tear up the sheets of blue letter paper, as though the hurtfulness written in them could be reduced to unreadable tattered shreds as well.

"If you're so unhappy with me, then you can go and live with your mother in America," he says.

The coldness in his voice terrifies her. She feels adrift, panicked, as if way out at sea and all alone on her rubber float. Suddenly, the prospect of leaving her father is too strange and frightening. A vacuum opens up inside her, a huge emptiness, and she doesn't know how to satisfy it.

You can go and live with your mother in America, he has said to her. These, the exact words she has ached to hear from him for so long.

"I won't stop you anymore," he continues without waiting for a response from her. "Or, if you prefer, you can go to boarding school in England first, and leave for New York when you turn sixteen. After your O-level exams. It's entirely up to you."

He gets up, puts the chair back at the desk, and leaves the room, letting the door slam shut behind him. For the rest of their holiday, her father, and her stepmother, grim with hurt and anger, barely speak to her. She's been given the silent treatment, the perfect antidote to her wounding words.

•   •   •   •   •

She was twelve that summer. What had she undone? She'd be leaving her father, her home, her school, her friends. But wasn't this what she'd so longed for? What happened? Why did she suddenly feel so scared? Was it the prospect of going to a strange home, in a strange city, in a strange country? Or to a mother she hardly knew? Faced with so many unknowns, the passage to her future loomed up; a long dark tunnel, the light nowhere to be seen.

Had he ever regretted his ultimatum? In the end, she hadn't. She's glad she made the decision to go to boarding school first, even if for the wrong reasons. At the time, she'd rationalized boarding school as her no-man's-land, a place where that old enemy she called betrayal, could never play a part. She would live with neither her mother nor her father.

Looking back, she is simply grateful for the education she received there.

But those early days in New York turned out to be unexpectedly difficult. Before she came, she hadn't really thought of how she would settle in. Since she didn't have to learn a new language, as her parents and grandparents had had to, she figured she'd wake up in New York the day after arriving and carry on with her life in much the same way as she'd always done. But Culture stood for all the foreign words. It lived in *West Side Story* and *Bye, Bye Birdie.* It lived in the black and white Hollywood movies she'd watched on TV all those rainy Saturday and Sunday afternoons in London. It lived in the way people spoke to each other and in the altered meanings of the words she didn't quite get at first. And most of all, it lived in the way she and her mother had forged their renewed relationship, a structure built more on guilt and insecurity than love and understanding. She remembers sitting on her bed in her tiny room, a neglected schoolbook in her lap, the same few records playing over and over on the bright red console, while she watched the cars in the street outside her window come and go, their headlights aglow, like search beams in the night.

Mali and her mother had lived at cross-purposes that first summer. But how could it have been otherwise? she wonders, thinking back on it now.

Neglecting her assigned reading of *Crime and Punishment* for her new school, Mali spent her days hanging out with her newly made friends at the park, where the girls practiced their dance routines to pop music that blared from transistor radios and the guys played basketball. At lunchtime they all piled into the small luncheonette down the street to eat tuna fish sandwiches on white bread and drink chocolate egg creams. In the middle of the afternoons, the Good Humor truck rang its bell. In the evenings, someone threw a party, and they slow-danced and smooched to the Ronettes and the Shirelles, those love-sick songs adding to the heat and magic of her first summer.

But she'd had a tough time adjusting then too. She couldn't quite grasp the reality of her being here. And there was no one to share her younger life with. No one to remember who she had been at ten, twelve, or fourteen. Always relegated to the outside of things, she could only look at the world and at herself as if through a frosted-glass window.

$$\bullet \quad \bullet \quad \bullet \quad \bullet \quad \bullet$$

What had her mother felt then? Perhaps she had been nervous for Mali as she navigated this sudden, new, and unaccustomed freedom. Would she be able to prevent Mali from getting into trouble? And was her mother afraid of what Hirschel might be thinking of her; worries of his disapproval, her constant companions in those early days? Mali never knew. She only sensed in her mother a vague disappointment and frustration, as Mali had when she was six or seven. Always made to cry too easily, she would hear the usual refrain from her mother: Why can't you be more like . . .?

CHAPTER 37

September 16, 2014

Last week I had an appointment, My Sweet. I was so tempted to skip it, ignore it, and pretend that my body, as it feels right now, doesn't exist. But I stuck to the rules and, like a good girl, kept my date. Just to let you know, though, I can't guarantee I'll do the same next time.

Back at my desk drawers again, I sort out my years as if I'm a farmer shaking the wheat from its chaff, or more probably, a cold-case detective, weeding, rooting, rummaging around all the clues and the bits and pieces of my life that have brought me to this very moment.

Ah! Here's a photograph of you and me. You sit on a bench, and I stand a little behind and to the right of you. Studying it, I try to remember when and where it was taken. No visible lines and crevices dent my face, as they do now. No poisonous, shadowy specters radiate from my core. In the picture, I wear my navy-blue blazer, the one with the brassy buttons, and from what I can tell, jeans and sneakers. You have on an oversized jacket, a man's maybe, dark green with blue squares and flecks of burnt orange running through the woolen material. I think you also wear jeans and sneakers. The sun shines. We both squint. I put the photo aside and continue to sort through the stack of paperwork I've pulled from the drawer. What a pack rat I am! I tell myself off as the pile for the incinerator grows way in excess of the papers I will need to keep.

I find more photographs in this drawer. Loads of old black-and-whites from wartime London. So many of the faces look unfamiliar to me now. I put them aside to go through later, when my drawer-straightening-out activity has depleted me of energy. Trying to be as disciplined as possible, I make myself go back to the unruly heap in the drawer and bring it to the dining table. As I sit, the papers spill from my arms and spread out onto the wooden surface. On top of the heap I find a travel agenda. The cover page reads: *Programm für den Besuch verfolgter und emigrierter Berliner vom 23. Bis 30. April 1991*. This was the schedule for the visiting, persecuted, and emigrated Berliners. Now I remember.

• • • •

I'd heard from friends that city governments in Germany were inviting German Jews back to the cities of their birth for one week. A form of restitution, apology, and to show how everything and everyone had changed. The individual cities footed the bill for the survivors. I called the German Consulate to find out more. Then I called you with all the details and asked if you'd be interested in coming with me. You said you'd love to. I remember that as the time for the trip neared, I became more and more excited at the prospect of showing you my childhood city. But I also worried. Would we, as mother-daughter and travel partners, get along? And then, of course, I wondered about the others in the group.

Ninety strong. Quite a crowd. And that number didn't include accompanying children, husbands, and wives. Like dandelion seeds, the Holocaust had blown us to the furthest reaches of the globe. We now called the US, Canada, Australia, Sweden, France, South Africa, England, Israel, Peru, and Uruguay, our homes. For many of the survivors, this was their first trip back to Berlin since they'd lived there so many years ago. For me, it was my second.

• • •

In my mid-thirties, I had a girlfriend, Ella, who had been through circumstances very similar to my own. She was dying to go back. She said she wanted to see how she'd feel being among the Germans in the city of her birth. She knew Berlin had changed, that most of the buildings had been bombed out during the war, and that she would most probably not recognize much of the city, if any of it. But for her, she said, she needed to find the nagging, lost fragments of her life. She begged me to go with her. We'll have fun, she said. We'll explore haunts as old-timers and sightsee as tourists. The best of both worlds. The comingling of the familiar and the strange. She found cheap flights and a reasonably priced hotel in the center of town. Ignoring any initial misgivings I had about the trip, I gave in and agreed to go with her. Once the arrangements had been made, I began to feel more positive and even looked forward to our adventure.

Except, now looking back, I realize that I wasn't at all prepared for the ghosts I came face to face with at every turn. Although my German was fluent, I felt too frightened to find the words I needed, to speak the language, to make myself understood. Traveling from New York with my British passport and speaking German as fluently as a twelve-year-old native, were clues as obvious to me as taking out a billboard to advertise myself as a Surviving Jew. I feigned incomprehension whenever I was addressed. In hotels, restaurants, and shops, I only spoke English, even when I knew the persons with whom I was conversing struggled to find the right words and gestures to make me understand them.

At the end of our day, Ella and I would sit in one restaurant or another, plates of Sauerbraten, red cabbage, and spätzle steaming in front of us, sore feet slipping out of our shoes, the travelers' guidebook open on the table between us. We'd read aloud to each other the blurbs describing the monuments and buildings we saw. We'd talk about the outings to our old neighborhoods and schools that we'd sandwiched between visits to the art museums and torture dungeons. Then, after discussing our plans for the following day, we'd put away the guidebook and finish our dinners. Invariably our talks would then lead us back to our past, to the Berlin we needed no guidebook for.

I told her about my parents, she told me about hers. We drank. We became morose. Then we talked about the schools we attended, the bullying, the friends and neighbors who turned away from us. And the dreadful loneliness we both experienced.

One morning, as we gathered our jackets and cameras for another day of touring, I suddenly became frozen in place. Sitting at the edge of my bed, I was my young self again, alone and holed up under a blanket in Opa's study. Terrified, I'd buried my head in Schani's fur so I wouldn't hear the heavy march of the Gestapo, their tall, black boots stomping up the stairs to our apartment. Or hear them banging down our door. Or have to anticipate, for even one second, rough hands pulling me up, dragging me away from everyone and everything I had ever known and loved.

Ella came and sat next to me on the bed with a box of tissues. She put her arm around me. I'm sorry, she said. Don't be, I told her. I'm glad we did this . . . this facing of our demons, and that we did it together.

Neither of us able to move, we sat on the edge of that hotel bed, each in our own silent world, blowing our noses and blotting the tears from our eyes. The longer we sat, the more painfully aware I became of my old longing for that other life, the one in Berlin that should have been mine. But then I also couldn't stop thinking about the man behind the hotel desk. How could he have let this happen? Then I thought of the chambermaid who cleaned our room. The waiter who served us dinner. The saleslady in the shop. The policeman directing traffic. The proud, young mother pushing the bright and shiny new pram, her sleeping baby tucked warm and cozy inside. The woman rushing home to make dinner for her family, a basket of meat, bread, and vegetables clutched in her hand and weighing her down. The teacher at school to whom we entrust our future. The librarian, guardian of the classics. The zookeeper, custodian of the uncivilized, wild, and dangerous. The fireman, protector from heat and destruction. The streetcar conductor. The ordinary and the exceptional man, woman, and child in the street. How could each one of them have turned a blind eye to what was going on around them?

And what if I'd been one of them? Would I have turned a blind eye too? I think back to those enlarged, grainy black and white photos at the exhibit at the New York Public Library. It can't only be through historical perspective we understand our lives and the choices we make. Can it?

• • • • •

Like a bad shuffler of playing cards, I've now spread out the mound of paperwork on my dining table and found more of the correspondence from our Berlin trip in 1991. That photo of you and me was taken on the one and only good-weather day of the entire week—no rain, no cold drizzle—just clear skies and warm sunshine. George, one of the gentlemen from our crowd who'd come by himself from Los Angeles, had snapped this picture of us. We both look good in the photo. Happy.

Afraid of losing it in the shuffle or, worse, down the incinerator chute, I get up and bring the photo to my bedroom. I lean it up against the most beautiful picture of my mother. Three generations of mothers. Then I move the photos of Julia and Steffi next to the photo of you and me and here we are, four generations of mothers. What luck we have had to bring us here. What amazing luck, is all I can think at the moment.

I go back to the paperwork on my dining table. I wonder how your memories of our week together in Berlin differ from mine.

•   •   •   •   •   •

Der Regierende Burgermeister von Berlin, our host, put us up at the Hotel Ambassador on the Bayreuther Strasse, just a few steps from the Kurfürstendamm. Perfect location. Our room, small and simple, had two low-to-the ground platform beds with feather blankets neatly folded at the foot of each one. Between the beds a low nightstand held a built-in radio and a digital clock, its bright red letters lit up and set for the wrong time. How very un-German, I'd thought. A short cord connected the black telephone to the side of the bed closest to the door, the bed you chose for yourself because you didn't want to be sleeping facing the wall. Every morning before calling room service for *Brötchen mit Aufschnitt und zwei Känchen Kaffee, bitte,* you'd move the phone to the floor and push it as close as possible to where I could reach it without having to get out of bed. Opposite our beds and attached to the wall was a beige carpeted booth with a wooden table, where we ate our breakfast. When our meal arrived, we had to move the copy of *Berlin Programm Magazine* and the picture book, *Welcome to Germany,* off the table.

Truth is, we didn't always feel welcome in Germany. In fact, specific instances made us quite paranoid and at times even indignant. One of those indignities happened on our way to meet George at the zoo. We were strolling along, arm in arm, on the Kurfürstendamm, enjoying the mild weather and chatting when a middle-aged woman dressed in a brown coat, matching hat, and brown lace-ups on her feet came toward us. She walked directly in our path, and for a few moments, we couldn't disentangle ourselves from each other and move on to our separate and opposite destinations. We danced on the sidewalk, moving from side to side, always in the same direction as the other. The small woman had a nasty, pinched look to her face and reminded me of a teacher I'd once had as a little girl here in Berlin. Instead of laughing, which I think most people do in these situations, she snarled at us and said, in German, of course, "Get out of my way, you foreign pigs." I stopped dead. We happened to be outside the KaDeWe, I remember, the biggest department store in Berlin. Stunned, I couldn't believe what I'd heard. As I turned around to watch her walk away, I noticed a news van parked in the public square behind us. Without another thought, I strode back toward it. I had to let them know about this Berliner woman and her intolerance that apparently had not changed since Hitler times. Had you walked with me? I don't think so. Probably too embarrassed. I didn't care. I knocked on the door of the van. A nice young man appeared. Two or three other people sat inside. Although in the middle of a broadcast, he listened in sympathy to my story, almost cooing in his commiseration. But what could he do? he said, holding onto the handle of the door, and trying to close up, bit by bit, the open space between us. I shrugged my shoulders. What could I have expected? I wondered of myself. That he would broadcast the event over the radio waves of Berlin for everyone to hear? The Jews are in town, be on your best behavior. What could he have done, really? Nothing, I conceded to him and then, to myself. I shrugged my shoulders again and took a step back so the nice young man could shut the door—quite firmly, I might add—leaving me speechless outside his cocoon. I walked back to where I'd left you looking in at the windows of the KaDeWe. I felt a fool and needed a Scotch.

We went to a café on the Kurfürstendamm, sat outside, and people-watched. A young German woman in her early twenties sat by herself at the table next to ours. Do you remember her? Attracted to us, she began a conversation with me in English, thinking us Americans. But still fuming and indignant over the encounter with the woman in brown, I responded to her in perfect German.

"You speak German," announced the young woman, quite taken by surprise.

"Yes," I began. "At one time in my life," my words spoken in a purposefully slow and deliberate way, "I was as German as you. But my life, as I knew it, ended when Hitler came to power. Ended when I was still a child. All and only because I am a Jew."

At first the poor, young woman just stared at me, her pretty face expressionless, her hands fidgeting slightly in her lap. Then she smiled, probably out of embarrassment or of not knowing what else to say or do. "I'm so sorry," she eventually said, and feeling badly myself, I let our conversation move on, in English, to a more comfortable place, the Berlin of the 1990s and the complicated merging of east to west. When we got up to leave the café, I gave the young woman my phone number and told her to look me up if she ever came to New York. She kissed me goodbye on both cheeks and hugged me, as if I were a long-lost friend.

Slowly, my shame and any thoughts of the woman in brown began to melt away with the Scotch and the warm sunshine.

We had arranged to meet George at the zoo. We found him pacing in front of the monkey house, a large Leica and loads of additional lenses hanging around his neck.

"Come and sit," he said to us, pointing to the rows of wooden benches lining either side of the pathway. "I want to take your picture."

You went to sit on the green bench. I stood in place, stuck, as though in a quagmire, unable to move one way or the other. Then, all at once, I found myself filled with hate and anger. I was a kid again, on a park bench with my best friend Marion, playing at having a conversation with Hitler, but terrified, at the same time, we'd be found out and arrested on the spot for sitting on a *green* Aryan-only bench. The few benches the Jews were allowed to sit on were *yellow* with Stars of David stenciled in black all over them. A guarantee there'd be no misunderstanding, no confusion, no mix-ups as to where our Jewish behinds belonged. But I always wondered who would be stupid enough to sit on a yellow bench, stupid enough to admit to being Jewish, when no one asked. Of course, this was before Jews were mandated to sew yellow Jewish Stars onto their clothing. So, so lucky my parents and I got out when we did.

"Come on," George said, gently trying to guide me by the arm to where you sat.

"I can't do it," I said. "I can't bring myself to sit on a park bench here in Berlin. Just the idea of it makes my stomach turn. I'm so sorry. I didn't imagine that after all this time . . ."

"Don't worry," he said, putting his arm around me. "All of us here have our little quirks and idiosyncrasies, our memories, our nightmares. Go and stand next to the bench and a little behind Mali. Will that be okay?"

And that's what I remember about that photograph of you and me.

They put on a great amount of fanfare during our stay in Berlin, a lot of speeches by the mayor and other city bigwigs. I guess I don't blame them. They tried hard to show . . . what? How people in Germany had really changed?

And here is the schedule of events for that week. On our first day, we were taken to the Jewish Community Center, where they served us lunch and we met with the Jewish luminaries of Berlin. To those of us, surprised at the existence of a Jewish Community Center here, they explained that many Russian Jews came to Germany in the eighties when Russia finally allowed them to emigrate. And what good news that the Jewish community thrived once again in Berlin. On one excursion, we went to see the prison, where dissenters and Jews were sent in the time between the two world wars and utilized, most especially, by Hitler and his henchmen as they rose to power. It was more like a stone dungeon, items of torture still hanging from the ceiling and jutting out from the walls. Another day, a coach drove us to Wannsee, the birthplace of the Final Solution. Such a pretty place for all those gruesome ideas to take root.

Do you remember the afternoon you and I took the S train at the Zoologischer Garten station and traveled north for approximately thirty kilometers to Oranienburg, the closest station to the Sachsenhausen concentration camp? We had a bit of a walk from the station to the camp, as I recall. The damp of a threatening rain seeped into us through our inadequate jackets as the wind bit into our faces on that cold, grey day. Small, pre-war houses lined both sides of the streets we passed.

As we walked, I asked if you could imagine the truckloads of prisoners being hauled down this wide, unpaved, sandy road leading to Sachsenhausen. I told you I could. All too clearly, I could envision the people in their houses, peeking out from between drawn curtains to see what all the ruckus was about. But I couldn't imagine how your Opa had felt or thought, jammed into the overcrowded truck with so many other Jewish men. Did he think it the beginning of the end? No. I can't reconcile that thought with him. Opa was a strong man. He'd been an officer in the

First World War. He'd told me his stories. And I remember, as a kid, poring over the books of tiny, sepia war-time photographs. Mostly of him in uniform posing with other officers. In the first album, if you didn't realize a war raged, you'd think the photos boasted a touring vacation. The men, dressed up in uniform, smiled for the camera while they played chess or dined in the mess hall, or listened to a duet for piano and violin. A few pictures showed well-dressed women, too. And shepherds with their mountain goats. The next album pictured snowy battlefields, burial grounds marked by large crosses, trenches, soldiers with their artillery, and even a wounded trooper being carried on a stretcher by two men from the Red Cross. I don't know where those pictures had been taken. Italy? Serbia? The photos, framed six within a page, were then bound and covered in beige linen. Opa had his own horse during the war, just like in the play, *War Horse*. He'd been so proud of that. He'd been a fighter. And that, he'd once said to me, was what had helped him to survive his weeks at Sachsenhausen. He told me only one story from that hell.

The prisoners rotated chores, such as bringing the filled coffee urn, mostly water, from the kitchen to the canteen at mealtimes. When Opa's turn came, he went into the kitchen to pick up the coffee as usual. Not to bring any undue attention to himself and since speed was always of utmost importance with the guards, he raced back from the kitchen to the canteen, the urn unbearably heavy and hot in his arms. But as Opa crossed the threshold of the canteen, the guard at the door purposefully stuck his foot out in front of Opa, causing him to trip. The urn slipped from his grip and crashed to the ground. Opa fell too, landing face down in the puddle of scalding, spilled liquid that quickly became a muddy mix on the dirt floor. Although stunned at first, he knew he couldn't stay down. That would've been the end of him. He knew this from his training as an officer. He knew this from what he'd witnessed in the camp. He jumped up, the coffee still dripping down his face, his prison uniform soaked through. Cold with the mud, he stood as straight as possible, his chest puffed out, and brought his hand up to his forehead in a salute. The guard must have been surprised by the gesture because, Opa said, he left him alone after that.

Never stay down, I'd heard him say so many times. No matter how badly you're hurt, always pick yourself right up. This, his ultimate lesson for me. Never stay down, no matter what. I heeded it, consciously or unconsciously, for most of my life, I'd say. Only, now that things inside my body have changed, I can no longer stick to his advice. No, not anymore.

From time to time, through the years, I have thought of Opa in that overcrowded truck. Did the men talk to each other? Console each other? Or did they suffer their fears in silence? But then I remind myself that they couldn't have even begun to imagine, not even in their wildest thoughts, what lay in store for them at Sachsenhausen. There was no precedent for what they were to endure, no history to fall back on, to understand, to put into any kind of meaningful context.

Oma and Opa said very little in my presence about his weeks there. I remember him coming home in the taxi, his shaved head, his shrunken hat. He'd become very thin and I, very scared. Perhaps that's when the reality of our situation began to sink in for me. Perhaps that's why, on waking every morning, I'd had to run for the bathroom to throw up. And now, as all this ancient history is coming back to me, I do remember that he told me one other story.

For many of the November prisoners, as they were referred to, release came just before Christmas, 1938. They'd had to relinquish everything they owned: cars, businesses, homes, jewelry, furs, and artworks. The day they let him go, Opa walked out through the gates of the concentration camp and onto the wide, unpaved, sandy road, the one you and I had walked along. He saw people peeking out from behind closed curtained windows, curious and afraid. But suddenly, a young woman came running out of her house toward him. She pressed a sandwich into his hands. Had she realized he was penniless and given him the money for the taxi too? And then what had the driver thought, bringing this half-starved, weakened man home? How could Opa have ever looked at life again in the same way as before? This is what I can never push from my mind.

Since I have no recollection, no knowledge of his experience in the Sachsenhausen concentration camp, I have decided, after much deliberating (do I really want to know all about it, at this late stage of my life?) to once again do the research to find answers. In a little book called *Crystal Night*, written by Rita Thalmann and Emmanuel Feinermann, I read that the detainees of Operation Crystal Night were put to hard labor, digging ditches, or working at construction sites or sawmills. The worst job entailed working at the brick works, where the men had to gallop with sand and sacks of cement on their shoulders from morning until evening, with only one fifteen-minute cigarette break at midday. They weren't even allowed to stand up straight.

On their third day of confinement, the camp commandant made an announcement:

You have been interned here because of your hostile attitude toward our people and our State. This concentration camp is not a prison or a gaol. Neither is it a sanatorium or a rest home. It is a centre for National Socialist education. You must first accustom yourselves to rigid discipline. Punishment will consist of twenty-four blows on the backside to make you hear the music of the spheres, or 'dry hanging', solitary confinement, assignment to a punishment brigade, standing to attention at the main gate of the camp, and so on. In the event that you should contemplate escape, you should know that you will not be shown any mercy: bang— one bullet and the matter is closed. My brave young SS men know how to shoot.

Surely, he had stood on the *Appelplatz* for roll call with the other November prisoners when this speech had been delivered.

A memory of Opa, the way he used to look in better times, comes back to me. As a young child, I would lie sprawled on the carpeted floor at his feet. Books piled all around me became an improvised castle for my princess doll, and he—debonair and stylish with smoothly shaven cheek bones, high and shining in the lamp's light—would sit at peace in his armchair, his eyes closed, his head tilted back, one leg crossed over the other, a cigarette held between fingers that tapped and danced on the arm of his chair in time to Beethoven's Sixth or Schubert's Spring, the grey smoke twirling upward, waving in time to the music, too.

A sharp divide had existed in his life, as well. On one side of it, a family man with a wife, a child, a business, and the usual worries of a sole provider. His life had been a comfortable one. Goethe, Schiller, and Ibsen lined his bookshelves. He prided himself on the many recordings he'd collected, including those of Mozart, Beethoven, and Schubert. A huge fan of the opera, he also loved the theater. Dinner with friends was a weekly ritual. Summer holidays were spent at the beach by the North Sea and then in the Tyrolean Mountains for a couple of weeks in the winter. On the other side of the divide, and from one day to the next, or so it must have seemed to him, he became a wanted man. Rounded-up with thirty thousand or so other Jewish men in Germany, he was imprisoned into a cruel and surreal world, where only sadists, thugs, and thieves ruled. Where everyday logic, humanity, and decency had been rooted out, the very qualities themselves deemed diseased and rotting.

All for the crime of being a Jew.

A long driveway led to the camp. Do you remember it? Over the gatehouse, those all too familiar words: *Arbeit Macht Frei*. Train tracks didn't lead to this gate—only a wide-open road paved with flat stones, and the growing weeds that pushed up through the cracks, as if struggling to give life back to the dead below. Once inside the gate, a sign commemorated all the people who had been imprisoned here. Dated between 1945 and 1950. The Soviets had built the memorial, an obelisk, standing tall and silent and sheltered by the darkness of the clouds above. But to me, it felt like a desecration, a betrayal, leaving only the hardened dirt below my feet, the silent, sad witness.

At the center of the camp, we had difficulty envisioning it the way it had been. The sparse, barren patches of grass covering the hilly land were the dead color of straw. One or two of the prisoner barracks still existed. Others had only foundation footprints to show where they had once been. At the bottom of a hill stood the remains of the concrete execution trenches and a few leftover brick ovens. Bleak and horrifying reminders. Back toward the gate we saw the huts that had housed the medical teams and doctors, who performed experiments on the prisoners. Inside, exhibited on tables, were the objects of torture and experimentation. Drawings on the walls showed the plans for the execution of those experimental surgeries.

This happened after Opa's imprisonment there. When the Final Solution had been put into place. When Jews were openly thought of as lower than life itself. I can't ever stop wondering how they could've done all those horrific things to each one of those millions, whose only guilt was to be born with Jewish blood. This is the question I can't help asking myself, again and again.

Somehow, a little part of you always expects the place you leave behind to be exactly that same place when you go back, no matter how much time has elapsed. In my case, I had hoped for a different Berlin. But I wound up thinking it hadn't changed, its spirit still apparently the same, as I discovered the day we went to see where I'd lived and gone to school in the Grunewald.

From the outside, the Lesslerschule looked much the same in 1991 as it had in 1938. But now, according to the sign outside the gate, it belonged to the athletic department of a university. When we went in, a man came forward, and asked how he could help us. I explained that I had attended this school in the nineteen-thirties. As I stood there, I remember I'd felt a slight twinge of nostalgia at first, looking around at the desks stacked with papers, and the trees beginning to bloom outside the large window. I even thought I could hear kids in the schoolyard shouting to one another, a ball bouncing against the outside wall, and our headmistress, our lovely headmistress, her young forehead rumpled in a constant state of worry and dread, telling us to go home, two by two.

"Oh yes, I remember," the man said, his tone too matter of fact. "It was the Jew school."

The Jew school? Not the Jewish school or the school for Jewish children or even the school for Jewish kids. *The Jew school.* I couldn't believe what I'd heard. On cue, I could taste the bile rising from my stomach. I had to get out of there. I grabbed you by the arm, pinching you accidentally in the process, and quickly thanked the man for his time. I pushed you toward the door and we ran from the building. Out on the sidewalk, I shook with fury. You put your arms around my shoulders, wanting to give me a hug, but your over-stuffed messenger bag became awkwardly trapped between us. We laughed. I thought of Oma then, and how valiant and brave she'd been through all those frightening years in Berlin.

Now I think to myself: If it had been me, I would have crumpled.

CHAPTER 38

October 26, 2014

It must be very late. Most of the lights in the windows of the apartments opposite have faded to darkness. Only a few still shine, looking like oddly placed dots on domino tiles. Mali takes her empty cup back to the kitchen, fills the kettle and, while waiting for the water to boil, goes in search of Philip's book again.

She starts with the hutch by the dining table. In the drawers, she finds outdated paperwork, insurance policies, and brokerage statements. Six pretty platters, in bright yellow, lean against the back of one of the shelves. A small daintily painted bud vase attracts her attention on the shelf below. She turns it over. Made in Dresden. Her grandmother's birthplace.

Next to the bud vase is the brightly colored sugar bowl she and her mother had been shamed into buying in Berlin. Picking it up, she looks for the chip in the lid. She notices now that her mother must have painted it over, but the blues don't match perfectly. Then turning the bowl over, she sees the name, *Anastasia,* printed in large block letters. Above it is a signature she can't read, and below it, the name of the town and country, *Salins-France.*

Restitution, good will, and proof of the city's transformation—the blurbs Mali remembers. It boasted a week packed with tours and lectures and visits to museums, as well as enough downtime for individual exploration and touring. Family members not only welcomed but encouraged to come along. At their own expense, of course. Mali agreed to accompany her mother. It was April 1991.

The sugar bowl incident, as Mali came to think of it, happened at Casa Nova, a china shop on the Kurfürstendamm. They'd passed it many times on their walks in Berlin, even stopping once or twice to look in at the shop's window display. Then one day, they were drawn inside. Perhaps by a selection of new items shown in the window. Though more than likely, a need to warm up or escape the drizzle that had besieged them for most of their week there. Mali saw the sugar bowl exhibited on a table in the middle of the store. Something about its colors—cobalt blue with purple, red, and bright-orange flowers—attracted her to it. She went to pick up the lid by its little button-shaped top. But her hands were stiff from the cold, and to her horror, the lid slipped from her icy fingers, and clinked to the floor. Next thing she knew, a group of four or five women salesclerks surrounded her. Hands on their hips, they pointed and *tsk-tsked* at her and at the damage she'd incurred. Mali had to pay the fifty-six Deutsche Mark for the sugar bowl, which was then swaddled in bubble-wrap and tape and carefully placed into a shopping bag.

Feeling like two naughty schoolgirls, Mali and her mother left the store, certain this would have never happened in New York. Perhaps, they had even half-joked to each other, word had leaked out that the Jews were back in town.

Armed with a fresh cup of steaming coffee, Mali regains her spot on the couch in the living room. She leans her head against the back of the couch, closes her eyes. She doesn't remember as much about Sachsenhausen as her mother did. What she can also never forget, though, were the undulating mounds, like waves, in the empty field, the dead color of the grass, and those weeds pushing up from the dry, inhospitable earth. She remembers the grey of the sky, too, the grim bleakness, and how the ever-dampening cold had enveloped them that day. She'd tried to sense the sadness of the earth and what it had witnessed. She'd tried to connect it to a place she felt positive she would find deep within herself. But she couldn't find that place.

What had they talked about afterward, on their way back to the station at Oranienburg? She thinks there were no words. She thinks they walked back quickly in silence.

She does remember the horrid little woman in brown, but not the photo taking with George at the zoo. Now, she can't even picture him. She'll have to look through the box of memorabilia. But she does recall their hanging out with a man, once or twice, when they had a free afternoon or evening. Most of that week, they were kept busy.

Their first night in Berlin, dinner for the survivors and their guests was served in a private room at their hotel. Long tables were set up, name cards placed on each white dinner plate. Not a thing left to chance. Their hosts, the mayor, and other local officials of Berlin, made many speeches, punctuated every so often by applause from their guests. Mali couldn't understand the German too well. She looked around the room, studied the survivors, and tried to gauge their feelings by the expressions on their faces and to imagine what it must be like for them to be back in the city of their childhood after so many years. Then she looked at the younger generation, the adult children. Had they only come for moral support? Or to satisfy their own curiosity? To see firsthand, as Mali had wanted, the buildings, the parks, and the streets she had seen in her mother's yellow-aged, black-and-white photographs?

Those pictures show a happy child: laughing as she hugs a huge paper cone filled with candies for her first day of school; or playing in the sand at the beach by the North Sea, tanned with white-blond curly hair, her face pointing up, her eyes squinting into the camera; or walking in a snowy park all bundled up in a woolly coat and hat. Once meticulously glued in chronological order to thick, taupe-colored pages and now haphazardly shoved between the leaves of the photo album, their off-white scalloped edges curling inward, these photographs stubbornly remain the testimonies to that other life.

Black-and-white enlargements of Berlin, set up on easels and displayed around the dinner tables, showed old, bombed-out buildings, synagogues, remnants of the Jewish Quarter. There were city maps too. She sat at her place at the table and watched the survivors search the brand-new streets lined with modern shops and apartment blocks, all the old and familiar reduced to rubble by the Allied bombs during World War Two.

How beautiful it used to be.

Can you imagine?

A constant refrain, this question, like a Greek chorus or a punctuation mark placed solidly at the very end of every story.

Can you imagine?

Mali tried.

She had tried to piece together the Berlin of her mother's childhood: the *wursty* stand at the corner; the Jewish schools they were made to attend after they were banned from the ones in their neighborhood; the different apartments they had to live in, each one smaller than the last; the Tiergarten; the zoo; the parks; the buildings their fathers had worked in; the marvelous cafés, where they met their friends; the wide sidewalks; the department stores; the way of life *then* in the before; and the way of life forever afterward.

Mali understands the before and after, the demarcation, like the crease of a turned-down page in a book, of a time and place in life. For Mali, the seesaw is unbalanced in the opposite direction. Her childhood memories—the craggy mountain peaks—are only just visible through the otherwise thick, white, puffy cloudiness of the time before her mother left. She doesn't have photos to mull over, no one to reminisce with, no testaments to that other life. She only has her memories, those inaccurate recorders that stretch and contract, as though heated one moment, cooled the next. But the afterward, the other side of that irreversible crease in the page, is all too clear.

Before her mother left . . . before Hitler came to power. How could she equate the two? the voice in her head shockingly demands. There is a connection, though. She's convinced of it. Hitler robbed her mother of her childhood. That's certain. Mali has been robbed of happiness in hers. That's murkier.

A strange trip in so many ways, she found she had to constantly remind herself she was here . . . here in Germany, in *Germany*. She berates herself now for not having paid better attention, for not remembering more. Her mother's cigarettes, her neatly folded shirts and sweaters always perfectly packed in plastic bags, her charm, her never-tiring energy, and her beauty that attracted people to her, men, and women alike; all these stupidly got in Mali's way. Whenever her mother introduced her as her daughter, she wondered whether those looks of astonishment were for her mother looking so young or for Mali looking too old to be her mother's daughter.

And Mali, on her side—wishing her mother to be a little more similar to the others; maternal with their naturally grey hair, unmade-up lined faces, and eyes that sparkled with love and warmth—couldn't help becoming more and more impatient, snapping at her when she misunderstood or couldn't hear what was being said. What had made Mali that mean? That relentlessly un-giving? Or was it that unforgiving?

After their week in Berlin, they boarded the train for Dresden. It was May 1st—May Day—and the station in Berlin was deserted, as was their train. They were lucky to end up with a compartment all to themselves. Just outside the station were rows and rows of tracks, coming and going in all directions, a geometry lesson in curves, angles, and straight lines. Above them, wires crisscrossed. And at the far end on the outer tracks, cattle cars, hitched two or three together, lingered like sleeping beasts on the sidelines. She couldn't help mixing up the view from her window with that picture in her head of the train tracks leading to Auschwitz. Even the stations they passed looked familiar to her. And when the train rattled by a forest, she envisioned herself looking for hiding places there. But this forest had no undergrowth. The tree trunks were bare, their bases painted a ghostly white. Then how did the forest hide the people on the run?

In Dresden, they went in search of her great-grandparents' delicatessen. They found the curved pedestrian street, the Fressgasse, but not the store. They walked the wide, long, concrete promenade to the River Elbe. Tall square blocks of apartments lined both sides. The Frauenkirche in the square, the museums, and the opera by the river, stood in blackened disrepair as though the bombs had only been dropped on Dresden the day before. The Semperoper, the opera in Dresden, was where my parents used to go on dates, her mother had said. Funny to think of it that way, she added. Next, they went in search of Weissenhausstrasse No. 17. It was where my grandparents lived, her mother declared, as if she'd needed to believe the memories floating in her mind's eye weren't just bubbles. The street existed, renamed now, and because a block of new apartment houses had been built where the house might have been, they couldn't figure out its exact location. A time in her history, gone forever.

Mali imagined the city beautiful in her great-grandparents' day. The magisterial buildings on the bank of the river, so different from the drab utilitarian structures built after the war, to house the people, to fill the bombed-out gaps. All sense of beauty had disappeared, it seemed, with Communism.

After a couple of days in Dresden, they got back on the train, heading further south to Prague. No bombs had been dropped here. Everything remained intact, even the topsy-turvy gravestones in the Jewish cemetery.

Standing back-to-back with her mother, in a narrow hallway at the Jewish museum in Prague, Mali felt as though the high walls were closing in on her. Dizzy, she could barely breathe. Jam-packed, hardly any white space between them, so much hopeful artwork filled up the area. All of it created by the children in Theresienstadt. Their paintings and drawings and sketches . . . of butterflies, pots of flowers, endless blue skies, puffy white clouds, deep yellow suns, radiating . . . everything beautiful in the world, everything they could remember.

"Can you imagine?" Her mother's words rose in a whisper behind her, just loud enough to be heard.

Here was the story of *Brundibár*, the children's opera. Written and composed in Prague in 1938 and performed fifty times in the camp. Performed for high-ranking officials in the Nazi party. For visitors from the Danish and the Swedish Red Cross. For dignitaries from other countries.

Had the children been able to take solace, Mali wondered, and to believe in the opera's message that if all the good hearts came together, they could conquer all the evil ones?

If only it were that simple.

Poets, artists, composers, musicians, writers, and children of all ages with infinite promise and endless possibilities.

Can you imagine? Her mother's words reverberating inside her head, thundered at the silence in this hallway.

Mali tried to take it all in, to reconcile, make sense, understand the terrible waste of all these brilliant futures. But how?

Her mother still talked behind her. What was she saying?

"Can you imagine . . .? The loss . . . impossible . . . unmeasurable . . . unbearable . . ."

But how could she imagine?

No new words had been invented to describe, to define this evil. Our vocabulary fell short, failed miserably, to give us a word for this horrific sub-existence.

And what are her mother's words telling her now?

CHAPTER 39

September 19, 2014

A few days ago, while visiting Elizabeth in her apartment, I came across an article in the paper regarding a man I believed to be the little boy my grandfather had adopted from a Jewish orphanage and brought to America for the daughter of the woman he'd become involved with. He's written a book, a memoir. He sent me a copy. But I'm getting ahead of myself here. The article in the paper was actually an interview. He told how he'd been saved from the Nazis by a wink and a giggle. I knew from the description it had to be him. I contacted his publisher. Although he was on book tour in the Midwest, I got to tell my story to his editor, who said she would give him my phone number. By the way, his name is now Philip Schwartz. The day after I spoke to his editor, a dozen yellow roses arrived at my door. *With love and gratitude from Philip*, the card read.

In a way, I'm sorry time ran out before I could meet him, but in another, I think I was relieved. Perhaps that's why I never mentioned finding him to you. Don't be hurt by this negligence. In truth, I was afraid to see him, and then for him to see me. I don't know. Besides, what would have been the use of it? To dredge up the terrible ugliness and horror all over again? In the end, I guess I just wanted to remember him the way I knew him—the little orphan boy who'd come to stay. It's one thing to write your memories in whatever chaotic order they come into your head and quite another to have them teased out of you. I'm sure if I'd told you I'd found Philip; you'd have insisted I meet him.

Philip's roses are magnificent. Every time I come back into the apartment, I'm caught off guard by their beauty. I'm convinced they possess a secret power to lure the light directly from the window behind them, to their yellowness, brightening up the petals even more. Philip's book sits face down on the table beside them, one of the roses pressed to mark my place. His picture stares up at me. He's different from how I would have imagined him to look. The photo must be fairly old, because by my calculation, he should be in his mid-eighties by now. The face in the picture is relatively young. He has dark curly hair, hazel eyes that smile out of a roundish face. He looks like a kind man, someone with whom, under different circumstances, I'd love to sit with, Scotch in hand, and talk and talk and talk until we have no more words for each other. I've begun to read his book. It's slow going for me with my poor old eyes, and I must admit, his language is sometimes dense and hard to read. The legal issues he's concerned with also make it more difficult for me to understand.

The letter he sent with the book is so sweet. I'm including it:

September 15, 2014

My Dearest Eva,

It's a miracle we're both here, still alive and kicking at this ripe old age of ours! It's even more of a miracle that we will meet each other again after almost eighty-odd years. It's practically impossible for me—you must excuse me for using this expression of the young, but it fits too perfectly— to wrap my head around. Ever since I heard from Rachel that you'd contacted her, I've been trying very hard to remember those months I lived with you and your wonderful parents in Berlin. I can still hardly believe it. My head is truly in a tailspin. Please excuse my digressions. I'm too excited to think straight.

Of course, I remember your white poodle and the races we had with him up and down your street. I also remember we'd go swimming every sunny day during the summer months, until we were banned from the pool. You were so upset. And there was that horrid little girl, the Esskind, *who came home from school every day to eat lunch with you. Germany's answer to forced charity, or was it its socialism? I don't recall her name. She wore glasses and her teeth seemed too big for her mouth, or was it her face? She acted very mean to me, probably because being an orphan was* still one rung lower from being too poor to afford her own lunch. And she could, and did, lord it over me.

I have such fond memories of your mother, and her taking me to the shops in the West End. We must have gone during the week, while you were at school. She said I had to look well-groomed and handsome for my trip to America. She bought me lots of pants and shirts and sweaters, as well as underwear and shoes and socks. Fun-loving, your mother always laughed. I liked her. She would call me her little man. After our shopping expeditions, we'd stop at the Café Dobrin for a treat. Anything made with chocolate, I devoured. We never had decent food to eat at the orphanage. At the Dobrin, we'd sit at a table by the window. Soon we'd be surrounded by your mother's friends, who totally forgot I was sitting there with them as they jabbered away. I didn't mind. You can imagine me in seventh heaven, munching away at my chocolate pastry, and watching the goings on outside the window, making up stories in my head about the people passing by. Do you remember teaching me the names and makes of cars? And the game we made of it? You always won. So I would also practice the game while I sat by the window in the Dobrin. Ironic, isn't it?—that for the first time in my young life, I felt as free as the birds gliding and swooping around in the sky, while your mother and her friends—huddling together around the small café table, heads bent, voices in whispers—tried to reimagine their lives, as each day new restrictions were put into place, squeezing them, like giant vises, into ever tighter places than the day before.

Your mother also took me for my first visit to the barber, where they cut off all my unruly curls. Afterward, we went to a photography studio, where they took photos of me from all angles. And when I came home, you laughed your head off at the way I looked—a shorn sheep, you said, and laughed some more.

I can picture your friend, the little Catholic girl. I've forgotten her name. Do you remember her? You were so jealous of her looks. She had a very pretty face, I'll grant you that. And her long, straight, blond hair. But I thought you the most beautiful girl I'd ever seen. There was never any contest as far as I was concerned, though who'd listen to a six-year-old orphan boy who knew nothing of life and beauty?

Your father, quite different from your mother, was very strict, and I must admit, he scared me. He hired a tutor to teach me English. Then he made dozens of recordings of my voice. It had to be perfect, he said, at his wit's end with frustration, but trying not to lose his patience with me. Table manners, obviously not a high priority in the orphanage, were something else I needed to be taught as well. Your parents worked like crazy with me. You would have been excused from the table long before, and I'd have to sit there, straight as a ramrod, learning which utensils to use, how to spoon my soup, away from me, always away, and how to hold my knife, cutting, not as if I were disemboweling a wild animal, and how to hold my fork as a utensil, not a stabbing tool. Little did I know, then, that the learning of these boring lessons in social aptitude—while I'd just wanted to be excused from the table so I could play with you—were hammered into me with the idea of sending me away to America to save my life. I thought your parents angels. I'm sure I never thanked them enough.

I'm so ashamed, so sorry I never found you. I hope you will forgive me. Rachel has filled me in on her conversation with you. It's incredibly amazing, isn't it?

For the next couple of weeks, I'm on tour with my book, after which I will go home to San Diego for a few days, and then I'll be in New York for another round of book readings. We will have to meet. I'll have Rachel give you my dates and the hotels I'll be staying at. Does she have your phone number? Do you have email? I can't wait for us to meet again.

All the very best, from your six-month, short-term, baby brother.
Philip

I can tell you, Mali, I made a mistake contacting his publisher and speaking at such great length with Rachel, his editor. What was I thinking? I didn't tell you I'd spoken to Philip because I didn't want the rush of enthusiasm, that inevitable "Oh, you must see him, you must."

Thinking of all those details I'd have to update him on makes me cringe. I don't want to be the bearer of sad news. Not now, so many years later. Imagine how he will feel when he learns the fate of Stella, the pretty little Catholic girl, stoned to death with gravel-packed snowballs just for the sin of being a Jew-lover. Or that our *Esskind*, Maria, cried when she could no longer come home for lunch with me because her Führer forbade it. And all those friends huddled around the café table at the Dobrin? Wolfe, the immigrant Jew from the East, his Berlin-born wife, Lily, and their daughter, my best friend Marion, all murdered so cruelly and beyond all reason at Auschwitz.

As I write now, and think of them, I don't know myself how to bear it. I'm sickened. I go back to Philip's letter and I read it, again and again. His words, as kind and loving as the picture of his face on the back cover of his book, seem so filled with optimism, somehow. I think he believes he can still change the world, pierce that ever-widening, ever-frightening circumference of silence.

• • •

Having plowed through all these memories, it occurred to me the other day that I also spent very little of my childhood with my mother. Before our lives became unbearable under Hitler, she hardly ever stayed home. We had a nanny to take care of me and a maid to keep things going in our large apartment. After we emigrated from Berlin to London, I was evacuated to the countryside and saw very little of her. Then a couple of years after the war ended, my parents moved to New York. I remember missing my mother terribly. And now I wonder, did I expect your father to fill in for her, take care of me, like a mother? Shower me with the love and attention I missed as a child and hungered for, so desperately? Is that what had happened?

CHAPTER 40

October 26, 2014

Mali sits on the Turkish carpet in her mother's living room by the box of photographs. She picks out the loose and random moments of her mother's life, holding them up in a guessing game of time and place and people—a game that stumps her more often than not.

But here's her father's old will, buried among her mother's old photos. It's ancient. 17th July 1956. So outdated, it's laughable. And not much to it. The page of legal mumbo-jumbo basically claims Mali is his only inheritor. A final paragraph asserts there are to be no provisions for Eva, his ex-wife, Mali's mother, the reasons set out in a separate statement. The statement isn't here, though. She wonders why. Probably just more graphic, more detailed legalese to do with her betrayal. But what's the will doing here in the first place? Had her father given her mother a copy . . . at the time, or years later when they were finally on more friendly terms? To prove that even though Eva got nothing out of the divorce settlement, Mali would.

This reminds her of a cold November day many years later. Mali and her mother were sitting across from each other at Mali's kitchen table, two half-empty cups of coffee in front of them. Her mother had just come back from seeing old friends in London. She'd also gone to visit Hirschel. She'd asked him about his will to make sure, she said, that Mali would inherit what Eva didn't. Her mother repeated his answer for her, and she had no difficulty hearing her father's voice. Tell Amalia, he'd have said, using her full name, which seemed to carry more weight, more deadly seriousness than her nickname, Mali. Tell her not to worry. There'll be plenty for her when I'm dead and gone. She could see how his mouth would have turned into a sneer, as he spat out his angry words. Words as sharp and painful to her as they had been on that day in her hotel room on the French Riviera when she was twelve. How had he lost contact with the person she was, his own daughter? How could he have thought she'd put her mother up to that question?

She feels herself becoming sleepy, woozy. Too many memories crowding her brain, fighting for prominence. She falls asleep and dreams she's in her bed at home in Connecticut. Quick, heavy footsteps beat the uneven flagstone path beneath her bedroom window. She turns her face toward the sound, to help her make sense of it. The footsteps stand still. Then a noise, a shuffle, as if he were wiping his feet on the jute welcome mat. A loud knock raps on the door. She gets out of bed, goes to the bathroom, grabs a towel, wraps it around her naked body, and tiptoes from the bedroom to the stairs, all the while holding her breath. The rapping stops. She breathes again, takes one step down. A man's voice talks in muffled tones on the other side of the closed front door. She strains to listen. The rapping begins again. The voice sounds urgent. What's he saying? She leans into the white wall, stares at a faded, rubbed-out child's handprint, the only mark on the whiteness, and flattens herself, as though she can melt into it, like a run-over character in a cartoon. She wants to run, to scream. No voice comes. Her legs won't move. They're locked in place, as if nailed to the carpet. Her head spins. The man's voice cries out: Delivery, special delivery. She can't think what it could be. She's not expecting anything. Again, the sound of his feet stumbling, and his voice, louder and angry now too. Her heart thumps so violently, she thinks it will jump out of her chest, a jack-in-the-box. He pounds on the door again. Then stops. The screen door slams back on its hinges. He paces outside the door. Then abruptly gives up, his retreating footsteps echoing on the flagstone path. Wrapping the towel tighter around herself, she goes down the stairs to the front hall, peeks through the window. A large, brown cardboard box stands on the wooden decking outside. Marked with stenciled black lettering in an alphabet she can't read, they look like passport stamps from a faraway country. Flaps hang over the sides of the open box, crushed reams of paper fill it over the top. She opens the door, takes a step forward, peers inside . . .

Her dream suddenly jolts her awake. She's dreamt this before.

CHAPTER 41

October 3, 2014

The truth in life, My Dearest, Darling Mali, is that no matter the number and variety of rehearsals you conduct inside your head, things never quite turn out the way you picture them in your imagination, the way the little newsreel in your daydream makes its roundabout progression from one episode to the next, and back again to the first.

I'd overslept on that cold and rainy late-December day in 1988. Rushing through my morning coffee and only glancing at the paper, I hurriedly showered and dressed. More out of sorts than usual, I made my way through prickly sheets of iced rain to the hospital. When I arrived, David was sitting, propped up with multiple pillows. At first, I thought that by some miracle he'd gone into remission. How stupid could I have been? We talked for a while, an hour maybe, then he told me to go home and rest and not to come back until later in the day. I'd been in such a rush leaving the apartment in the morning, I'd totally forgotten to pack my book and Walkman device, and besides, he seemed so much stronger to me, I agreed to go home and come back later.

Only there was no later.

When I got home, the first thing I did, the very first thing I always did, was to check the answering machine. Usually I had no messages. This day, however, the little red message light blinked furiously at me. I pressed play. I dropped my umbrella and bag to the floor, and suddenly feeling very heated and sweaty, I unbuttoned my raincoat, and stripped it from my body, unable to stand the weight of it on my back any longer. I sagged to the floor. My heart pounded, as the dreaded voice rang out from the machine and echoed into the loneliness of my apartment. David's nurse left her telephone number and said to call as soon as I got her message.

He must have known, was all I could think of then. He must have garnered all his strength, all his resolve, to make me believe he could get better. And I believed him. Had I been that naïve? Or that unprepared, or unable to accept his death that I would've believed in any show of bravado he might have put on for me? What became so painfully obvious, as the days drew on afterward, was that he didn't want me there at his end. And, even to this day, so many years later, I will never understand that. Perhaps there is shame in dying.

•   •   •   •   •

I wrap my woolen shawl around my shoulders, stand at my window and watch the traffic up and down York Avenue. The rain is pouring now, trilling as it splashes the aluminum railing on my balcony. The streets glisten, reflecting traffic's red, white, and green lights. Opened umbrellas, as if they're the colored dots of hope, brighten the city's grey landscape. Today, I'm glad I don't have to be anywhere. The TV in the den is loud with newscasters spitting out the near and far-away disasters of the day. I can't help but think back. It's what I do best these days. Probably because, at my age, there's more in that direction than I can even imagine in the other.

My doctor's office has just called. The doctor wants to see me, the sweet-voiced receptionist said, almost apologetically. The results of my latest tests must be in. I want to tell them it really doesn't matter anymore. My life is lived. I don't though. I have an appointment for next week. Maybe you'll come with me?

CHAPTER 42

October 27, 2014

As the sky lightens up, a rosy redness lines the far-side of the river, as though a fire rages beneath the belly of the world. Mali yawns and gets up to look out at the life below her. A few cars drive by. The market across the street has just opened. A delivery truck double-parks outside.

She did go to the doctor with her mother. Rather than the grave news they'd expected, though, the doctor told her she was doing well.

On that late September afternoon, one too beautiful to miss, they'd walked back from the doctor's office, stopping at Joe Fresh on the way. Mali moved through the store, picking out skirts and shirts to try on, while her mother sat on a couch outside the dressing room, waiting to give her opinions of the various outfits Mali modeled for her. She tired easily that day. Mali should've realized.

She turns from the window now. More of Philip's rose petals have dropped to the table, their stamen leaving orange, dusty trails on the wooden surface. A half-filled mug of leftover coffee from the night before sits beside the stack of her mother's letters. The blue blanket lies bunched up on the yellow leather couch where she finally fell asleep. She'd managed to stay up for as long as it took to finish reading her mother's pages, then crashed.

Michael will be here soon. She should hop into the shower, make herself breakfast, begin sorting through her mother's things. Begin. Yes, she must. But instead, she finds herself drawn back to the window again.

More people have come out to the street. She needs to see this life now, *this* ordinary, everyday life of today.

Poor Philip. She thinks he must've been very disappointed to have missed her mother. From his letter, he seemed to remember more than he'd let on to Mali when they'd spoken. He probably didn't want to go through it all again. But now it's all behind him. No one else will remind him of where he came from. It can all be neatly stacked and put away. Unlike this messy box of old photographs sitting here by the couch.

The top of the sun peeks out over the horizon, a crescent of brilliant yellow. The river shines with sparkly reflections like a multitude of mirrored shards bobbing up and down with the current. Mali turns away from the glare at the window and walks around the apartment, turning off the little lamps as she goes. She should look for Philip's book again. She should check her email. In the kitchen, she fills the kettle, takes the English muffin and butter out of the fridge. Then, while she waits for the coffee to drip through the filter to her cup and the toaster to pop up her muffin, she walks through the living room. Scans the bookshelves once more for Philip's book. And gives up for now. She'll look again later. It will show up somewhere, she's sure of it.

Mali's drawn back to the box of photographs. She loves to look at the old places and times. As she begins to pull them out at random, her thoughts go back to her mother's strange words in her unfinished letter. She can't think why she would've written them, what might have prompted her to do so. It doesn't matter. Her mother was right: it's best to just let things go. She'll have to practice that in her old age. Even though, she must admit, letting go is something she's always had trouble with. She's no better than a hoarder, gathering all those wrongs into her and then, when the mood hits, spreading them before her, as if they are little treasures to be mulled over, one by one. She's not an easy forgiver. She is, after all, her father's daughter too.

She shuffles the handful of photographs she's pulled from the box and carefully lays them on the cocktail table, brushing away the rose petals to make room. She places them in columns, face down, as she would with cards in a game of solitaire. She's looking for inscriptions. There's only one in this batch: Wedding Day, March 25, 1945. She turns it over. Here are her parents, both in dark suits, standing on the steps of the synagogue they've just left. The tiny white hat and the netting that juts out in a halo from the crown of her mother's head and the black Homburg, slightly askew on her father's, are the only clues a marriage has taken place. Ignoring the camera, they're turned in toward each other, smiling and happy.

Is that what her mother had decided to do in the end—she wonders, as she stands the photo up against the vase of roses—just let it all go?

She brings up another batch and turns them over as well. Mostly, the same group of Jewish refugees, all in various poses, stand together with arms wrapped around each other's shoulders, or they sit in deckchairs planted on sand or grass. Laughter creases their faces as they look straight into the camera. And someone always cuddles a poodle. She remembers several of these people. Hannah and Max, for instance. A few years older than Mali's parents and married before the war, they had been imprisoned together in the Warsaw ghetto, and afterward in Auschwitz. He had managed to escape from the ghetto, or was it from Auschwitz? The story Mali remembers is that, in escaping, he'd found eleven English soldiers lost in the Polish woods and had led them to safety. Later in London, in England, Hannah could never leave her flat without an apple in her bag, the fear of starving too strong to ever forget.

Of course, Mali hadn't known any of this back then. They had two boys. One a little older than Mali, the other a little younger. Both families used to get together for walks in Regents Park or Primrose Hill, then go to their flat on the Maida Vale for afternoon tea. She remembers being a child easy to cry and her mother's impatience with her. But oddly, she can barely remember much more from those early days. After her mother left, she never saw Max and Hannah again. Her father had wanted to eradicate those years, strip them of everyone they'd ever known. But she'd missed them. Every part of her life had changed the day her mother—dressed in her best navy-blue suit and shiny sequined beret—picked up her two suitcases, one in each hand, walked down the drive, and into the waiting taxi.

The toaster dings. The coffee grounds in the filter have dried with the last of the water pressing through them. She stacks the photographs into a pile and leaves them on the table. When she comes back to the box, after her breakfast and her shower, she pulls out another handful and lays out this new batch in the same way as before. Turning them over, she sees her children as babies and toddlers. And then her children's children from infants to school-age. What will the world be like for them? Will they be prepared? She stacks these photos next to the first lot and digs into the box again. This time she pulls out a letter. It's from her daughter, Julia, to her mother.

Dear Nana,

I'm sending you Leigh's story because I think you'll find it very interesting. He wrote the story for school. Don't ask me where he got the idea from. I guess all those times we sit around the dinner table, for one occasion or another, and your talk invariably goes back to Nazi times in Germany and the war in London—I mean, really, when does it ever not? — and there's Leigh sitting with us, busy playing Angry Birds on my mom's iPhone, seemingly oblivious to our chatter. But as you'll see from his story, he has imbibed—if that's the right word—all of it. You once asked me if, and then how, I would teach the Holocaust to my children. It's such a tricky thing. I think my parents might have been too vigilant in their teaching us. Afraid, I'm sure, that if they weren't, the Do Not Forget *legacy would die with their generation. Well, it seems that the Holocaust has become an integral part of who we are, as a people, even of my nine-year-old son. I've copied over his story for you and have made a few corrections in tense, grammar, and punctuation. Otherwise it really is all his.*

It Was a Time of War

It is a balmy day in Germany. Derek, who is 18 years-old, is awakened to terrible sounds he's never heard before. BOOM! BOOM! Explosions so loud they hurt his ear drums. He jumps out of bed, thinking the worst possible thoughts: I wonder if people are getting hurt. What is happening outside? Derek rushes down the stairs and opens the front door. He sees fire everywhere. People are crying, running, and screaming frantically. Derek realizes that the soldiers have invaded his village. Nazi soldiers are dragging all the children into the streets . . .

The doorbell buzzes. Mali drops Julia's letter on the table and runs to open the door. Michael stands there. Alongside him is a borrowed cart from the building's super, filled with flattened cardboard boxes, a tall pile of newspapers for wrapping, and a giant roll of tape. In his hand, a grande latte for her from Starbucks.

She helps him unload the cart. They stack the boxes by the dining table.

"So, how're you doing?" He looks around. "I can see you got a lot done." A grin spreads across his face.

She shrugs. She smiles too. Takes a sip of her coffee.

"But I'm ready to pack it up now," she says.

"First, I'll bring the cart down to the super. Then, when I get back, we'll begin it together. Okay?"

Holding open the door for him, she watches him maneuver the cart along the hallway to the elevator. Only after she hears the elevator door slide shut does she go back inside.

At the little table in the entryway, where she's put her mother's keys, she suddenly feels as if the paintings on the walls, the bric-a-brac, the books, are beginning to close in on her again—but now it's as if she's looking at the room through a wide-angle lens, everything seeming to be far and near at the same time. She's dizzy. She tries to push herself forward, but her legs won't let her. They're locked in place. Ghosts have surrounded her, taken her hostage. "Listen to them," she hears her mother's voice, wraithlike, though resolute. Mali shakes her head, takes a deep breath, and makes her way further into the living room. Now the lens is making everything seem farther and farther away from her. Then gone, like her mother.

Before she had lost consciousness and after her request not to be resuscitated, her mother had turned her head sideways on the white hospital pillow and said, "I'm sorry." Sorry? Sorry for what? Oddly, her father had said those exact same words to her the last time she saw him in London, before he died. Were they sorry to be leaving her? Sorry for all the goodbyes in her childhood, for all those courageous, held back tears?

Held back tears. As a kid, she hadn't been very good at it. She'd always tried to be brave, especially for her mother and for her father. But then she would feel a hotness, a stinging behind her eyes; and as though from a fiery spring, deep inside her, the tears would well up, and before she knew it, they'd be streaming down her cheeks. Anything would set her off. And sometimes, nothing at all.

Despite her father's lectures on the importance of education, the value of gaining knowledge—the one and only thing no one could ever take away from her—learning remained painfully elusive. As hard as she'd tried to concentrate on the subject being taught, her mind would become like a topsy-turvy Chagall painting, and soar high above the neat rows of wooden desks and chairs. Always in search of her mother, it went to another place in the world—a place where mothers and fathers and children belonged together, possessing one history, one language. When her mind returned her to the classroom, she would find everyone staring at her. What's the matter? one or the other would ask. Why are you crying?

She never could find the right words to tell, to explain the sad longing she'd had for her mother; or the aching inside her that was as constant as the rise and fall of her own breathing.

Rise and fall . . . rise and fall. Only a week, and it feels more like a year, since she'd sat by her mother's side in the hospital, stroking her motionless hand and watching for any slight change in her closed eyes, her unconscious face, or the short signs of life between her shallow breaths. Rising and falling.

A music therapist had come to the hospital floor one afternoon. She went from room to room, singing and playing on her guitar. What should she play? she'd asked, as she came into her mother's room. *You Are My Sunshine,* Mali said. The song she'd chosen had no particular significance for them—it'd just come to Mali without thought. While the therapist sang and strummed the tune on her guitar, she watched her mother and tried to stop the tears beginning to well up in her eyes. Although her mother showed no visible change or sign, Mali hoped her mother could hear the music, take in the words.

The words. Yes. Mali remembers now. Her mother *had* been her sunshine. And when she'd left all those years ago, she had always looked for her mother's face, that ray of brightness, everywhere she went. And she would find it. On the faces of strangers walking toward her on the street, or in queues at the shops, or waiting for the 143 bus at the top of her road. Yes, her mother was with her everywhere in London—fleetingly—but with her, everywhere.

Now she was both afraid to witness her mother's last breath and to miss it.

When she got the call at home from the nurse at the hospital, she couldn't help but ask herself, over and over, if there hadn't been something she should or could have done to save her. She'd felt so inept, so useless.

Was she supposed to have sat by and just let her go? For good this time?

Almost all the petals have dropped from their stems. From where she stands now, the bare stalks appear to her like raised arms, and the two shriveled rose buds, still stubbornly holding on, like closed fists. Is her mother still reaching up to her? Or has she finally had her say? Mali comes to the table. Yellow petals blanket the pile of mismatched notepaper, as if to safeguard all the words written on them. Or perhaps, she thinks, as she blows away the petals from her parents' old wedding photograph, Julia's letter, Leigh's story . . . perhaps . . . they're here to say, it's all right now to bury the memories, the hurt.

"And to let it all go," she says out loud to the empty apartment.

She blinks, and the tears she has been holding onto finally fill her eyes and fall.

ACKNOWLEDGEMENTS

There have been teachers, along this journey, who not only taught, but inspired and encouraged me as well—from my early days at the University of Bridgeport with Jeffrey Skinner and Dick Allen, to classes at The Writing Institute at Sarah Lawrence College with Joan Silber and Myra Goldberg, and then to Suzanne Hoover at the Westport Writers' Workshop.

I have also been very lucky in finding a home at the Fort Lauderdale Writers' Group. Everyone has been so supportive and generous with their critiques and encouragement!

The Women's Fiction Writers Association has been a wonderful resource for me. I have learned so much from my fellow writers, and from my mentor, Karen O'Neal Jones, who has provided me with unstinting cheer and support.

Thank you to my editor, Pamela Taylor, who did an incredible job proofing my manuscript.

I am deeply grateful, thrilled and honored to be a part of the Black Rose Writing family of authors.

And finally, I am most thankful for my family—my husband Peter, my daughters and sons-in-law, Jordie and Rory, Nikki and Paco, and my grandchildren, Sammy, Devin, Lucy, Harley, and Maeve—who have never lost faith in me and whose love I cherish beyond all words.

NOTE FROM THE AUTHOR

Word-of-mouth is crucial for any author to succeed. If you enjoyed *Circumference of Silence*, please leave a review online—anywhere you are able. Even if it's just a sentence or two. It would make all the difference and would be very much appreciated.

Thanks!
Jacquie Herz

Thank you so much for reading one of our **Historical** novels.

If you enjoyed our book, please check out our recommendation for your next great read!

Z.O.S. by Kay Merkel Boruff

"...dazzling in its specificity and intensity."

–C.W. Smith, author of *Understanding Women*

View other Black Rose Writing titles at
www.blackrosewriting.com/books and use promo code
PRINT to receive a **20% discount** when purchasing.

CPSIA information can be obtained
at www.ICGtesting.com
Printed in the USA
LVHW041434261221
706788LV00004B/15